Identicals

A Novel by

William Brennan Knight

Published by Altron Services
Copyright © 2022 by William Brennan Knight

Printed in the United States of America
First Printing, 2022
Published by Altron Services
ISBN: 978-1-7339698-3-3

www.authorwbk.com

Books in The Suicide Society Series:

Desolation (Prequel)
The Suicide Society
Rational Insanity
Kill it to Death
Resurrection of Death

Other Books By:
William Brennan Knight

The Suicide Society Series:

To Michelle: Watching you triumph over the most challenging adversity has been inspirational. Be true to yourself, and appreciate how valued you are to others and the world. For you, the adventure is just beginning. May the wind always be at your back, and most importantly, be the ball...

Chapter One

Jack raised his foot and moved it past the red line.

If he did the math right, it had to be over a thousand. That's how many weekdays he stood on this platform in about the same spot, waiting for the 7:16 from Arlington Heights to the OTC. Once he arrived downtown, he always grabbed a cab or an Uber to make the rest of the trip to 625 N. Michigan Avenue. Yet, in the blink of an eye, everything changed. Now, he walked to the bus stop every morning where he would catch the 125 on the green line to save money. His routine was so ingrained he imagined he could do it blindfolded if there weren't so many people rushing to their destinations who would get in the way.

The experienced travelers were easy to pick out because they inched forward with impatient energy. Today, the bitter cold distorted their faces, and the heavy condensation of their breath made temporary thick streams of fog that clouded the platform. The sound of the wheels grinding steel on steel was still about twenty seconds away, but the veterans felt the vibrations long before the noise

1

arrived. By the time the train made the last curve and came into sight, the subtle fight for position was in full swing as the travelers crowded onto the center platform, looking as pitifully desperate as they probably were.

The train slowed, but even at a crawl, it could still crush anyone who stepped in front of it. Jack moved his foot farther past the red line as the train decelerated, now about thirty-five feet away and closing. The omnipresent gray tint that clouded his vision began to lift, and the true color of his surroundings emerged and brightened the scenery.

For a brief moment, he felt alive.

Within ten feet of the train's arrival, his foot moved past the platform and now hovered over the track area.

Maybe this would be the day.

His forward movement was almost imperceptible, but just before the front of the Brookville monster reached him, he glanced to his right and saw a woman staring. She was slender and attractive, but her business suit was a bit too tight, which accentuated her curves, probably on purpose. *Sales or a corporate climber* was his instant judgement.

Their eyes locked for a moment, and they exchanged a trove of information in that instant. He sensed a hint of panic on her part. Not that she particularly cared if he died, but the prospect of watching his body impacting with the train would be unpleasant. More importantly, she would be very late to her destination as the police investigated the scene.

Her eyes shifted down to his foot, still hovering ever so slightly above and past the platform. He moved it back behind the red line, and he noticed her exhale. They smiled at each other awkwardly, and she quickly moved away from him as the train finally stopped. The doors slid open directly, and he boarded just as the gray shading returned to cloud his vision.

***

The walk to O'Malley's from the bus stop wasn't very far. In fact, if he looked over the tops of the two-and-three-story bungalows surrounding the bar, he could see the gleaming high rise in the distance. His old office had a panoramic view of the city, but he always hoped to make it over to the lake side. Of course, like all the other goals in his life, that one was crushed on the day everything changed.

O'Malley's was more Boston than Chicago with its brass railings, dark cherry wood and stained-glass accents that tried to conjure up an atmosphere of an authentic Irish pub. The place was inhabited by professionals and neighborhood residents, but they usually came rolling in around noon for lunch. Tommy looked up and then over at the wall clock. 9:30 in the morning was early even for his best customer.

"Whaddaya know, it's Jackie boy." The bartender was large and portly, sporting a thick handlebar moustache several shades darker than his curly auburn hair. He had one of those faces that said mid-50s, yet he was closer to forty-five.

His name was Alfred, but he shed that a long time ago. Everyone called him Tommy, but nobody except the bartender really knew why.

Jack walked over to the end of the bar towards his regular stool. By the time he arrived, a cup of hot, black coffee was already waiting for him. He looked up at Tommy, who smiled and nodded. The bartender was a veteran, and there was no way he was going to tolerate a customer getting that kind of head start. The first drink was poured at 11:30. Those were the rules.

"I had to leave the house on time today. Juanita is getting suspicious. I could have stayed at the station, but…"

The bartender puffed out his cheeks and expelled the air slowly. "I get it, Jackie boy." He picked up a glass and absently started drying it. "Any job prospects? We're in good times, ya know. It shouldn't be too hard for a seasoned peddler like you to find work out there."

Jack ran his hands through his hair. "I gave those bastards twenty-two years of my life, Tommy, and they kicked me to the curb. I have a setback, and they kicked me to the fuckin' curb."

The bartender grabbed a menu, pushing it in front of Jack. "Hey, you look like you haven't been eating. Pick out something, and I'll cook it up for you. We got steak and eggs on there. It might do you some good, Jack." He started to wipe the bar down even though the acrylic surface was already clean and shiny as a mirror. "Yeah, that's rough, Jackie boy. But… well, as much as I appreciate the business, no one's gonna pay you to sit in my bar every day. Ya know, just sayin'."

4

Jack took a sip of coffee and glanced briefly at the menu. "Twenty-two damn years. You get down on your luck, and nobody cares. Kick you to the curb; that's what they do." He looked up. "I made them a fortune, Tommy. They were just a couple of geek engineers working for Carrier when they started the supply company. Give them credit. They came up with the idea of consolidation, but they didn't have a goddamn clue how to sell it." Jack slurped at the coffee and set the cup back down.

"For sure, Jackie boy, for sure. What did you say you wanted for breakfast again?"

Jack looked at the menu in earnest. "Okay, Tommy, the steak and eggs look good."

For the next hour and a half, the skilled bartender used every tactic he learned on the job or in bartending school to delay the inevitable. The eggs and steak took twice as long to cook as they ordinarily would have. He indulged Jack in his misery and played the role of the sympathizer without ever piercing the protective veil. "The Subject" never came up. Anyone who entered Jack's personal space knew he was harboring something so raw and ugly it couldn't be discussed even after all this time.

"They could have given me some warning, ya know? I've been a little down on my luck, sure, but all those years of delivering the numbers. You think that would have meant something."

Tommy stopped wiping the bar down and began to speak but thought better of it. Jack noticed.

"What is it, Tommy? You have something to say?"

"Never mind, Jack. It wasn't important... Hey, take a few more bites of that steak, okay?"

"No, no, go ahead. I want to hear it. Don't hold back."

Tommy sighed. "Look, Jack, it's none of my business, but maybe you should talk to someone. Maybe a professional who deals with these kinds of things. You know, a counselor type. Could something like that be helpful?"

"A shrink?" Jack's back stiffened. "You sound like my wife, Tommy. A *shrink*? There's nothing wrong with me. I've just hit a little streak of bad luck. It'll be over soon."

The bartender sighed and nodded. They both glanced at the wall clock at the same moment. It read: 11:32.

"C'mon, Tommy, set me up," said Jack with a note of desperation. "My mouth's as dry as the Sahara, and the coffee and water aren't doin' it for me." He pushed the breakfast plate forward, signaling he was finished.

"Hold that thought." Tommy held up a finger and walked into the back room as though he just remembered something important. In reality, it was another technique he used to get his patrons to slow down without having to confront them. About ten minutes later, he re-emerged with a shrug. "Sorry, Jack, that was a call I had to make. My mom's going in for surgery Thursday, and I needed to talk to the doctor."

"That's tough, Tommy. Hope it's not serious."

6

"Gallstones," said the bartender as he set a glass down in front of Jack and did a long pour. "She has to get her gallbladder removed. It's pretty routine, but she's seventy-two, so…"

"Yeah, I miss my parents, but when I hear all the old age horror stories, I'm glad they never had to go through any of that shit." Jack picked up the drink and took a long sip.

"I get it," said Tommy. "It's part of why I moved back to Chicago. My sister unloaded on me about how unfair it was to put it all on her. The guilt worked."

The bartender encouraged the banter to slow Jack's drinking, but the first double still went down quickly, and the second was polished off shortly thereafter. Fortunately, by 11:45, some of the lunch crowd started filing in, which meant Tommy could spend time with his other customers. Even with all the delaying tactics, Jack was already well on his way to a decent bender. Tommy welcomed more people into the bar because that meant more talking and less drinking, which in Jack's case, was a good thing.

As they came in, usually in small groups, Jack acknowledged the early regulars with a wave. He knew most of them by now. Pablo was a Gulf War vet who never got past the flashbacks. Tony was a kid who wasn't quite right in the head. He was on permanent disability, and his family got him set up in a two-flat on Chestnut and then pretty much washed their hands. Once upon a time in the '90s, Earl owned a big contracting company, but he became a right-wing conspiracy nut and had a nervous breakdown just after the business went belly up. Earl just hoped his money didn't run out before he died.

Jack finished waving and nodding at Earl when the door opened, followed by an icy blast of wind. An old woman walked in, her face shrouded by a thick scarf and a large babushka pulled down over her eyes. She wasn't familiar but seemed to know the layout of the bar without speaking or looking at anyone. As though she had been here before, she walked over and sat at the most remote corner table, slowly unwrapping one of the scarves.

Jack tried to remain inconspicuous while watching her. She clearly was uncomfortable and out of place. Her stature was thin and gaunt to the point of emaciation. Deep stress and worry lines zig-zagged across the sagging skin on her face. She looked out the window as if lost in a trance or dream of some sort. Tommy walked out from behind the bar and went over to her table, talking to her briefly.

Turning back to the business at hand, Jack finished his drink and signaled he was ready for another. The clock read 12:32, which meant Tommy would shove a burger and fries off the grill in front of him within the next half hour. In their unspoken agreement, Jack knew he better take a few bites if he wanted to continue drinking through the rest of the afternoon.

A few more people came in off the street, blowing into their hands to fight off the cold. It was raining intermittently, and the lake effect was mixing in some snow. A perfectly miserable January day in Chicago. The snowy slop on the street grew dirtier as the cars slushed through it, one after another.

Even as he watched the unfolding weather, Jack couldn't keep from glancing over at the old woman. On a typical day, he might make occasional small talk with a few of the regulars, but for the most part, they learned to leave him stew in his misery. He was such a downer, and he drove everyone away. So, it wasn't unexpected that the normal din of chatter dialed down a notch when they saw him pick up his overcoat and walk over to her table.

"Mind if I join you?"

She looked up and regarded him for a moment before motioning him to sit. Without saying a word, she turned back to the window. Jack continued to have the odd feeling they met before. Something was vaguely familiar. Maybe it was her body language, which suggested they shared more than just a chance encounter.

"My name is Jack," he said as he stuck out his hand awkwardly.

She ignored the gesture and continued staring absently at the street outside. "You don't need to introduce yourself; I know who you are," she said in a tone that was subdued and somber.

He shifted in his seat and opened his mouth to speak but reconsidered when he saw Tommy approaching with her drink.

"Here you go, ma'am. A tall bourbon, neat. That will be seven and a quarter." Tommy smiled as he set the drink on a napkin and took a step back, but she didn't move. After an awkward silence, he said, "Ah, the drink, ma'am. It's seven-twenty-five.

9

Should I start a tab?" Again, she made no attempt to pay or answer.

Tommy looked over at Jack, who shrugged slightly before saying, "Just put it on my tab, Tommy." The bartender gave him a thumbs up and looked back at the woman with just a slight shake of his head before slowly turning and walking back to the bar.

Jack engaged in some one-sided small talk, but she never answered or even acknowledged he was speaking. After several minutes of awkward silence, he considered how he might get away from this uncomfortable situation. He moved his seat back and stood up when she said, in barely a whisper, "I told you, I know who you are."

The unsettling sense of connection returned, and he was drawn back to his chair. She turned toward him and pulled away the scarf that hid her eyes. They were deep, vivid blue but had a hint of orange around the cornea. Were they infected? He had never seen anything like it. She locked onto him, and he couldn't break away. The nagging feeling he knew her intensified and crawled through his body until chills caused instantaneous sweat to bubble up on his back.

He knew her; he was sure of it. "Where did we meet? You look so familiar," he said quietly.

"When it happens, you must show up and pay your debt, you pissant," she said in a shaking, agitated voice.

Jack frowned and pulled back. "What are you talking about? And what did you just call me?"

With a trembling hand, she reached into her purse and pulled out a crushed pack of cigarettes.

Struggling to light one, she took a deep drag, ignoring city ordinances and the signs that prohibited smoking in Tommy's bar. She moved in closer. Her breath stank of nicotine and rot. "Did you hear me? When the time comes, you must show up and pay your debt. You can't get away from it, pissant!" She reached over and grabbed his arm with surprising strength. "Pay your goddamn debt!"

Jack recoiled and tried to stand up, but the chair skidded backwards and nearly toppled over. He regained his footing and moved away from the table, never taking his eyes off her. "What the hell is wrong with you, lady?"

"Remember," she said in a voice loud enough for everyone to hear, "you can't get out of it. You must be there and pay your debt, pissant."

When he reached his bar stool, Jack opened his wallet and pulled out two twenties he laid on the bar. Tommy ambled over as Jack slipped on his overcoat. He leaned in while shifting his eyes between the woman and his regular.

"Hey, what happened over there, Jack? That one's got the look, almost like crazy Tony. Something is wrong with her... Hey, are you alright?"

"Yeah, yeah, I'm okay. Just a little shook up. I need to get some air. Anyway, the trains are always running late this time of year. I better get going."

"Okay, Jackie boy. Maybe you'll get a job offer tomorrow, yeah?" Jack nodded as he got up from the stool and turned toward the door.

"Thanks for the drinks and the company, Tommy," he said while keeping his eyes glued to the floor and away from the woman.

"Not a problem, Jackie boy," Tommy called from behind him. "Good luck to you. It's a damn tough life, and sometimes, it gets even worse. Be safe out there."

Jack paused with his hand on the doorknob. He would have turned and asked Tommy what he meant, but for some reason, he needed to get out of the bar. His muscles were tight, and he could only breathe in short, shallow gasps. Blood coursed through his veins like sludge through a restricted sewer pipe, and his heart pumped so slowly he was certain every beat would be the last.

I'm having a panic attack.

With enormous effort, he was able to force his hand to push the door open and stumble outside into the cold, heavy winter air. Before the string of entry bells sounded, he thought he heard her voice in the distance.

"Show up, and pay your debt. No matter what, you better be there, *pissant*."

Chapter Two

The gray hue in their home was darker than anywhere else. Jack believed that was because tragedy clung like moss to the walls, ceiling, furniture and every crack and crevice in the house. It hung in the air and invaded his body with each breath.

It's your fault, Jack. It's all your fault.

Even now, he found it impossible to look at Juanita for more than a few seconds at a time. In another life, another reality, there remained a faint memory of her face, so full of life, and how it would light up when she caught him staring at her. In those moments, she recognized the love he radiated as sure as if it was tangible matter. Hugs, kisses and lovemaking were only an affirmation of all they felt and shared every day together.

And yet, it all ended in one dreadful moment. Twenty-five years flushed down the crapper in a New York minute.

"Dad, can you help me with my astronomy project? It's like half my grade, and I haven't even started." Leighton was the middle child, but at thirteen, he was a full participant in the grief and anguish that suffocated each one of them. He might be slightly more resilient because of his youth, but the nightmares still visited him regularly. Unlike the rest of the family, counseling seemed to help, but the psychologist said Leighton continued to harbor many dark memories and feelings he found hard to express.

"When is it due?"

"Two weeks. I probably should get started on it."

Jack nodded. "Sure, but not tonight, okay? I'm feeling tired and a little under the weather." None of that was true, of course. The overwhelming depression coupled with his blossoming hangover meant that tonight's routine would be no different than yesterday's. He would retreat to his den and escape into a bottle of scotch as soon as he could get away from the dinner table.

That Jack had spiraled down into a cycle of alcohol-fueled self-pity was an unpleasant family secret that was growing increasingly difficult to hide. His drinking was the proverbial 1000-pound gorilla in the room, ominous and threatening, but off limits for discussion. After all, *he* was the one suffering the most, right?

Jack watched Leighton's shoulders slump as he went back to moving the food around his plate. He looked at his other son, Bryson, eighteen, and then back at Juanita.

"What?" he said. "Why are you all looking at me like that?"

"No one is looking at you," said Juanita. "We're just eating dinner."

"Yeah, without talking… Bryson, how was your day?" Jack noticed his son's back stiffen as he chewed more slowly, which delayed his answer by almost a minute.

"Fine. My day was fine."

"Well, tell us what you did."

"I went to class. A few of us hung out at the rec center after school."

Jack laid down his fork and folded his hands. "So, you're wasting time in the rec center while I'm busting my ass to save for your college tuition. Have you seen your grades lately?"

"Not now, Jack. Leave him alone." Juanita's tone was sharp and curt.

"I'm just trying to figure out why someone with a D average has time to spend in the rec center instead of hitting the books. It's my money, so I have a right to an answer."

Bryson wiped his mouth and threw his napkin on the table. "Your money, your money, that's all you have, isn't it? Well, don't worry, you won't have to pay anything for me. Once I graduate, I'm out of here."

"Oh, really? You'll do no such thing. You'll finish high school, and in the fall, you *will* be attending DePaul. That's final."

Bryson slid the chair back and stood up. "No, I'm not going to college. I just want out of here. This place makes me sick to my stomach." He paused as the tears welled up in his eyes. "I can't be around you anymore. You're just a…"

Jack got to his feet and approached his eldest son. "I'm a *what*, Bryson." They were only inches apart, and neither was backing down. "I said you're going to finish school. There is no more discussion. Now, get up to your room and start

15

studying, and do something about those shitty grades."

Bryson stood toe to toe with his father as the tears leaked out over his lower eyelids. He looked away and shook his head but still didn't give any ground. "No," he said softly. "I'm leaving this living morgue. If I stay here, I'll kill myself. I can't let you bully and browbeat me over your guilty conscience anymore. And one more thing. Your breath stinks like you've been drinking."

Jack drew his arm back with an open palm as Juanita screamed, "No!" Even as he prepared to strike, Bryson didn't flinch. At the last moment, Jack stopped his backhand just before it made contact with his son's left cheek. They remained glaring at each other for some moments before Bryson turned and walked away. The front door slammed, and Jack remained in place, stunned at how quickly the confrontation escalated.

Juanita glowered at him and projected such venom it scorched his soul.

They don't understand. None of them understand what I'm going through. I just want to get away from all this.

He stumbled toward his den. In the background, Leighton cried softly. Just before he closed the door, Juanita spoke in a whisper, but it carried throughout the house.

"God, I hate you, Jack. I hate what you're doing to us."

Jack woke with a start and lifted his head from the desk. He was still in his den, slumped over with his hand wrapped around an empty glass. The fifth of scotch he drained was lying next to him on the floor.

The inside of his mouth felt like it was stuffed with cotton soaked in turpentine. He sat up and immediately felt a sharp pain in his lower back and a pounding in his head. His brain tried to decide which one hurt worse. The headache won out, but figuring he could kill two birds, Jack reached into his desk drawer and pulled out a bottle of Advil. Four, no six pills later, he struggled to his feet and walked slowly to the kitchen. That Juanita might be in another room was too much to hope for.

"You're going to be late." She raised her eyes momentarily and gave him a once over. "Did you sleep in your clothes?"

Jack didn't answer. He picked up a piece of cold toast and tried to eat a few bites, but the wad of cotton in his mouth resisted. For a moment, he wondered if he could keep it down. The acid in the orange juice made his stomach curl, so he was left with a glass of water from the dispenser on the refrigerator. He gulped and slurped as the liquid ran out the corners of his mouth and dripped off his chin.

"For God's sake, Jack. Have you lost every shred of dignity?"

He set the glass down but didn't face her. "Don't play dumb, Juanita. You know exactly what's wrong with me."

"Go ahead, tell me, Jack. Tell me why you've lost your self-respect. I'd love to hear it."

"Stop it. I don't want to talk about it. Please, not today."

She whirled around to face him directly. "You never want to talk about it. It's been a year and a half and you still won't talk about it. I know you blame me. Why... why don't we just get a divorce and be done with it?"

"You know why." He pointed a finger at her as his eyes flashed. "I'm trying to make the best of it until Leighton finishes high school."

"Five more years of this... I don't know if I can take it," she said.

Juanita looked at her phone, and her voice slipped back into its usual emotionless monotone. "There's an open house at two, so I probably won't be home for dinner." She was halfway up the stairs when he heard her say, "And clean up before you go to work. You smell like a bum."

"Love you too, dear," he called after her.

Somehow, Jack found the strength to brush his teeth, but the thought of showering was too taxing. For a brief instant, he considered telling his wife he lost his job, but that would only lead to another argument. With his head throbbing, he just wasn't in the mood.

Juanita stopped doing his laundry a couple weeks ago, so yesterday's attire would have to pull extra duty. He found a clean shirt hanging in the closet, so hopefully, his fellow passengers would be spared the worst of his odor. As he walked to the door, he almost forgot his briefcase, so he went back into the study to retrieve it. That's when he noticed something was out of order.

Did she go through my things? His eyes reached the credenza when he saw the photo in the gold frame.

That bitch.

He strode over with purpose and grabbed the picture while simultaneously opening one of the drawers. He shoved it inside like it was something radioactive and slammed the door shut. The veins on his neck bulged, and his jaw muscles worked as he stormed out of the den and into her home office.

"Can you get any lower? What is it you want? Do you want to torment me into a total breakdown?"

Juanita looked at him and frowned. "What are you talking about?"

"You know exactly what I'm talking about. The picture. The goddamn picture."

"Get a grip, Jack. I haven't been in your den for weeks. It stinks in there."

He pointed his finger directly at her. "Keep it up. Just keep it up." He turned and walked toward the front door.

Just before he opened it, he swore he heard Juanita say, "You're so fucking hopeless."

He stopped and went back into the kitchen. "What did you just say to me?"

"Nothing, Jack. Get going, or you'll be late for work."

Where else was there to go?

Jack stood on the platform waiting for the 9:15. The temperature was in the low twenties, and there was just enough wind to drive the cold through his trench coat, deep into his bones. Here was another day with nothing useful to do, but he just wasn't up to explaining why he lost his job to Juanita. Last time he checked, there was still enough money in savings to pay the utility bills for at least a month, maybe two. At some point, he would have to deal with all of it, but not today.

The 9:15 squealed as it turned the corner, and as was his routine, Jack inched up over the red line. He closed his eyes and listened to the sounds, converting the Doppler effect into distance in his mind. One foot raised, he kept moving it farther out until it was clear of the platform.

Just one more step. Take it, Jack. Take it.

The engine passed him as it braked, and the train squealed before coming to a full stop. Jack opened his eyes as the automatic doors released.

The 9:15 was only half-full, so he had an entire bench seat to himself, which was a rare pleasure. He stretched his legs out, and once they were underway, he cozied up against the window. Jack found the motion of a moving train very soothing, and still hung over from last night's bout of drinking, he soon dozed off. Somewhere between Mount Prospect and Des Plaines, he felt a strong poke in the ribs. A second, harder strike caused him to sit up.

Through bleary eyes, he looked over at a man who had taken the seat next to him. Most likely, he was one of the drifters who traveled on the trains all day. His smell was worse than Jack's own, some combination of body odor and filthy clothes. As his eyes gained focus, Jack noticed the food crusted in the man's beard and a scar that started next to his left nostril and ran down through his upper lip.

A scar just like Chuck's…

"Excuse me," said Jack, "but there are a bunch of empty seats in this car. I'd like to stretch out and get some sleep."

"To forget?" The man asked in a low, gravelly voice.

"Forget? No, I'm just tired, that's all. Now, could you move?"

"Movin' ain't gonna do it. Runnin' ain't gonna do it. That's not the solution, but you already know that."

Jack looked at the man for a moment. He bore an uncanny resemblance to his older brother Chuck, who died ten years ago from drug addiction that led to a brain aneurysm. "Look, let's not cause a scene here. You want this seat? Fine, take it. Just let me out and I'll find a different one."

"Runnin' ain't gonna solve it. Gotta face it; face the music, brother."

Jack tried his best to stand up before pushing past the man's locked legs. By the time he reached the aisle, his body was so awkwardly contorted he almost fell face first to the floor. After regaining his balance, he repositioned and started walking to another car. A strong hand reached out and grasped his wrist.

21

"Ya gotta be there, Jack. Ya gotta listen to the old woman. Remember to be there on time and do the deal. The whole thing falls apart if you ain't there. None of them can get out of this hell until you show up and pay your debt."

"Let me go…" Jack turned around and pulled his arm, but the grip remained firm.

"Yer only gonna get one shot. Ya better hit the mark, buddy. Listen to your big brother. Don't be late. Whatever you do, don't be late."

Chuck?

"Whaaa?" Jack lurched forward in his seat as his brain tried to untangle the dream from reality. After some moments, he sat back and took several deep breaths.

God, Jack, are you losing it? I got to stop drinking. I swear, I gotta stop…

The door to the train car opened, and the conductor stepped in briefly. "Next stop, OTC. End of the line."

Jack looked down at his watch. He was asleep for nearly an hour.

Inside the Ogilvie Transit Center, he joined the group of aimless gawkers sitting on a bench in the middle of the main concourse. They all had the lost look that came with an unexpected absence of purpose. How many of them were hiding? Maybe they were afraid to tell a spouse they lost a job or tell a parent they dropped out of school. The big bench in the center of the Great Hall was a place to pass the time and think about what to do next.

It was almost eleven, and most of the people with goals in life would be heading out to an Uber to make their lunch appointments. For Jack, the decision on where to go next was an easy one, simply because there were no other alternatives. He walked to the 125 green line almost on autopilot. O'Malley's would already be serving lunch, and Jack had nothing but time and a growing thirst.

***

"Jackie boy!" Tommy looked up from the bar and waved as his regular walked in. "Great to see you, buddy."

Jack ambled over to his preferred bar stool. Legend had it—mostly perpetuated by Tommy—that John Belushi sat in that very seat almost every night when he was in Second City.

After he bellied up and settled in, Tommy walked over and put both hands on the bar and leaned in. "You got good news for me today, Jack? The company realized it made a mistake and begged you to come back, right?"

Jack waited until Tommy finished pouring him a double. He swirled the liquid in the glass before downing it in one long swallow. He motioned for more and chuckled sarcastically.

"Naw, I'm still fired. It's just... I can't tell the missus, Tommy. Things haven't been great since, well, you know... Telling her I lost my job... I just can't bring myself to do it."

For just a moment, the bartender's rigid guard dropped, and his expression softened in a way that conveyed sympathy. Just as quickly, he recovered from the lapse and donned the well-rehearsed look of concern that was almost like a uniform he wore as part of the job.

"Yeah, that's a tough one, Jackie boy. We have a lot of guys who come in here with the same problem. Lota heartache on Michigan Avenue. It's a place of dreams and nightmares. You'll take some time to get on your feet, but you'll bounce back." He looked up at the clock. The battle between Jack's thirst and Tommy's need to regulate his customer's consumption had begun.

As usual, Jack impatiently waited for a refill. The look Tommy gave him as he poured a single shot into the glass conveyed a message to slow down. Bartender and customer usually got along well except for one dust up, and that was right before Jack got fired. Tommy wouldn't serve, and Jack got mouthy. The threat to ban him from the bar permanently was enough to settle the issue.

Jack sipped at his second drink.

As the regulars rolled in, Jack found himself in a more sociable mood than usual. With drink in hand, he ambled over to the far end of the bar, occupied every Friday by a few retired sanitation union workers. Each day, they frequented a different bar in the neighborhood, drinking away their pension money and mostly waiting to die.

"Hey, Jack, take a seat, buddy. We was just talkin' about doz damn Bears. Glad the season's over. Dem bums disgrace the uniform." Timmy Shaunogan was the leader of the group and also the loudest.

"They need a quarterback," said Earl while sitting at the bar nursing a jack and coke.

"They always need a quarterback," said Jerlo Griffin, the man who once had the highest seniority in the sanitation department. Griffin was also the one with the largest pension, so he always ended up buying more than his fair share of the drinks. Those who benefited from his generosity always laughed at his jokes. "Those assholes in the front office could screw up a wet dream. Well, at least there's always baseball." His companions murmured, chuckled and shook their heads while toasting each other.

"So, Jack, we don't talk much anymore. You have any luck on the job front?" They all knew the answer but still enjoyed baiting him.

Jack took a bigger swallow of his scotch. "Naw, it's tough out there. HVAC is a small industry, and all the competitors I kicked the crap out of hate my guts. I can't go back to a counter job. There's no fucking way…"

"Yeah, I understand," said Julio Grossman, a short bald guy two seats over. "That type of shit that happened to you will fuckin' ruin your life. You'll probably never get over it."

Instantly, the conversation died. The others looked at Julio with various degrees of incredulity. By now, everyone knew, but Tommy made sure no one brought it up. Overhearing the remark, he was quick to refill Jack's glass with an extra shot on the house. Tommy glared at Julio in a way that could have melted iron.

Jack got up from the seat and mumbled, "Just forget it." As he made his way back over to his regular stool, the door opened. The old woman walked in wearing the same coat and scarves from the day before.

Chapter Three

On stiff legs, the hag hobbled over to the table she occupied yesterday. Slowly, she unwrapped the scarf that shrouded her face and rubbed her hands to shake off the cold. Tommy eyed her suspiciously, but he came around the bar with his pad and pencil and took her order.

Without turning away from the new 4k smart TV Tommy installed over the bar a few months ago, Jack kept watching her out of the corner of his eye. Some old world series replay was showing on ESPN, and he found the game mildly interesting because he had no idea how it was going to turn out. Bottom of the 11th inning, bases loaded, and someone named Edgar Renteria was at the plate. The count was 0-1, and the pitcher was in the stretch. Just as he released the ball, Jack felt a hand on his shoulder. He flinched, and when he turned, the disheveled woman stood close.

"We need to talk," she said in a low voice.

Jack looked at her, and everything else tuned out. He didn't hear the normal bar chatter or the roar of the crowd as Renteria's single drove in the winning run.

"No, I'd prefer you leave me alone," he said. "Yesterday, you made me very uncomfortable."

She poked a finger in his chest as her expression hardened. "Listen to me. We need to talk. You'll be sorry if we don't." She motioned over to her table. "Go."

Warily, Jack rose from his bar stool and followed her, mindful that both of them were under Tommy's watchful eye.

"Did you listen to what I said?" she asked as they sat down.

Jack raised his glass and savored his drink. He didn't want to push it, so he glanced at the clock and mentally calculated that this one would have to last another fifteen minutes before Tommy would provide a refill. "I heard you, but you made no sense. What do you mean, 'pay my debt'?"

She gave him a once over. "Looks like it's the same jacket as yesterday... You sleep in it?"

"None of your damn business," he snapped and took a much larger swallow than his measured allotment allowed.

"I bet you're not sleeping too well these days, are you, pissant?" She reached into her purse and pulled out a smoke.

"You can't smoke in here..." She ignored him and lit up. The appearance of the flame and smell of the burning tobacco attracted everyone's attention, including Tommy. Yet, no one said a word, and the bartender went back to the business of shining glasses and talking to customers.

"Look, pissant, I know where you're at. You're all in it together. Everyone has to do their part or none of it works. I know you're going to take it; I could see that coward's look in your eyes the first time I saw you. You're too weak to face up. That's why you've got to be there and pay your debt." She took a long drag on her cigarette. Jack couldn't tell if she was tearing up or if she suffered from an old-age-related medical issue. As she raised the glass to her lips, he noticed her hands shaking badly.

"What the fuck are you talking about?" he asked.

She shook her head. "You'll find out soon enough. What you need to know is on the paper I'll give you."

He looked over and decided in that moment she was crazy. Whether it was alcohol, drugs, Alzheimer's or just good old mental illness, there was no point in continuing to subject himself to this smelly, old bag lady. He reached for his overcoat, which was slung lazily over the chair next to him, but her bony hand snaked out and grabbed his arm.

"No! You don't leave until you understand. When the time comes, I hope to hell you remember." She rose from the table, picked up the scarf and wrapped it around her face. "You better keep that paper I give you, pissant. And for God's sake, don't be late."

"Wait a minute," he said as she scurried toward the door. "What paper? Who *are* you? What's your name?" She sneered and flipped him off as she left the building. The frigid blast of air that rushed in was especially cold, and Jack shivered either from the weather or a growing sense of fear.

He picked up his coat and walked back to the bar. For several minutes, he tried to figure out what just happened. Shaking his head and writing off the old woman's ravings to some sort of psychosis, he held up his glass and shook the ice cubes. Tommy came by and poured a refill. For several minutes, Jack sipped at his drink and tried to forget her. The '98 Stanley Cup finals were on the TV now, but he couldn't focus. Her warning kept repeating over and over in his head.

You better keep that paper I give you, pissant. And for God's sake, don't be late.

***

Jack stood out on the platform, hunched over to shield himself from the frigid cold. To some extent, he was grateful for the weather since it always had a tendency to sober him up. He called it a day earlier than usual at O'Malley's. The drinks didn't set right after his latest encounter with the old woman, and anyway, it started snowing. Jack lived in Illinois long enough to recognize a blizzard in its early stages. If he didn't get out of Chicago soon, who knew how long the transportation systems would be gridlocked.

The train was crowded with suburban people looking to flee the city before the worst of the storm hit, but Jack was still able to get a window seat. Every part of the process would slow down as the heavy snow started falling. Passengers needed more time to board and disembark, so each stop would take twice as long. Even the train itself moved slower in this weather. By the time they reached Jefferson Park, almost all the seats were full. Jack just hoped they would get to Arlington before someone took the open seat next to him.

Almost as soon as the thought passed through his mind, the train stopped at Gladstone Park, and the doors swished open. After an unusually long delay, a large man with perspiration issues lumbered up the two steps into the car. He surveyed the remaining empty seats and began making his way to the back of the train.

No… No, not here... Please.

With a total lack of grace, the heavyset passenger flopped down next to him, breathing in rattling gasps and wiping sweat from his brow

I'm freezing my ass off and this guy is sweating.

They pulled away from Gladstone slowly, and the train moved at a crawl as the snow continued to accumulate. The blizzard unleashed its full fury, and there was nothing to see but a cascade of white. Jack pressed up against the side of the car and slouched down in his seat to become more comfortable. His eyelids sagged, and his mind drifted until he felt an elbow in his ribs.

"Excuse me," said his new traveling companion. Jack looked over as the man wiped away more sweat.

"Yes?"

"Could you move to another car? I like to occupy the entire seat whenever possible."

Jack's face reflected his disbelief at the audacity. "If there aren't any seats in this car, there's no reason to think any of the other cars will be less crowded. So, no, I'm not moving. Why don't *you* check out another car?"

Inside his open coat, Jack could see stains under the traveler's fleshy armpits spreading spontaneously while he wiped at his brow feverishly. "It's difficult for me to travel from car to car. You are slender and more nimble."

"I'm not moving," said Jack defiantly.

The fat man grunted and wiggled, spreading the flesh of his bottom so Jack was pushed farther towards the window. "I've tried to be polite, but now I'm no longer asking. You smell of alcohol. If you won't move, I'll call the conductor."

Jack stared at the heavyset man for a moment and shook his head. "You worthless fat piece of shit."

"Now you're fat shaming me, and your tone is threatening." He swiveled his head to look down the aisle before raising his arm. "Excuse me, Mr. Conductor. Excuse me."

Jack shook his head and looked out the window. "Un-fucking believable."

"This man. This *horrible* man called me a fat piece of… Well, I won't say the word. And his tone was threatening. I'm disabled, and I politely asked him to move. He also has been drinking. I feel uncomfortable and vulnerable sitting next to him."

The conductor nodded and turned toward Jack. "Sir, I'm going to have to ask you to move."

"Are you kidding me? Why can't *he* go sit in the handicapped car?"

"I couldn't walk all the way to the *accessible* car," the contentious passenger said. "This is as far as I could make it with my disability." He looked up at the conductor. "Don't Retra's rules for disabilities mandate that I be given priority seating?"

The conductor nodded. "Yes, in fact they do." Then, turning back to Jack, "Sir," he said in a voice that suddenly sounded authoritarian, "I'm once

31

again going to have to ask you to vacate your seat to this gentleman. There are hanging safety straps at the front of the car you can use."

"Are you *kidding* me?" said Jack, as his voice rose to meet the intensity of the conductor. "I have to stand the rest of the trip because of this guy's weight? Forget it. I'm not moving."

"Sir, do we have an incident here? Should I call the authorities and stop the train?"

Jack sat for a moment, staring at the conductor. "Unbelievable," he muttered as he rose to a three-quarters standing position and wiggled his way past the monstrous mass of humanity between him and the aisle. Once free, he gave the conductor a look of death and started walking to the front of the train.

"I told you he would back down." Jack heard the conductor talking behind him.

"Yeah, he's a pussy alright. Weak-kneed coward," answered the fat man in his high-pitched voice. Jack stopped in the middle of the aisle, and his back stiffened.

"Well, what would you expect from a guy who would let something like that happen to his family?"

"I know," replied the fat man. "And the yellow asshole didn't do a damn thing to stop it."

Jack turned and raised his arm, pointing a shaking finger at the pair. "You shut up. You both shut up."

"What? You gettin' upset, Jackie boy? Maybe you want to do something this time instead of sitting on your ass and letting it happen?" The conductor's face contorted into a scowl of disdain.

32

"Just be there on time and pay your debt, Jackie *boy*," said the fat man as he leaned over and stuck his fleshy face into the aisle. "We can't have you spoiling things for everyone, now can we?"

Jack turned and charged toward them, his hands clenched into fists, ready to punch both of them until they took it back. He cocked his arm and readied to throw the first blow.

"Whoa, whoa… Sir, sir… Are you okay? Hey are you okay?"

Jack sat up straight like he had been hit with a cattle prod. "What? Whaaa…" He looked around to gain his bearings. "I—I'm sorry. I…"

"Just take it easy," said the hefty traveler beside him. The man smiled, which shifted the fat in his face to his cheeks and neck. "You were having one heck of a nightmare there. You seemed to be in some distress. Punching the air and such. I hope you don't mind that I woke you."

"No, no," said Jack. "I appreciate it. Sometimes I have these dreams…"

The thickset man waved him off. "No need to explain. I just wanted to make sure you were alright."

Hearing the commotion, the conductor approached from the other end of the car. "Everything good here?" he asked with a look that expressed concern, perhaps about Jack, but probably more about a potential disruption on his shift.

Jack nodded. "I'm fine. Sorry for the ruckus."

"No problem at all, sir." With a tip of the cap, the conductor moved on and walked through the connecting door to the next car.

33

Unsettled, Jack sat back in his seat and pushed up against the window as far as he could, but that only gave the plus-sized man more room to spread out, and he instantly occupied the vacant inch of separation.

"My name is Tucker Lutz, but everyone calls me, Tuck," he said while extending a large, soft paw. Jack reached over awkwardly and shook it. The man grasped his hand and squeezed an uncomfortably long time. His eyebrows arched in an odd way before he let go. Jack did his best to hide his revulsion as a thick layer of sweat transferred between the two men. As inconspicuously as possible, he wiped his hand on his trench coat.

"I'm Jack," he replied. "Jack Clausen."

"Nice to meet you, Jack Clausen... You fleeing the city early like everyone else, huh? Looks like we're going to get hit with a cyclone bomb."

Jack smiled. "Yeah, every weather event has to be a catastrophe now, right?"

Tuck laughed. "Bad news sells."

"Ain't that the truth."

They rode in silence to the next stop. The *thumpity thump* of the tracks was especially loud as they slowed and approached the station at Norwood Park.

"I'm Park Ridge," said Lutz. "I bet you're Arlington Heights."

Jack's eyes widened a bit. "Yeah, as a matter of fact, that is where I'm getting off. You must have a bit of psychic in you."

"Actually, a little more than a bit. I'm a clairvoyant... A professional clairvoyant."

34

"Wow," Jack turned and regarded Lutz directly. "That's wild. You get paid to talk to dead people?"

Lutz laughed. "No, you're thinking of a medium. A clairvoyant sees into the future."

"I see. So, you tell people what's going to happen to them?"

"Not people so much as companies," said Lutz. "Giving a CEO of a major corporation a glimpse into the future can provide a huge edge. I get paid a fair amount of money to give them guidance."

"That's actually quite fascinating," said Jack as the conductor called out, *Edison Park*. "Can you read anyone's future?"

"No, it doesn't always work, which is a drag because I lose a lot of money. But I won't fudge. If I don't get a vibe, I tell them."

"How can you tell if you 'get a vibe'?" asked Jack.

"It has to do with the earth's harmonic. Sometimes, there's a deviation."

"What? C'mon, a radio frequency?"

"More like a musical note. And yes, Jack, it's for real." Lutz tried his best to shift his body around, but there wasn't enough space. "It's called the Schumann frequency, and it has resonated at 7.83 Hz for thousands of years and affects everything: plants, animals, rocks and people. The resonance has been constant for as long as we could measure it. At least until recently."

"What's happened to it?" Jack suddenly found himself more than mildly interested.

"It's started to fluctuate. It's risen to as high as thirty-Hertz and as low as three-Hertz. Somehow, I can sense these changes, especially in people. If someone is resonating lower than 7.83, I can feel it, and that's when I might get a glimpse into their future."

Next stop, Park Ridge

Lutz looked up the aisle at the conductor and began the arduous process of getting out of his seat. He grabbed the support pole, and with an effort that was painful to watch, hoisted himself to his feet. With difficulty, he reached into his shirt pocket and took out a business card.

"Here, Jack, take this. You're resonating at a very low frequency. In fact, it's so low, I've only experienced it a few times before. It's—troubling." Lutz paused and seemed to struggle finding the right words. "Look, if something unusual happens, and you want to talk, call me at this number, okay?"

Jack reached up and took the card. "What is this? I don't understand…"

"I'm not really sure." Lutz looked over his shoulder as the doors opened. "Hey, I have to go. But as I said, if you need to talk, call me."

The rotund man waddled down the aisle, and with great effort, conquered the steps that took him down to the platform. As the train pulled out from the Park Ridge station, they locked eyes a last time, and Jack was certain he saw fear in the face of his traveling companion.

***

Friday nights were always difficult because it meant he would have to spend the next two days with Juanita and the kids. As awkward as their lives had become, there was no way he could leave the house and travel downtown without raising suspicion. His weekend routine devolved into intense drinking and isolation in his den. On the occasional Saturday night, he might talk Ray Cohen into picking him up and driving over to Chauncey's Tavern in Mount Prospect under the guise of playing cards at a friend's house.

Recently, Cohen was less and less available, and although Jack called him a dozen times when he got home, Cohen didn't return one of the phone calls.

So, he was left here with Juanita in a blizzard.

Great.

Well into his third scotch, Jack heard his wife's footsteps approaching. *Thump, thump, thump* in a distinctive pattern he had become familiar with over the past year and a half. These days, she always walked with purpose, like she was late for an appointment.

She entered the room holding up several sheets of paper. "Where are our savings, Jack? Where the *fuck* are our savings?"

He gulped at the scotch and slammed the glass down. The proverbial jig was up. "You suddenly have an interest in our savings and investment accounts? When everything was good, you could give a shit about our finances. As long as you got a new Lexus SUV every other year and your credit cards were never turned down, life was good."

Her eyes smoldered as she stared at him. "Where did the money go, Jack?" She pulled an envelope out of the stack and flung it on his desk.

"We're four months behind on our mortgage payments? They're threatening to foreclose."

The ominous looking envelope sat on his desk. He backed away from it like it was toxic waste. "Yeah, so I fell a couple months behind on the mortgage, so what? I'll work something out with the bank. It's not like we're being evicted."

Juanita wiped at her eyes and put her hand up to her forehead. "I don't believe this. When were you going to tell me we're broke?"

With his eyebrows raised, Jack poured himself another scotch. By now, the effects of the first two drinks revived the buzz he started at O'Malley's, so his speech was slightly slurred. "So, you've been spying on me? Wonderful. What else did you find out?"

"Isn't it enough that I found out we're losing everything, Jack? I also know you've been leaving the house every day and ending up at a bar downtown." She collapsed into the chair across from his desk. "I called Walt today. You lost your job. Were you even going to tell me, Jack? How could you do that to us?" Her eyes welled up.

"Don't start with the tears, Juanita, and don't give me the martyr act. I see those anti-depressants you pop like candy mints. You've been as cold as a well digger's ass since..."

"Since when, Jack? Since when?" She slumped farther down in the chair. Her sallow skin looked more pale than usual, and in that moment, Jack realized she had aged ten years in less than two.

"Since *it* happened."

"What happened, Jack? ...Say her name."

Jack sat silently and lifted his glass. With the quickness of a pouncing cheetah, Juanita rose and leaned over the desk, slapping the glass out of his hand and sending the liquid splashing in all directions. "RosaMarie, Jack. Your daughter's name was RosaMarie."

Chapter Four

The mere mention of her name always sent Jack into a kind of dark dysphoria. His skin grew damp and clammy. He stood up and walked over to the bar, and with shaking hands, he reached for a fresh glass.

"I know her name," he said softly.

"Then why won't you ever say it? It's been over a year and a half, Jack. I—I can't live like this anymore. None of us can live like this."

"You sent her outside…"

Juanita's eyes seemed to sink deeper into their sockets. She shook her head and looked away. "I know you blame me. I do. But you said you were just going into the garage. You were supposed to be right outside."

"Why didn't you check? You could have walked outside the goddamned door and checked."

She held up her hand. "You know what? I'm not doing this anymore, Jack. I'm just not doing *any* of this anymore." She turned on her heel as he opened his mouth to speak, but she was already going up the stairs before the words filtered through his alcohol-saturated brain.

Snapping on the TV, he tried to find something to help pass the time as the booze worked through his system and further numbed him. Out of the corner of his eye, he saw movement from the kitchen. It was Leighton. The kid was standing at the far end of the counter staring at him. Jack considered getting up and shutting the door, but the effort was too much.

"You got a problem, boy?" he yelled out.

Leighton continued staring as he backed up slowly. "No, Dad. I was just looking to see what you were doing."

"Quit staring at me, and get the hell out of here... Little creep." Hearing the words and the tone that accompanied them, Leighton sprinted out of the kitchen. Some pitter-patter up the stairs and slamming of the door.

He got the damn message.

A half hour and two scotches later, Jack's head rested on the desk as he drifted back and forth between a drunken stupor and blacking out.

"Jack!"

Startled, he sat up so suddenly he hit his arm on the edge of the desk. "Owww! Shit, Juanita, what is it?" He hadn't noticed she was standing in the doorway with two suitcases.

"I'm leaving, Jack. It's reached the point where I can't take it anymore. You're hurting the children and ruining all of our lives. I won't stand for it."

"Hurting the children? How the hell am *I* hurting the children? That's ripe coming from you, Juanita. How much more can you hurt a child than what you did to..."

"Can't even say her name, can you?" At that moment, Leighton streaked past his mother to the door.

41

"When are you coming ba… Hey, Leighton, get over here!" Jack rose from the desk too quickly, and the resulting rush sent him spinning until he crashed down on the wood floor, hitting his head smartly. He reached up and touched the point of impact. When he looked at his hand, he saw it was covered in blood.

"Goddamn it. Juanita, get me a bandage."

"Get your own bandage." She looked at him with loathing.

"Leighton, I said get back here." Jack got unsteadily to his feet and walked over to the desk. He rifled through the drawers until he found a cloth for cleaning his reading glasses. He dabbed at the blood on his forehead. "This hurts like a son of a bitch."

"Before I go, there's something I need to tell you, although I doubt you'll care."

"What, Juanita? I'm bleeding for God's sake. What can be so goddamn important?"

"I think… No, I'm pretty sure Bryson is doing drugs. I don't mean just marijuana. I think he's doing crystal meth or something even worse."

Jack dropped the cloth on the desk and looked at her. "What? Why would you say that? Bryson's a good kid."

"No, Jack, he *was* a good kid. Have you seen the type of people he's hanging around with lately? His whole circle of friends has changed. You know his grades have gone to hell, but did you ever wonder why? And yesterday, I found this." She reached into her pocket and pulled out a small, dirty pipe covered in thick yellow tar and burn marks. "He's smoking something. It's bad, Jack. I tried to talk to him about it, but he started yelling at me, and I thought he was about to get violent.

"Here, let me look at that." Jack grabbed the pipe out of her hand and inspected it. He put it up to his nose and took a whiff. "I'm no expert, but you're right, it's a drug pipe." He sniffed again. "Not marijuana, that's for sure."

Juanita snatched the pipe away. "Don't you get it? Bryson's in trouble. We're all in trouble. We need help."

Jack went back and flopped down in his chair. "More therapy, Juanita? More damn therapy? Talking about our dirty laundry to people who give you their fake sympathy and send a big bill? I'm done with that." His speech was thick, and certain consonants were badly slurred. "When will you be back?"

"I don't know, but I'm taking the kids with me, Jack. Don't bother to call or try to track me down. I'll figure out how to get Bryson the help he needs without you."

"Juanita, there's a fucking blizzard outside. You can't take Leighton out in this. I won't have it... Come back here right now."

He heard her heels clacking as she moved across the wood floor.

"Bitch!"

Jack poured himself another drink as the front door closed with a slam. For a moment, reality pushed through the fog, and he got up to go after her. Their marriage was crumbling, maybe already beyond repair. This might be his last chance to salvage it. He made it as far as the living room before thoughts of RosaMarie flooded into his mind. The images were as fresh as the day it happened. He slumped against the wall with the original Chagall and slid down to the floor, moaning as he tried to get the memory of her dead body out of his mind.

***

Jack felt something pleasant happening between his legs. Then there was a gentle tugging on his eyelids. He tried to open his eyes, but a paste-like crust had glued the upper and lower lids together. Using his fingers, he pulled on the thin membrane until the bond broke, and his eyelids finally parted. At first, his vision was blurry, and his eyes were dry and irritated. A full moon on a clear night illuminated the landscape, and eventually, everything came into focus in shadows and shades of gray that bordered on black.

Somehow, he had managed to crawl into bed and remove his clothing. In fact, he was completely naked. Lying on his back, his legs were bent at the knees and hung over the edge of the bed. Something red and sticky was smeared across his stomach.

Paint? Blood?

Jack tried to fight through the haze of a particularly heavy night of drinking, even for him. He vaguely remembered calling Juanita several times, but he couldn't remember what she said or if she even answered. A soft mewing sound came from somewhere near the foot of the bed.

He jerked reflexively as two hands caressed his legs. "What the..." Looking down, he saw her slithering up from the floor until her head was above the footboard. Long, gray hair hung down over her face, and she reached up and grabbed his flaccid member and slowly stroked it. Numbed and seemingly paralyzed, Jack remained in a kind of catatonic fog as he desperately tried to process the situation.

Mumbling "No," several times, he found himself torn between wanting to pull away and letting her continue. He hadn't had sex since RosaMarie died, but even so, a menacing feeling grew in the pit of his stomach. Propping himself up on an elbow, he looked down at her. The skin on her body looked like crepe paper. Fat deposits jiggled under her arms, and her head jerked up and down as she worked.

"Hey," he said groggily. "I don't think this is such a good idea." She quickened her pace, took him deeper and used her hand. Jack lay back in the bed for a moment and covered his eyes with his forearm before sitting back up. "No, don't... I—I don't think." He could feel the pressure rising in his loins as she moaned and sped up the pace.

There was no turning back as he reached the point of no return. Jack cried out and released, but she did not back off. In that moment, darkness enveloped him as a cloud covered the moon, and the room plunged into an inky blackness. She pulled away as he finished, and in the same instant, he felt a sharp pin prick on the outside of his lower left calf, somewhere in intensity between a bee sting and dog bite. Soon after, he felt another on the opposite leg.

The bitch is biting me

After two more punctures on his hip and outer thigh, he knew the woman was not alone. Even before the thought could register, several more savage bites followed, and he howled and flailed his arms at the invisible aggressors.

Jack recoiled in disgust as his hand made contact with what felt like a child's bald head but slick and sticky as though it was covered in oil. At that moment, the cloud moved past the moon, and in the ominous gray light, he saw at least a half dozen small, semi-human beasts chewing and sucking on his flesh.

No more than three feet tall, their bodies were thick and squat with wide eyes set into oval faces. Short arms connected to narrow shoulders on one end and oversized hands with fat digits on the other. They were indeed bald, but the scalp skin appeared weathered and leathery.

Aware that he was watching, they stopped chewing and looked at him as one. Grins simultaneously spread across their faces, which revealed rows of pointed miniature teeth that almost looked machine filed. On first glance, they appeared identical, and as he looked closer, Jack was unable to distinguish one from another.

From below the end of the bed, the woman stood up, a sickly smile spread across her face as ejaculate leaked from the corners of her mouth. Jack gasped as he looked into the eyes of the same old woman he encountered at Tommy's bar. She raised her skeletal hand and extended a forefinger. Her eyes flashed as she spoke.

"You must be on time, pissant. Pay your debt and be on time…"

She twisted her hand around and used the same forefinger to beckon him forward, and against his will, Jack rose from the bed. Somehow fully clothed, he followed behind as she disappeared into a swirling cloud of gaseous mists. His mind screamed, *stop*, but he couldn't summon the willpower. The smell was fetid and rotten, and it seemed like he continued walking for an eternity, although his sense of passing time was distorted and unreliable.

Finally, his vision cleared, and he found himself standing on an unfamiliar urban neighborhood street. He assumed he was still in Chicago because he caught a whiff of lake air coaxed out from the stew of old buildings and rotting garbage. He could only see a few houses clustered together on a deserted street of mostly empty lots. Wherever he was, Jack sensed he was unsafe.

Up ahead, he found the old woman and quickened his pace so he wouldn't lose sight of her. She stopped in front of a drab, white house with peeling paint and rotted wood. Tentacles of something that looked like black mold ran up the side of the building to the roofline. Turning back, she again motioned for him to follow. They started up the broken and cracked walkway, climbing the stairs to the porch before going inside.

Something about this place was oddly familiar, although Jack couldn't quite remember why. His attention was drawn by movement in the kitchen, and as his eyes shifted, he saw a woman sitting in a corner up against several filthy broken cabinets. Her breast was exposed, and a baby's lips were attached to her nipple, sucking vigorously. She

47

pulled the child closer as she saw Jack in the hallway. The baby must have sensed someone was in the room because it stopped feeding.

Except it wasn't a human baby. Its body was streaked with thick, red veins, and its ears were grossly misshapen and much too large for its head. As Jack continued to stare, the child turned in his direction and hissed. The beast's eyes flashed an iridescent green, and it bared a set of jagged, uneven fangs.

The old woman moved toward the first bedroom, and Jack hurried to catch up. As they passed the threshold, he saw a man chained to a bed with a hood over his head. As the whip cracked viciously across his back, he shuddered with pleasure brought on by the pain as blood splattered across the walls. The dominatrix laughed and raised her hand high, readying the riding crop yet again.

The second bedroom carried an odor so revolting, Jack choked on his own rising bile. A body lie propped up on the bed, eyes wide open, staring straight out the door. Its skin was shriveled, and the tone was a blueish black. Jack was certain he was looking at a decaying corpse until its eyes blinked, and its face contorted into a mask of misery.

Finally, they reached the living room, and the hag moved away and sat on an old stained and worn green couch set against a sidewall. At the back of the room, seven small creatures, who looked exactly like those in the pack that attacked him, stood shoulder to shoulder. They were smiling uniformly, but it was clear their expressions were forced and unnatural.

"Who are you?" he asked. "Why did you bring me here?"

"Choice, Jack. Make choice. Soon," said the one in the middle of the group. His speech was clipped, and his pronunciation of "Jack" sounded more like "Jick."

"What choice? What are you talking about?"

"Choice, What choice Jack want? Very big."

"I don't understand. What do you mean? How did I get here?"

The old woman tried to clear her throat, but the phlegm was too deep and impacted. "It was your fault, pissant," she croaked. "Both times; your fault. You caused it all, so you have to make it right. You must be on time. Be-on-time."

She repeated the phrase, and soon the small creatures joined in, and it became a chant. "Be-on-time... Be-on-time..."

"What is this?" Jack said as he backed out of the living room, past the two bedrooms. "Leave me alone. Leave me the fuck alone!" He reached the kitchen just in time to watch the child-beast open its mouth and bite down hard on the woman's breast, tearing flesh until it separated from her body, hanging ragged and bloody in the child's mouth.

The woman screamed, and Jack shuddered in disgust and fear as he pushed the front door open. The grayness outside swallowed him up and sucked the air from his lungs. Suffocating and unable to breathe, his vision blurred as consciousness slipped away.

He cried out again and again. "Help me! Help me! For God's sake, please, somebody help me."

He lashed out and slammed his fist into something solid, which triggered his pain centers. Slowly, his awareness rose just above the level of unconsciousness. Curled up against the headboard in his bedroom with the sheet pulled up over his exposed body, Jack started to hyperventilate. Just before he passed out, his bladder emptied.

Chapter Five

The bedroom brightened with muted color as sunlight crept through the window and night slowly transitioned to day. Jack dozed in and out of consciousness, but the pounding in his head became more incessant and demanding until it could no longer be ignored.

Without opening his eyes, he rolled toward the edge of his bed and sat up. The throbbing intensified, and he rubbed his temples and smacked his lips to generate some saliva to clear away the disgusting taste in his mouth. He squinted down at the floor. Two 750 milliliter bottles of scotch lay side-by-side, one completely drained and one half empty. He wouldn't remember opening the second bottle.

"Some party," he muttered while reaching for the Acetaminophen on the nightstand. "I gotta quit the booze. These goddamn dreams." He pulled out four pills, thought better of it, and took out two more. Stumbling to the bathroom, he grabbed a glass on the sink, filled it, and swallowed them all in one gulp. He considered leaving without looking but gave in to the temptation. With a sense of dread, he turned around and gazed at his reflection in the mirror.

Facially, he was no worse off than expected. The lines and wrinkles were more pronounced, and the bags under his eyes looked angry and swollen. All in all, considering the quantity of alcohol he ingested, there wasn't much to be surprised about, but when his eyes wandered down to his torso, he gasped and backed up until he hit the towel rack.

Moving closer to the mirror, he slowly ran his hand across his chest until he reached the raised bumps that defined the outer edges of the first contusion. Small, and about the size of a half dollar, the circular wound showed deep bruising with a cascade of colors in different shades of blue, black, red and yellow. About sixteen inches down and to the left was another identical to the first, and a third occupied the space between his navel and waist.

Jack went into the bedroom and stood in front of the full-length mirror Juanita used for dressing. The abrasions covered his legs and groin area, and they were all virtually indistinguishable from each other. Significant bruising and blistering, but no skin was broken. In all, he counted seven of these wounds, all on his front side.

Fighting a rising panic, he walked out of the bathroom shaking his head and running his hands through his hair, a nervous habit he picked up in his teens. An ill-omened feeling welled up from the pit of his stomach, and a cold sweat broke out across his back.

"What the fuck is going on here?" he mumbled out of fear and frustration. The little men, or creatures, or whatever they were in his dream, couldn't have been real. No way. Yet, what else would explain these abrasions that looked like an anaconda had given him seven hickeys?

Slowly, Jack made his way to the foot of the bed, remembering where he first saw the old woman in his nightmare. He leaned over and peered at the floor just past where the bed's legs were positioned. A large damp stain had set in the sheet right near the outer edge of the mattress, and dried whitish tracks ran down the side of the footboard and pooled on the floor. With one knee bent, he inhaled and took in the unmistakable scent of his own semen.

The headache instantly abated in the same way a broken leg negates the pain of a pulled muscle. Stark naked, Jack ran from the bedroom and down the stairs, chortling and breathing heavily. When he reached the ground floor, he didn't know exactly what to do.

Call the police? And say what, exactly? How can I possibly explain this to anyone?

Juanita... I need to call Juanita.

He went into his den and picked up his cell phone. As he hit "recent calls," the list popped up, and he scrolled down: *Juanita, Juanita, Juanita... My God, I called her twenty-three times last night? I—I couldn't have... I don't remember talking to her at all. Voice mail.* Jack shuddered at the thought of the messages he might have left her in his alcohol-induced rage.

He went to the bar in his den and walked over to the liquor cabinet where he knew there would be several fresh bottles of scotch.

No, I can't... Not now.

53

His closet was empty, so he dressed in the same clothes for a third day. Jack scrubbed up the drying puddle on the floor and pulled the soiled sheets off the bed. The tasks took his mind off his headache and gave him time to rationalize what happened last night.

Okay, so he obviously pleasured himself in his alcoholic stupor. That wasn't a first, but why would he have included that busted down hag in the fantasy, and how could he explain the bruising all over his body? There had to be some explanation better than those small monsters biting him in his nightmare. Could his blackouts now include self-abuse?

As the effects of the alcohol and last night's strange delirium slowly faded, recent memories settled back in. One day closer to losing the house, he now faced the prospect of moving forward alone. Juanita was gone, probably for good, and she took the kids. He imagined she went to Algonquin, where her parents lived. The thought crossed his mind that he should drive out there and talk to her. In another place and time, Jack wouldn't have hesitated.

For an instant, an old feeling flickered inside him. A memory of the angst born from the all-consuming love he felt for his wife. In the early days of their romance, he remembered being borderline obsessive. No matter where he was or what he was doing, Jack couldn't stop thinking about Juanita. A missed phone call could mean she didn't love him anymore. A broken date meant she was probably with someone else.

RosaMarie.

That's all it ever took for any pleasant thought to be instantly purged from his mind. The moment passed, filled in by the hollowness that smothered any sense of feeling in the present. If he drove to Algonquin, he would have to see Paul, his father-in-law, and there was no adequate way to express how undesirable that confrontation would be. Juanita's dad never liked him from day one, and RosaMarie's passing turned an unspoken dislike into open contempt.

No, a far better solution was to kick back on the couch and binge on Netflix, his weekend habit for the past year and a half. He was tired, a permanent condition resulting from either depression, alcohol or both. The counselor, the last one Juanita dragged him to before he said he'd had enough, told him that if he didn't accept treatment, his spiral would ultimately result in his death and the destruction of his family.

He remembered telling her that he was beyond caring, and the session ended abruptly.

Around 11:45, he got up from an unsatisfying nap and sought out the refrigerator, looking for something to eat. A couple slices of bread surrounding some packaged ham and cheese would serve as breakfast and lunch. Jack got most of his calories from alcohol, but he still needed to satisfy the grinding in his stomach with real food every now and again. After a few bites and a couple antacids, he lay back down on the couch. The clock read 12:18, and he drifted off for a few minutes. Sleep was uneven and didn't refresh him at all, but at least the nightmares left him alone.

Less than fifteen minutes later, Jack woke up and looked at the clock. 12:32 meant the drinking lamp was officially lit, and he rose from the couch and wandered into the den. As a last vestige of self-respect, he talked himself into believing that if he didn't drink before noon on the weekends, he couldn't be a *real* alcoholic.

With shaking hands, he ignored the nausea and poured the first drink of the day, but some of the liquid spilled onto the bar. When he finally brought the glass up to his lips, he swallowed the scotch like a man in the Gobi desert dying of thirst. The spirits ran down his esophagus and warmed him inside. By the second drink, he stopped shaking, and the demons reluctantly receded into the background, at least for a while.

When you're a drunk, the actual art of drinking takes the place of any hobby, job, family or other endeavor that might be considered constructive. Jack found himself alone in a big house, which only intensified his depression. His family might be gone for good, but to be honest, he found their absence was a relief in some ways.

Now, he wouldn't have to hide his drinking from Juanita's watchful and judgmental eye. No kids running around bothering him to play baseball or go fishing. He had the peace and quiet a boozer craves. With his feet up on the couch while staring blankly at some Netflix original, the alcohol worked its magic, dulling the pain and numbing his emotions.

For the next six to eight hours, Jack would do the familiar slow burn. By now, he knew that once he started drinking, the day only ended when he passed out. That's passed out as in blacked out. If he maintained any sort of cognition after he drained the last drink, the recriminations would crush him. The alcohol might push the feelings aside, but the demons remained just off stage left, ready to pounce if they found an opening.

The morning guilt was overwhelming enough, but caught in the snare of the drink, the ugliness unleashed came from a place so dark and hopeless he struggled to find a reason to go on. That's when thoughts turned to the .38 caliber pistol he kept in the glovebox of his car. Sometimes, late at night, when hellhounds returned with a fresh set of memories, Jack would sit at the desk with the gun raised to his temple, simultaneously trying to talk himself in and out of pulling the trigger. So far, the nays had won the day, but the ayes were steadily gaining ground.

That's why it was better to drink into oblivion.

Somewhere between the fourth and fifth episode of "The 4400," his cell rang. He smiled smugly as he rifled through his pockets until he found the device. No doubt Juanita calling to apologize and smooth it all over. Juanita the accommodator; Juanita the compromiser. He loved and loathed her most prominent personality traits. When the screen lit up, he pulled back a bit.

Bryson?

Bryson never called his father unless he was in trouble or needed money. Whatever the bad news might be, Jack wanted no part of it right now. He rejected the call and poured himself another drink.

Call your mother, kid. She's got all the answers.

The pizza came at six, which ended up being a bit awkward because the delivery person was one of Bryson's old friends. Jack couldn't quite remember his name. Tommy or Timmy... Something like that. Tommy or Timmy shuffled back and forth uncomfortably as Jack fumbled through his pockets to find his wallet. The kid would certainly smell the stench of the booze and body odor, and combined with the appearance of the clothes Jack slept in for the last couple of days, he would know Bryson's dad was on a bender. For just a moment, Jack felt a twinge of guilt, but it passed quickly.

"Look, Mr. Clausen, just forget about it. Keep the pizza, and pay me next time."

"Right, right," Jack mumbled. "I'll make it up to you next time. Double tip."

"Yeah, sure, Mr. Clausen. Next time."

Hardly waiting for the kid to turn around, Jack slammed the door and staggered back to the living room, tossing the box on the cocktail table. He picked up his second slice when the phone rang again. This time it *had* to be Juanita come to grovel. He looked down at the screen.

Bryson again.

Something bad must have happened. Ever since the—accident, Bryson changed. He was the athletic kid in the family but never spoke about sports anymore. Jack couldn't remember the last time he saw Bryson's jock friends hanging around the house. They were replaced by a different group, and these new kids had a defiant, rebellious look in their eyes.

That crappy ringtone he chose just wouldn't stop. Jack dropped his pizza, picked up the phone, and hit the end call button.

I'm not in the mood to deal with any shit. Why won't they ever acknowledge what I'm going through? Why can't they see I just want to be left alone.

With drooping eyes and an empty glass, Jack turned over with his face against the back of the sofa and his legs bent at the knees. The bottle of Laraby's single malt sat on the floor about three quarters empty as the TV droned on in the background. The clock read 9:30 pm, the usual time Jack typically passed out every night. By experience, he knew that ingesting more than half a bottle of scotch without a pause overloaded his liver, and his body would have trouble metabolizing the poison. Yet, that was the minimum quantity he needed to send the demons into temporary retreat.

While he snored, Jack was aware he entered a dreamlike state. Most nights, this was a bad sign because it meant he hadn't fully blacked out. Tonight, in the grip of semi-consciousness, he knew "The Dream" was coming.

She stood looking at him with that sweet innocence he had come to love. Her wavy red hair flowed down to her shoulders, and the smile that melted his heart every single time flashed across her face.

"Daddy, do you have time to play with me?" she said with that combination of purity and hopefulness. If he didn't have the time, she might be disappointed but wouldn't let it show. RosaMarie was an old soul that way.

Even at five years old, she had empathy for others and put their needs ahead of her own. Her kindness,

59

understanding and insight were developed well beyond her years. For some reason, Juanita never saw it the way he did. She truly loved all her children equally, but for him, RosaMarie was his favorite. He hid it as best he could, and many times, he felt guilty because of it, but he couldn't deny that he loved his daughter in a way he could never love his sons.

Today, in his dream, he had the time to play. It was Saturday afternoon, and there was nowhere he would rather be than in RosaMarie's rich world of fantasy. Whether she chose an adventure with her Pooh Bear characters, a dress up day as prince and princess, a tea party or a story reading session, Jack knew he would have more fun than she did.

"Sure pumpkin. I promised, didn't I? A promise is a promise."

As he entered her room, he saw the small figurines positioned in a semicircle just outside a plastic castle he remembered assembling last Christmas. RosaMarie used the full set this time. Tigger, Pooh, Owl, Eeyore and a host of others from different shows and movies. He saw Donald Duck, Mickey, Minnie and a few he couldn't quite place.

Dropping to his knees next to her, he picked up Donald, shook his head, puffed out his cheeks and vibrated his larynx. "Whaaaaaa. I'm mad because everyone likes Mickey more than me!"

RosaMarie howled with laughter and picked up the Mickey figurine. "Don't be mad, Donald, I'll be your friend."

So it went for the next half hour as the story unfolded in a different way than the many other times they played the game. With every laugh and giggle, they created a memory that would last longer and have more meaning than any photo or video could ever provide.

The story was reaching a climax as the group, led by Pooh Bear, entered the castle to rescue the princess. Just as Tigger confronted evil Queen Grimhilde, a single bell on the grandfather clock chimed three times. He froze. The monster was coming… Soon.

"Jack. Jack, are you up there?" Juanita's voice. He didn't want to answer.

"Yes, I'm with RosaMarie." His words were wooden, and his lips, lungs, throat and jaws worked against his will.

"Jamal is here. Could you come down and talk to him?"

He didn't want to go, and he looked over at RosaMarie, who just shrugged. "It's okay, Daddy. Go talk to Mr. Egebe. I'll have to finish without you." She picked up Minnie Mouse and a turtle he didn't recognize and continued the imaginary discussion where he left off.

His feet and legs worked on their own, defying instructions from his brain. Each step down the stairs was excruciating, and as he approached the foyer, he saw Juanita casually chatting with his neighbor. They both looked up as he grew nearer.

"Hey, Jack," said Jamal while giving a wave. "Do you have a few minutes to show me that new mower?"

The muscles that created the bogus smile hurt, but against his will, he nodded. "Sure, follow me." He turned to Juanita. "We'll be in the garage. Just a couple minutes."

She smiled and waved them away, eager to get back to her spreadsheet.

He led the way out to the detached garage and workshop behind the house, and they huddled around his sleek, new self-propelled riding mower.

"What a beauty, Jack," said Jamal as he smiled and nodded. "A Craftsman, no less. That engine is a monster."

"Twenty horse and some special transmission. I think I could beat the BMW off the line for at least ten feet." A sense of pride washed over him, but something was wrong with all of this.

Fighting through a growing sense of panic, he patiently ran through every feature, from the zero-turn radius to the mulching kit, and he finished by inviting his neighbor to hop on and experience the seven-layer, reinforced leather seat.

"Next time you need to cut your grass, give me a call." He noticed Jamal dropped his head and shuffled awkwardly.

"Well, that's the thing, Jack. I hoped you might let me... You know, I was wondering if I could cut my grass with it today?"

"Today? I — I'm not sure, Jamal. I..."

"C'mon, Jack, be a pal. Let me give it a spin. My lawn's a mess, and the old push mower won't start."

Faced with the choice of letting a friend use his new mower or pissing off a neighbor, he crumbled. With a quick nod, he got into the captain's seat and motioned for Jamal to climb on the back. When they arrived at Egebe's house, he parked in the driveway, shut the mower down and started giving a quick operations lesson.

A few minutes later, as he watched the machine lurch forward with Jamal driving, his heart continued to sink, and a growing feeling of dread enveloped him.

Halfway through the cut, he saw Juanita running toward him in the kind of slow motion you see in the movies or on a sporting replay. Instantly, he knew what had happened. RosaMarie left the house looking for him while Juanita thought he was still outside in the garage.

The child took a wrong turn and got lost, and he would never see his daughter again.

Images of her mangled, damaged body flooded his brain like he was watching a gruesome picture slide show on a fast speed. The bruises, the blood, the broken bones, the cuts and the tattered clothing tore at his soul and ripped his heart to shreds all over again.

He gasped and groaned as the intense emotions caught in his throat and squeezed it in a vice grip. He stumbled forward, and yet, the grief and self-loathing wasn't intense enough this time. Something wasn't right here...

...Where is that damn phone ringing coming from?

Chapter Six

Wait a minute, is this still the nightmare? Or...

Jack lunged forward and nearly fell off the couch. He swiveled his head, expecting to see Juanita or the kids. The phone stopped ringing for about twenty seconds and then started again. A water bottle was on the coffee table, and he grabbed it and took a long swallow.

What the fuck? What time is it?

He swung his head around until he found the grandfather clock. 3:45 a.m.

This isn't going to be good.

Through bleary eyes, he picked up the phone and looked at the screen... Juanita.

"Yeah," he stammered.

"Jack." Her voice was a dull, flat whisper. "It's Bryson. I'm at Lutheran General."

"What? Wait... What's wrong? Tell me what happened?"

"He's overdosed, Jack. It's very bad. Two of the people that were with him dropped him off at the emergency room. It's—it's heroin."

In an instant, Jack sobered up as adrenaline coursed through his body. "... Heroin? Are you fucking kidding me? Not Bryson. No fucking way."

"Not now, Jack. You've got to get here. Are you... Can you drive?"

"I—yes, yes I can drive." Jack knew his blood alcohol would be well over the limit, but that wasn't a consideration. "I'll be there as soon as I can."

He grabbed the keys on the way out the door. The BMW's tires squealed as the car lurched forward, and Jack maneuvered the side streets without an error. Lutheran General was a twenty-minute drive, but he was determined to make it in fifteen.

He pounded on the steering wheel when he found himself caught behind a semi at the stoplight on Dempsey, but he swerved around the rig directly into oncoming traffic. Only the quick reflexes of the terrified driver in the other lane averted a head-on collision. With just a glance in the rear-view mirror, Jack sped on, praying that no one got a good look at his license plate.

The car shuddered as he hit the speed bump in the hospital's parking lot. His fine-tune motor reflexes were a mess, and he ended up parked diagonally across two spots. Gulping air and sprinting into the lobby, his dulled mind tried futilely to process the situation.

"My son is here. I need to see him."

The admitting nurse flashed a momentary look of distaste. "What's his name, and what's yours?"

Jack glanced down and imagined she was reacting to his appearance and smell. Right now, he didn't give a shit about her impression of him. His gaze hardened.

"Bryson Clausen, and I'm his father, Jack. I want to see him right now."

She glanced down at her sheet. "He's in ICU. Third floor. Get off the elevator, take the second right and go down to the end of the hall. There's a large button. Push it. They'll have to buzz you in."

"Which way is the elevator?" She raised her arms and pointed to her left without looking in that direction.

Jack sneered at her as she returned the sentiment. He turned and ran down the hall until he found the elevator. The wait was interminable, and he kept punching the button, but at last the doors slid open. There was something surreal about the painfully slow ride up to the third floor.

He stepped out of the cab and turned toward the double doors of the ICU just as they burst open. A gurney rolled out like a scene from a hospital-based TV show, except the patient had a sheet that covered their head and extended down the length of their body.

Wow, I come up here just as they wheel out a stiff... Poor soul.

The automatic doors remained open long enough for him to avoid buzzing in, so he walked up to the desk. The lights in the reception area were purposely darkened, which made the environment all the more foreboding. At the far end, he saw a technician or doctor in a white lab coat in front of a computer screen. As he walked up, he knew the white-smock saw him but remained glued to the monitor. His name badge read, *Scott Weeby*.

"Excuse me. I'm looking for my son. His name is Bryson Clausen."

Still no acknowledgment.

"Hello?"

The slender, balding man with spectacles hastily typed something into the computer before looking up. In the background, the soft hum of the servers and medical equipment played a somber tune.

"You didn't check in. Next time, make sure you wait at the door until you're checked in. There's a sign with explicit instructions."

Jack did his best to squelch his growing anger. "Yes, yes. My son, Bryson Clausen. What is his room number?"

"Three-thirteen... Over there." Scott Weeby pointed down one of the four hallways that branched off the main lobby. Jack nodded and walked away. In a crisis situation, odd and irrelevant memories are often imprinted on the minds of those most affected. From this day forward, he would remember the hollow sound of each footfall as it echoed down the empty corridor.

A dim light escaped through the curtains drawn across the sliding glass door of Bryson's room. When he arrived, Jack felt a knot in the pit of his stomach that tightened like the grip of a python. He struggled to breathe as he slid the door back and stepped inside.

His eyes immediately found the bed where Bryson lay on his back, completely motionless. The sight of his son's bloated face, bluish and grotesquely disfigured by the effects of the poison, tightened the grip of the snake around his chest to the point where breathing was nearly impossible. He couldn't pull himself away from staring at

Bryson's eyes, so swollen they were completely shut.

The tubes up his nose and down his throat twisted his mouth into a macabre, grotesque mask that made him appear like some gruesome gargoyle on the front of a gothic revival building. The rhythmic sounds of the ventilator sent a message that needed no words: Bryson was on life support.

Eventually, Jack's eyes moved to the far side of the room. In the low light, he could barely see the outline of Juanita sitting in the corner. Her shoulders slumped, and her long hair was uncombed. Occasionally, he heard her blow her nose into a tissue. She hadn't said a word to him since he arrived, so Jack thought it best to move to the other side of the room, where another chair was positioned near the bathroom.

For nearly forty-five minutes they sat silently, but the sound of the beeping heart monitor and the steady *whoosh* of the ventilator seemed so loud Jack was certain his eardrums would burst. He shifted uncomfortably in his seat and periodically looked over at her until he couldn't take it anymore. In a battle of the cold shoulder, Jack knew he was no match for Juanita. He always spoke first, and today was no different.

"What was it? What did he take?"

She slowly raised her head. When he met her gaze and saw the contempt in her eyes, Jack knew in that instant that any vestige of love that might have remained was gone forever. She would feel nothing for him but disdain and scorn from this day forward.

"Heroin. Heroin laced with fentanyl. When the paramedics arrived, his lips were blue, and he was foaming at the mouth. They hit him with three doses of naloxone, but he seized. By the time they got him into the ER, he was in a coma." The last words were nearly inaudible as she began to sob again.

"How could that be? We had all the drug talks. Bryson was the most anti-drug kid in his circle. I don't understand..."

When Juanita replied, her voice trembled with a quiet rage. "You don't *understand*, Jack? While you escaped by diving into a bottle of scotch, I've watched our children fall apart day by day. They wondered why you didn't love them anymore. Worse, they wondered why you had grown to hate them."

Jack looked over at her. "I don't hate my children. That's absurd."

"How much time have you spent with them since RosaMarie died, Jack? How many of Bryson's basketball games have you attended? How many of Leighton's baseball games? Did you know Leighton won a spelling bee at school and came in third at a district contest last month? Bryson has a girlfriend... Did you know any of that?"

He opened his mouth to speak but couldn't find the words. Instead, he slumped down lower in the chair just as the door opened. A tall, slender woman with olive skin and close-cropped black hair walked in. The stethoscope identified her as a doctor. She looked over at Juanita and nodded before turning to Jack and extending her hand.

"Mr. Clausen, I'm Doctor Sharma." Her handshake was firm and self-assured. She backed up, so she was able to address both parents.

"I want you to know we've done everything humanly possible to save Bryson, but the damage is severe. We've run electroencephalography and magnetoencephalography tests to accurately map Bryson's brain. He's suffered an extreme anoxic trauma, which occurs when the brain is deprived of oxygen for an extended period. Severe apoptosis set in, and I'm very sorry to say there is virtually no activity in his frontal lobes."

"I don't understand. What does that mean, exactly?" asked Jack.

The doctor sighed. "If we could have gotten to him sooner. Maybe..."

"What are you saying? Bryson's going to be alright, isn't he? People OD on drugs all the time, and they're just fine."

"This is different, Mr. Clausen. Bryson has very limited brain activity and nothing that would indicate he is capable of sentient thought."

Jack started to tremble as Juanita moaned in a loud, mournful, low voice.

"Well, save him for God's sake. You're a doctor. That's what you're supposed to do... Please, help my son." Jack began the sentence in anger, but it ended in a desperate plea.

"I wish I could, Mr. Clausen, but—but we have to make some very difficult decisions. Do we want to leave Bryson on life support, or do we want to take him off the ventilator?"

Jack sat slowly back down in the chair while maintaining eye contact with the doctor. "There must be other options. He... What if he wakes up?"

The doctor shook her head. "He won't. He will be non-responsive for the rest of his life. Without the ventilator, he would immediately go into cardiac arrest."

As the machines pumped, beeped, clicked and whirred, Jack fought against rising panic. Out of nowhere, Juanita screamed loudly. Instantly, his memory connected the sound to the exact moment she learned RosaMarie was dead.

Almost as though he was transported back in time, Jack stood in the living room looking at his wife as she wailed in a way that still chilled him to the bone every time he relived the memory. A guttural sound full of the unimaginable pain and sorrow reserved only for a mother who has lost a child. No woman should ever have to experience that type of pain even once. Juanita would experience it twice.

Jack looked over at her and then back to the doctor. "We need some time to talk this over. I don't think we can make this decision right now."

"Certainly, Mr. Clausen. It's unlikely Bryson's condition will change for the worse anytime soon. However, as much as I wish I could avoid this, I have to bring up the financial side of your son's care. I understand your insurance coverage ended on the 30th of last month. The bills for round-the-clock care in ICU are substantial, and if you choose to keep him on the ventilator indefinitely, long-term financial arrangements will have to be made.

If you would like, I'll arrange a conference with the financial department at the appropriate time."

Juanita raised her head and peered at the doctor through bleary eyes. "What do you mean our insurance ended on the 30th? My husband has health insurance through his employer." The doctor looked away. "Jack, you signed us up for the COBRA, right?"

"Not yet," said Jack in a whisper to no one in particular.

Doctor Sharma stood up and began walking to the door. "Look, you two have a lot to talk about." She walked over to Juanita and extended her hand, which held a business card. "Please, call me when you've made your decision. My cell phone number is on the back of the card."

She turned and nodded to Jack with pursed lips. "The consent forms are on the table near the door if you would like to read them, sign them or consult with your attorney. Again, I'm so awfully sorry."

Jack was staring at the floor when he heard the soft *click* of the sliding glass door as it shut. He was left with the crushing noise of the machines and the pungent smell of hospital disinfectants. The air inside the room grew thick as the tension mounted. Finally, he couldn't take it anymore.

"I need time to digest all of this. There isn't any reason to decide anything right now. I'll talk to you about it tomorrow."

"I don't want to talk to you tomorrow." Juanita's voice was flat and lifeless. "In fact, I don't want to talk to you ever again. Bryson's family and the people who love him will say goodbye, and he will be taken off the respirator." She shook her head and let out a soft sob. "You will sign the consent forms before you leave, but you will *not* come to this hospital tomorrow."

"Wait a minute." Jack's words were still slightly sloppy and slurred. "He's my son too. You have no right to push me out."

"I have every right," she hissed as she stood up. "You haven't been a father to Bryson since RosaMarie died. You made him and Leighton feel guilty and worthless as though it was their fault. And now I find out you lost your job almost a month ago? At least it explains why you came home drunk every day."

She reached into her jacket and pulled out a cell phone and thrust her arm out toward him. "Bryson's phone. I looked at the calls list, Jack. Three times he tried to call you last night. *Three fucking times*, but you never answered."

"I—I didn't have my phone on me. Didn't he try to call you?"

"No. Maybe he was too ashamed, or maybe he wanted to say something that was just for you, his father, but I guess we'll never know." She turned back to the door. "Say your goodbyes right now, but you better not set foot in this place again, and if you value your life, you'll get those papers filled out for that goddamn COBRA and pray they cover us."

"Juanita, I'm not right," he blurted out. "Something is wrong with me. I'm seeing things, and I'm having these bizarre dreams."

"Save it, Jack. If you think you're going to gain sympathy by feigning mental illness, you need to come up with a better plan. Face it, you're nothing but a goddamned drunk.

Alone and hollow, Jack was unaware how long he sat in silence looking at his son, broken and dying in a hospital bed. This was the lasting image of Bryson he would take with him forever. Perhaps not as murderous as the picture of RosaMarie's body seared like a brand into his mind, but almost as fatal.

Nurses came and went regularly. Most were polite, and one large Asian woman offered to get him water and some food as the first rays of the sun signaled a new day approaching. Jack was well outside of normal visiting hours, but those rules were stretched for people unfortunate enough to be in the ICU under such circumstances.

Unaware he had dozed, Jack was jarred by a gentle nudge and momentarily startled as he looked up to see the friendly nurse standing over him.

"Sir, can I get you a blanket or something? I brought you a bottled water and a muffin. It was all I could find at this hour."

"What time is it?" he asked.

"Sunday morning just past seven. Why don't you go home and try to get some rest?

Jack nodded, and she put her hand on his arm and squeezed before leaving the room. He walked over to Bryson. Only a few inches away, his swollen face was a sickly, pasty white, so different from his natural tan and golden complexion. Bryson seemed smaller, as though he shrunk in just a day. Jack reached over and ran his hand through his son's hair. He hadn't done that in years, and the curliness and coarseness triggered a memory of a day at the lake when Bryson was about ten. They had a great day together, and a hand that ruffled the young boy's hair elicited a huge grin filed away permanently in Jack's long-term memory.

He leaned down and kissed his son on the forehead. A teardrop splashed on Bryson's face and rolled down his cheek, almost as though it came from his own eye. Several more tears fell, and without warning, Jack found himself on his knees with his head buried in Bryson's chest, crying uncontrollably.

When there were no more tears, and the emotion was so raw it numbed him, Jack finally said softly, "Goodbye, my son. I love you," before walking over to the table where the consent forms were stacked in a neat pile. After scribbling his name and initialing twenty-four times, he turned toward the door, shuffling down the hallway to the elevator. Just before he got in, he reached for his cell phone. There were three messages from last night.

7:36: Ah, Dad, it's Bryson. Mom's with Leighton at a movie, and ah, it's getting kind of weird over here. I — I was hoping you might come and get me. Jeramiah picked me up, and I don't know where he went, so I don't have a ride.

8:15: Hey dad, I really need a ride. I'm getting worried. These guys are pushing me to do some stuff I don't want to do. I don't want to call mom about this... Call me, Dad, please? I want to get out of here.

8:55: Dad, I — I don't feel right. I just took some stuff, and I don't... Please call me. I need you to come and get me, Dad. I'm at this party in Elk Grove. I'm feeling funny and having a little trouble breathing. I'm... Dad, hurry.

Jack dropped the phone and crumpled to the floor in a heap. *I killed my son. My God, I killed my son.*

He had vague recollections of a nurse with a terrified look on her face leaning over him. A doctor came a few seconds later. The next thing he remembered was sitting in the hospital chapel talking to the doctor and a clergyman, but everything looked and sounded like it was under water. There was no telling how long he was with them, and he couldn't actually recall leaving, but somehow, he ended up in his car driving.

The trip home and the rest of the day would prove to be a blur, and when Jack finally regained some sense of consciousness, he was slumped over his desk with a glass of scotch in his hand. He looked at the clock, which read 9:23 a.m.

Bryson is dead. Except for the image of his son in the hospital on a ventilator, heavy drinking had wiped the balance of Sunday from his memory.

The sun was out even though dark clouds covered it completely. This was going to be another ugly winter day in Chicago. He got up and rubbed his eyes and stumbled into the downstairs bathroom. Splashing his face with water, he looked into the mirror.

The God-awful creature who stared back was a fright. His eyes were so red and bloodshot, he could have played the role of Satan himself. The long-term effects of the alcohol were startling. His pores had widened, and spidery red veins snaked up the sides of his nose. The lines around his eyes were deep and road mapped. His teeth were yellowed and buckling, and the black shadows around his lower gums exposed unattended decay.

Jack stepped back and looked away from his reflection. It took a moment for him to realize it was Monday morning. His son would be cremated today, and he wouldn't be there to mourn.

Why was he so intimidated by Juanita? Bryson was his son too, damn it, and he had every right to be there when his boy breathed his last breath. He should tell her that he wasn't going to listen to her, and he intended to be a full participant in the entire grieving process until Bryson's ashes were spread. That's what a real man would have done, even if it meant having a nasty conflict with his bitter wife and heartless father-in-law.

Yes, that's what a real man would have done... Instead, Jack walked into the bedroom and searched for the suit that had the lowest level of stench. If he hurried, he could make the 10:26 train to Ogilvie.

Chapter Seven

Jack arrived at Arlington with time to spare. The walk from the parking lot to the station usually took about five minutes, but today, it might be a little longer. His melancholy lifted, and he felt a sense of serenity, a state of mind he had almost forgotten. Several large maple trees lined Vail as he approached the building, and Jack stopped to admire them.

Even though they looked barren and naked in their dormancy, he appreciated what they endured to grow so tall. He glanced over at the end of the row and saw one of the trees was dead but hadn't been removed yet. The secret, he mused as he continued walking, wasn't the struggle itself, because every living thing experienced hardship, but rather, in the will to live. Perhaps the dead tree had enough of the constant battle against the elements over the years. Its DNA might have been as robust as its companions, but maybe its desire to continue living simply waned over time.

He walked through the station and exited trackside, encountering a few stragglers who were late for work and a couple teachers pulling field trip duty. Jack smiled politely as he made his way past all of them and continued to the far end of the platform. In the background, he could hear the train approaching, and he looked down at his watch. In about a minute, it would reach the leading edge where he stood, far removed from the rest of the passengers.

As the sound of the diesel engine grew louder, he closed his eyes. A quarter mile... 400 yards... 200 yards... The platform rumbled as the locomotive slowed.

With his eyes still closed, Jack instinctively knew when the engine was only a few yards away. He picked up his right foot and moved it forward. For a moment, he remained suspended in midair. Panic swept over him as his body fought against the conflicting instructions it received from his brain.

Falling.

That was the thought that registered as he started to lose his balance just as the train arrived. Like those who survive near-death experiences so often recount, time slowed, and Jack had a chance to review his entire life in the intervening milliseconds.

The images rushed by quickly: Growing up in Scottsdale; moving around the country as a military kid; his father in an alcoholic rage; college at Arizona State where he met and married Juanita and the birth of his three children all flashed and vaporized in a sea of white light.

The last few stills were filtered through the same dark lens that gave everything around him a gray tint. RosaMarie's tragic death lingered, conjuring up the toxic mix of sights, sounds and smells that recreated the essence of the tragedy. He was left with the disturbing vision of Bryson in the antiseptic hospital environment, brain dead and relying on machines to breathe...

"Please forgive me."

The gray hue faded to black, and Jack succumbed to the enticing allure of death, falling into the void. The intense heat of the engine singed his cheek, and the forged steel of the deflector kissed the heel of his shoe. Full impact was imminent.

The nightmare is almost over.

***

The hand that gripped his left arm was strong and unyielding. In a single motion, it jerked him back from the brink just as the Retra train rolled past. The unexpected intervention created a moment of confusion, and he stumbled backwards and fell onto the platform. The wind and noise from the train muted the reaction from the other passengers as they tried to figure out what just happened.

Jack looked around, stunned, trying to make sense of it. Out of the corner of his eye, he saw someone looking at him with curiosity. A small, squat man in a dark coat and fedora hat moved closer and smiled. His face was wide and angular, with broad ridges over his eyebrows, and his teeth were square at the gum line but pointed on the ends, giving the overall impression he might be carrying an extra chromosome. Jack recoiled as he stared into the face of one of the creatures he remembered from his nightmare.

Cowering and drawing in his arms in stunned confusion, Jack used his legs to inch backwards. "I remember you... You were in my dream, biting and sucking on my flesh... Was it you who pulled me back?"

The small man nodded. "Yes. Torto pull you back from train, don'cha know."

Jack grabbed his head with his hands and choked back a sob. "Why? Why would you do that? I was finally going to be free, and you ruined it... Why? And who the fuck *are* you, anyway?"

"Sorry," the smallish man shook his head. "Torto think Jack should live. Make him happy again."

"Trust me, you can't help me... Am I losing my mind? What is it you want?"

Torto's smile widened. "Daughter. Torto give back."

Jack looked up, and his gaze hardened. "Look, I don't have any idea who you are or what crap you're peddling, but it's not funny. How do you know about my daughter?"

"Talk somewhere. Jack and Torto talk. Torto maybe give Jack chance to fix and get daughter back."

"My daughter is *dead*. There is no bringing her ba..." Jack stopped mid-sentence. Something hijacked his mind and created pictures of RosaMarie, only it wasn't. She looked the same, but... older. Definitely older. The images weren't fuzzy or blurry like memories but more like portrait shots from a hi-def camera. In a matter of seconds, they stopped, and he was again staring at Torto.

"RosaMarie, soon seven now," he said. "Maybe be alive if Jack know Torto before."

Jack shivered against the cold. The wind picked up, and the sky grew ever darker. "Okay, where? Where do you want to go and talk?"

"Jack take Torto for ice cream. Torto like ice cream, don'cha know."

The thought of morning ice cream on a cold January day was incredibly unappealing, but Jack nodded and began walking toward his car with the strange, squat being waddling behind him. If he was to guess, the creature most likely was a man, but non-gender conforming probably fit better. When they reached his car, Torto had difficulty climbing up onto the running board, so Jack went to the passenger's side and awkwardly lifted him up and in.

They rode silently as Jack followed the GPS to the closest ice cream shop in Arlington Heights, which was closed, of course. Two more stops and a half hour later, he finally found "Terry's Delights," a place in Mount Prospect that served ice cream but really was only open for the coffee and doughnuts.

Torto moved quickly to the ice cream freezer and stuck his face directly on the glass. Jack grimaced as thick strings of drool leaked from the corners of the strange being's mouth. Torto groaned and made an odd purring noise as he stared at the ice cream.

The counterperson looked at Jack with an expression of curiosity and disgust as he reached over and handed him a latte. He walked slowly to the ice cream side as Torto started hopping from one foot to the other in anticipation.

"Can I help you?"

"Rock-y-Road. Torto have three scoops in cup, don'cha know."

The attendant hesitantly grabbed the scooper and started dishing the ice cream into the container.

"More," said Torto as the first scoop hit the bottom of the cup.

"More? What do you mean? You want four scoops?"

"No, big scoops. Torto get big scoops of ice cream."

Raising his eyebrows and sighing, the middle-aged man dug into the barrel while muttering. Two additional huge scoops later, he handed the cup to Torto. "That'll be eight thirty-five."

With his back turned to the counter, Torto walked over to the table where Jack was sitting. "Jack pay." Jack got up, rolled his eyes, and handed the server a ten-dollar bill.

Torto dug into the Rocky Road like he was inhaling an uncut gram of pure cocaine. With a fervor that resembled an addiction, he held the spoon in his fist and dug into the mound, cooing and clucking in a way that sounded almost orgasmic. Jack sipped at his coffee and watched in fascination as the merciless attack on the ice cream mound continued for several minutes. Torto gurgled and slurped, and when he finished, he scraped the remnants off the sides, tore the cup open and licked the surfaces clean. When there was nothing left, he groaned in a piteous way, and his shoulders slumped.

"Rock-y-Road Torto's favorite. All gone."

"I'm glad you enjoyed it," said Jack as he took another sip of his coffee. "Why don't you tell me why we're here? Why am I in an ice cream shop in the middle of winter with a character from my nightmare? And how did you put those pictures in my head? I have no time for fodder. You have no idea what I'm going through."

"Torto knows," he said with a shrug. "Daughter die, and now son die. Jack sad so he want to die too. Torto can fix."

"Yeah, fix my life, sure," said Jack as a single sarcastic chuckle escaped his lips. "I'm broken, and there is no fixing me. I just want to die. The guilt and pain are overwhelming."

"Torto fix."

"What are you, a drug peddler? Even self-medicating doesn't blot out the pain anymore."

Torto shook his head vigorously. "No, do over. Before girl die. If Jack not forget, he keep bad things away."

Jack leaned back and finished his coffee before standing up. "Okay, thanks for pulling me away from the train, I guess. It was nice talking to you, and I'm glad you enjoyed your ice cream, but I've got to be going."

Torto vigorously waved him off. "No, no, Torto tell truth… Here." He reached into his pocket, and when he extended his hand and opened it, Jack saw he was holding a rather large, yellow pill that appeared to glow with a kind of subtle fluorescence.

"Take pill. Wake up before girl die. If Jack not forget in time, he can save."

Jack reached out and took the pill, holding it in the palm of his hand. "So, you *are* a drug peddler, after all. I've never seen a pill that looks like this. What is it, PCP?"

"Take and see girl and son again. But then Jack owe Torto, don'cha know."

"Owe you? What are you even talking about?"

"Big, Jack owe. If not forget and save girl, Jack owe Torto. Must pay and be on time. Jack 'stand?"

"Sure. I take this pill, and my daughter and son come back from the dead in my acid trip. Then I owe you something. Yeah, I'll remember... Anyway, you need a ride somewhere?"

Torto shook his head. "No ride, but more ice cream, okay?"

Jack couldn't help but smile. He walked up to the counter and laid down another ten-dollar bill. "Give him ten bucks worth of ice cream," he said before heading out. Just as the chime on the door rang, he turned back to Torto.

"How did you know about my children, anyway? I never mentioned either one of them to you."

Torto smiled ear to ear, revealing those unusually straight, pointy white teeth. "Torto know Jack. Take pill, get girl back. Ros-a-mah-ree."

Jack stiffened, and a chill ran down his spine that raised goose flesh on his arms. "That's her name. Wait a minute; I'm confused..."

"Bry-son... Leigh-ton. Know wife Jua-ni-ta. Broken man. Broken fam-i-ly.

Jack inched farther out the door. "Okay, now you're freaking me out. Have you been stalking me?"

85

Torto shook his head vigorously. "No. Torto help fix. Take pill, Jack. Then pay debt, don'cha know."

"Yeah, sure. Whatever you say. You take care, pal, and I'll see you around."

Jack waved him off, turned, and walked away quickly. "Fuckin' nut," he mumbled under his breath.

Still mind numb and hopeless, he got into his car and started driving home. There was no point in taking the train downtown to Tommy's bar since he wouldn't get there until late in the afternoon when the rough evening crowd started filing in. He chuckled at the thought of caring about his safety when he came so close to committing suicide, but there were ways Jack didn't want to die, and getting beaten to death by an angry drunk was high on the list.

After stopping at the liquor store, he walked into the house and threw his keys on the table. He wondered if Bryson was cremated yet and checked his phone. No calls or messages. His son died, and they were burning his body, but Jack didn't even warrant the courtesy of a phone call or text. A surge of bitterness coursed through him, but he never considered the reason why no one bothered to contact him.

In his familiar spot behind his desk in the study, Jack poured the first drink of the day. His hands shook badly because the drinking lamp was an hour and a half late. He downed the scotch quickly and poured a refresher. Sipping slower this time, he noticed the silence. The grandfather clock in the corner ticked steadily, but there was nothing else.

No sound of three kids playing or a happy wife on the phone. Just the clock and the occasional squeak of the house settling.

Jack sat back in his chair and closed his eyes. He only had one decision left to make. His parents and brother were dead, and two of his children were gone. Juanita hated him, which meant Leighton was the only one left in the world who might shed a tear at his passing. A pang of sadness and guilt welled in the pit of his stomach when he thought about the poor kid. At thirteen, he would take it hard, but children are resilient, and Jack knew he would survive.

He may survive, but he'll never be right.

Back at the desk, he read through the life insurance policy he pulled from the filing cabinet. Juanita would receive a cool million when he died, even in the event of a suicide. It was the one bill he made sure was paid current. Juanita always said she thought the suicide clause was creepy, but Jack wanted it in there without knowing exactly why.

He only needed to decide how he was going to do it.

That damn curmudgeon.

He hadn't thought much about the strange little person since he left the ice cream shop, mostly because his mind wasn't really working properly anymore. Jack viewed his life from the same perspective as someone preparing to leave and move to another state or country. So far past this reality, he hardly recognized he was still in it.

To pass the time while liquoring up, he grabbed a photo album off the shelf. The tears flowed freely as he gazed at the pictures of the kids playing together, posing and laughing. Those were happy times. He flipped through to the end of the album. The last picture showed all of them at RosaMarie's fifth birthday, only two weeks before her death.

Jack closed the book and looked around. Forget waiting for the train the next day, he needed relief from this oppressive pain right now. A gunshot to the head came to his mind, but he quickly dismissed it. Since RosaMarie's death, Juanita was easily traumatized, and he couldn't imagine the impact on Leighton.

Damn curmudgeon.

He thought about hanging himself from the door, but he couldn't figure out how that would work. If he slid down, wouldn't it be too easy to just stand back up?

That left an overdose of pills. Jack didn't really like that option because it seemed cowardly, but at least his body would still be intact. Hell, maybe Juanita could pass it off as a heart attack. Somewhere, he had a prescription of antidepressants. Jack remembered trying them for a couple weeks, but they really didn't help. Only alcohol could blot out the intense pain.

Pill.

Without really thinking, he pulled the curmudgeon's large, yellow pill from his pocket. It still had that weird, fluorescent glow. If anything, it was brighter than he remembered it in the ice cream store. Jack held the pill up to the light from the window and stared at it. On a normal day, he might have called the police on the little guy. Certainly, he would have a story for Juanita. But on this day, reality was a dark blur, obscured by one foot in the afterlife.

Without really giving it much thought, Jack gulped the pill and washed it down with a long swallow of scotch. At best, the little being was a psychopath who gave him a poison pill. At worst, it would be a placebo, and he would end up searching for those antidepressants after all.

Jack was contemplating what he would do next when the first wave of nausea caused his stomach to clench. Soon, his limbs started tingling and went numb, and he lost control of his motor skills. He looked at his right hand and tried to will himself to lift his forefinger, but he couldn't. Almost immediately thereafter, his respiration grew shallow, and he felt his throat swelling. Breathing became difficult and then impossible.

His head slammed into the desk as he fell forward. Just before blacking out, he thought, *Good guess, Jack. I guess the curmudgeon was a psycho after all, but at least you got your wish. He killed you.*

Chapter Eight

Something about sitting in his office with a vague sense of discomfort...

That was the only part of the dream Jack could remember as consciousness grabbed the reins from the murky shadows of shallow sleep. He rolled onto his back, which caused Juanita to stir. She inched over and placed her arm across his chest, and he responded by covering her hand with his own and giving it a reassuring squeeze.

They remained in the same position for several minutes, connecting on the level Jack loved the most. The two of them wrapped up together, pushing out the rest of the world and the problems that kept encroaching on their time. He started thinking about today's agenda just as the alarm went off.

"Alexa, off," he said as he squeezed Juanita one last time before rolling over and getting up from the bed. As he stretched, the first thing he noticed was how good he felt physically. Remarkably good, in fact.

"You have something important today?" Juanita asked in a sleepy voice as she looked at the clock on her nightstand.

"Yeah, I have to track down old man Simmons. Apparently, he's taken his business elsewhere because Amtron gave him a better quote on equipment. That Gerry Rourke is a helluva salesperson, and the fact she's a knockout doesn't hurt with old lechers like Simmons." Jack rubbed the sleep from his eyes. "If we lose that account, Walt and Hans will have matching heart attacks."

Juanita got up and walked over to him, wrapping her arms around his chest and pressing her lithe body up against him. "Hey," she said while lifting his chin so she was looking into his eyes, "you may be the national sales manager, but you're still the best salesman they have, and Walt knows it. You'll probably keep the account, but even if you don't, there's nothing that will shake my faith in you... Got it?"

He smiled and pulled her close. More than anything else in life, he craved Juanita's approval. A word of encouragement from her and he felt like he could conquer the world. Gerry Rourke didn't stand a chance.

After a shower and shave, Jack selected his most effective power suit. The blue pinstripe had fourteen notches on it. That was fourteen wins and no losses. He was undefeated in this one, and it was the perfect day to bring it out. For some reason, he felt especially confident, almost as though he *knew* he would triumph. He dressed quickly and made it downstairs just as the kids were coming down for their breakfast. French toast Guatemalan style. Jack's favorite.

He barely reached the first floor when he caught his oldest child's eye. "Dad, we're going fishing tomorrow, right?" Bryson was a little over sixteen, and Jack was all too aware of the confusion and angst boys suffered at that age. A girl recently entered the picture, and he noticed Bryson's circle of friends had changed a little. Jack was keenly aware of both, and he was determined to keep his son on the right path. The B+ average remained intact, and Bryson still had the same warm smile and optimistic outlook he always had. Monitoring his son without becoming invasive and smothering was the challenge.

"Sure, I did say this weekend, didn't I? Where do you want to go?"

"Busse Woods. Lawrence showed me a hidden cove on the map no one knows about. He says the bass are huge."

Jack nodded. "Hidden cove… Yes, that's right. Make sure all the gear is ready and the reels have new line."

"But dad, you said you would come to my baseball game tomorrow." Leighton swallowed his cereal too fast and nearly choked as milk dribbled out the sides of his mouth. Before it was all over, Jack knew the middle boy would be the easiest to raise. Wickedly intelligent, Leighton had the confidence of an eleven-year-old going on thirty-nine. Teachers and counselors talked about how he was clearly gifted and had recommended he attend a private school. Jack and Juanita talked about it, but the tuition was a real issue. They were well off, but another $60k would hurt, especially with Bryson's college on the horizon. Juanita arranged an appointment with the school's scholarship director for next week.

"Ah, yes, of course." Jack slapped his forehead. "Don't worry, Bryson and I will be back in plenty of time for your game, especially if we're out the door by five thirty." He glanced over at his eldest son. "How about it, sport? Willing to get up an hour earlier so we can go to your brother's baseball game?"

Bryson rolled his eyes and curled his upper lip slightly, but he nodded anyway.

Crisis averted.

Jack's eyes moved over to his youngest child, who sat quietly eating her French toast while swinging her legs under the table. Her hair was a beautiful shade of red, and the curls were the perfect compromise between Juanita's tight black locks and Jack's stick straight brown hair. She turned her head and looked at him as that big smile crossed her lips, revealing a noticeable gap where she had recently lost her first tooth.

"Daddy!" As always, her voice and innocence melted his heart. He walked over as he did every morning and kissed her on the forehead.

"Morning, princess. What are you doing in school today?"

"We're going to learn how to spell our names and learn the numbers up to fifty... It's hard." Her brow furrowed, but even that expression was too cute for words.

"Kindergarten is tough, sweetheart," he said. "But you're a big girl now, so you have to really pay attention."

"I will, Daddy. I promise."

He knelt down so he was on the same level as she was. "What can *we* do this weekend,

RosaMarie? I'm fishing with Bryson and going to Leighton's baseball game. I'd like to spend some time with you."

"It's okay, Daddy," she replied. "I know you're really busy."

RosaMarie was far too wise for her age. From the time she became sentient, she always thought about how her actions impacted others. The selfishness stage Jack remembered going through with Bryson, and especially Leighton, never materialized. RosaMarie was the child who every teacher and adult she encountered praised. At school, she was the one who made sure everyone was included, just like her mom.

"I'm never too busy for you, princess. You name the time, and I'll be there."

"Okay. Maybe we can play characters tomorrow afternoon after Leighton's baseball game?"

"It's a date."

He turned to find Juanita standing right behind him. She hugged him and pulled him close. "My hero," she whispered and kissed his cheek.

At the door, he stopped and looked back at his family as they sat at the breakfast table.

Too perfect. I don't deserve this kind of happiness.

When he walked out the door, something odd and unsettling bubbled up in a way he couldn't explain. An uneasiness that suggested maybe his life really *was* too perfect.

***

Jack got in the car and immediately called Stephanie, his executive assistant. She wouldn't be at the office yet, but he needed to change his schedule.

"Hello, Jack." Steph was always available, and for as long as he could remember, she never let the phone ring more than twice before answering.

"Steph, did you get everything changed on the Boston trip?"

"I talked to Munson, but wouldn't you know, he has a vacation planned for next week. Family, I guess. No point in traveling to New England if you can't work with the regional. Looks like you'll have to hang out here for the next two weeks. Remember, you've got California and Arizona in October. I guess that means you get New England in November." Jack thought he heard the slightest chuckle.

"Haha, Steph. Goddamn Simmons sure messed up my schedule... Anyway, tell Williams I'll be visiting the branches here next week. I'm sure he'll be thrilled. He doesn't need to travel with me, but let him know I'm going to Schaumburg on Wednesday, okay?"

"Sure, Jack. See you at the office. Try to have a good day."

Jack used the train ride downtown to psych himself up, and by the time he reached Ogilvie station, he was brimming with confidence, which made his entry to the office all the more dour. The atmosphere was thick and gloomy, like a heavy layer of smoke after a grease fire. He looked over at Steph, and she saluted. Nine years working together, and anytime he saw her, he got the exact same salute and smile. He couldn't imagine his working life without her.

"They're waiting, Jack."

Of course they're waiting. The Simmons account.

He nodded and made his way over to Walt Offerman's office, not bothering to knock. Both partners were inside, and they glanced up at Jack as he took a chair at the conference table.

"How bad?" he asked.

"Simmons canceled the meeting," said Walt Offerman. "He called before hours and left a goddamned voice mail. Said the offer from Amtron was too good to turn down. Said it would save him a million bucks a year."

"Son of a bitch never even called me," Jack mumbled under his breath.

"This is a catastrophic hit," said Hans Morris to no one in particular. "Over twenty-five million in sales flushed. We're an independent distributor. We can't afford to take that kind of hit."

"That Amtron has been a pain in our ass ever since they moved in here," said Walt. "That exclusive deal they cut with Comfort King on equipment is killing us, and now they're ten percent lower than everyone else."

Jack stood up, walked over to the window and absorbed the stunning view of Lake Michigan. Every time he looked out Offerman's window, he was reminded just how badly he wanted to become a senior partner.

He joined SPS Supply when it was a small company with a few branches scattered throughout Chicago and one branch in Arizona. Their main office was out in Elk Grove in a modest strip center. He applied as a wet-behind-the-ears kid fresh out of Arizona State with a business degree who had

96

been turned down for every job in finance or investment banking he applied for. Bad economies sometimes make choices for you, so he jumped at the offer from Walt even though he knew nothing about the heating and air conditioning business.

At the time, he wasn't aware of the real reason Offerman opened a branch in Scottsdale. Walt mostly came down to golf, but occasionally, a woman who was not Walt's wife would show up at a cocktail party or dinner engagement. Jack never said a word about it even in private, which seemed to curry favor with Offerman. Over time, Jack's burgeoning success in sales earned him a promotion to store manager, and finally, western regional manager a few years later.

The west was booming, and with as much luck as skill, Jack happened to be in the right place at the right time. Sales rose double digits every year as new branches sprung up in Tucson, Mesa, Glendale and Las Vegas. On his fifteenth anniversary with the company, Walt and Hans called him to Chicago to see their new offices on Michigan Avenue.

While he was there, they offered him the newly created title of national sales manager. Within a month, Jack packed up his young family and moved to a fashionable area in Arlington Heights. Recently, he and Juanita had been talking about moving to Palatine, a mile marker in their road to success.

Yet, none of that would happen if Simmons bailed. He could feel the eyes following him as he said his goodbyes and walked out of Offerman's office and went over to his own. With a sense of urgency, he called Heating Experts and asked for

Simmons senior, but the old man wouldn't pick up. He asked to be transferred to Bobby, Simmons' oldest kid. Jack spent a lot of expense account money making the kid feel important. Trips to Vegas, fishing expeditions, golf, lunches, booze and even a couple hookers. The kid *better* pick up the damn phone.

"Look, Jack," said Bobby Simmons without a salutation. "My dad made the decision, not me. I was against it. But, you know, he still owns the company."

"Sounds like a power move to put you in your place, Bobby," said Jack. This was bare knuckles time, and Jack was playing hardball.

"Yeah, maybe. But it doesn't matter. He made the commitment and placed the first truckload order yesterday."

"He can cancel it as fast as he issued it. I need a meeting with him today. You owe me that."

"I can't, Jack. He said he doesn't want to see anyone from SPS Supply, especially you. Damn, Hans and Walt have been driving him crazy with all the phone calls."

Jack paused, and when he spoke, it was in a low, flat monotone. "You get me in to see him today, Bobby, or I swear... I swear I'll show him the pictures from Cabo."

He thought he heard a groan, and the breathing on the other end became heavy. "Fuck you, Jack. That's fucking extortion... You son of a bitch. You told me you destroyed those pictures."

"I honestly thought I did. I was going through some old stuff and found a file on my computer, but I can make sure I erase all of them for good this time... So, do I get my meeting?"

Jack waited. He knew in this moment that he must not speak until Bobby answered. "You're a motherfucker, Jack. I can't get you a meeting, but Big Bob is having lunch with Jimmy and me at Epstein's deli at eleven thirty."

"That's good enough. I'll be there. And, Bobby?"

"Yeah?"

"I lied. I destroyed those pictures years ago. I would never do that to you." The line clicked off as he hung up the phone.

***

Epstein's was a dine-in deli on LaSalle Street, about fifteen minutes away from corporate. Jack sequestered in the smaller conference room with the door closed, trying to plan his strategy. Big Bob was a gruff, no nonsense riverboat gambler, who started his business with five grand on borrowed credit cards and was now the biggest HVAC contractor in the Midwest. He had no time for bullshit, and if you were weak, he would leave tire tracks on your back.

For a meeting of this importance, Jack would have started planning weeks in advance, but he didn't have that luxury. Today, he would shoot from the hip. Without saying anything to Hans or Walt, he called an Uber and left the office, eventually arriving at Epstein's around 11:45.

Across the street from the restaurant, inside the lobby of a nondescript building, Jack waited and watched intently out the window. Just before noon, a company car pulled up, and Big Bob and his two kids got out and walked casually into the diner. Jack let ten minutes pass to ensure their orders were taken, which would make them a captive audience.

After entering the deli, he quickly sought out Big Bob. As he strolled casually up to an adjacent table, Jack made sure Simmons and the boys noticed him before he acknowledged them. He sat down slowly and pulled a menu from the holder.

"I don't fuckin' believe it," said Big Bob as Jack turned and feigned surprise. "Which one of you numbskulls told him we'd be here?" Both boys shook their heads vigorously.

Simmons looked back at Jack. "Look, I'm sorry, but the deal is done, Jack, and I don't want to talk about it. I can save a million bucks next year, and that's a lot of cabbage. The first order is already in, so there's no going back. Now, please, don't ruin my lunch."

Without being invited, Jack closed his menu and pulled a chair up to their table. "Honestly, Bob, mostly I'm disappointed, but yeah, I'm hurt too. We've done business for twelve years, and I've handled your account for seven. In all that time, have we ever cheated you?"

"No, that's not what this is about. I told you…"

"Remember five years ago during the last recession when you got in trouble and couldn't pay your bills? Who carried you, Bob?"

"Well, yeah, you guys did." Big Bob's volume and octave dropped considerably.

"Yeah, it was us. And do you know how that happened? Finance wanted to cut your ass off, and

100

you know who went to bat for you? Me. I put my job on the line and vouched for your character with Walt and Hans, Bob. Your *character*." Jack let the words sink in. "Ashad in finance never forgave me, and he's sticking this up my ass every day. I put everything on the line because I trusted you, and I saved your business, but now you fuck me in the ass and treat me like I'm just some damn street peddler."

"No, you're more than a peddler," said Bob while keeping his eyes turned down. "You came to both my kids' weddings. We've had you and Juanita over for dinner. We've gone on fishing and hunting trips together. But business is business. You understand."

"So, that's it, Bob? Business is business? Nothing else matters? Fuck relationships, and a man's word is worthless?"

"Look, Jack, I feel like a heel about this, okay? Yeah, I should have told you, but I didn't know how. It's just that Amtron's bid was so much better than yours. A million bucks, Jack."

"Yeah, and I'll bet that Gerry Rourke isn't hard on the eyes either."

"Well..." Bob smiled and shrugged.

"Yeah, she's one hot tamale for sure." Jack winked and elbowed his client in the ribs in a good-natured way as they both shared a laugh. "One hot tamale. I bet she shows a little leg when she comes over to make a sales call?" The laughing intensified as the boys joined in, and Big Bob rolled his eyes.

Jack let it continue, but then brought his palm down hard on the table. The laughing stopped immediately. "But I wonder, did she push the

101

Chicago Housing Authority contract your way last year, Bob? You retrofitted how many low-cost housing units with air conditioning? Wasn't it something like 3000? What was the size of that contract, Bob? About twelve mil if I remember right? More importantly, what was the profit margin because I don't remember you needing to negotiate? And do you recall *why* you didn't have to negotiate?"

Bob Simmons looked at Jack, but his eyes drooped, and the corners of his mouth turned down. His voice was hardly a whisper. "Because of you."

"Damn straight, Bob. Because of me." Jack jabbed a thumb into his own chest. "I worked with the city's engineers for over a year to write those specs. Those goddamn arrogant city engineers. Kissin' their ass so they would give the contract to whoever I told them to. And that guy was you, Bob." Now, Jack jabbed a finger into Simmons' chest. "And now you fuck me over because of some woman with big tits and a nice ass?"

The table went quiet. None of the Simmons men would make eye contact.

"I wasn't going to tell you this until the Vegas trip next month, but the city is ready to approve another 3000 units for retrofit." Simmons jerked his head up. Jack had his attention.

"Maybe I should call Rodnoir Mechanical about the new contract. Maybe they won't fuck me like you did, Bob."

Simmons looked terrible. His face was red, and he was sweating. His eyes narrowed into tiny slits, and they were wet with moisture. "Jack, what can I say? I can see I made a terrible mistake. Maybe you can get those equipment prices down a little, like at least five percent?" He held out his hand so his forefinger and thumb were positioned a half inch away from each other.

"I'll cut two percent, but I want a signed commitment for two years on equipment, Bob. That stuff she's selling is shit anyway, and you know it. You'll end up losing a million dollars in warranty costs. I'm doing you a favor."

"So, if we commit, we'll get the next phase in the city's retrofit project?"

Jack stood up as a big smile crossed his face. "I'll think about it. Let's talk it over in Vegas next month. I'll bet we can work something out. Oh, and I'd like to see the purchase order for that truckload on my desk by the time I get back to the office... You guys enjoy your lunch."

Simmons nodded and waved him away.

***

True to his word, Big Bob sent the order over so it was in the SPS system by the time Jack got back to the office. As he opened the doors, he wasn't prepared for the reception. The entire staff was perched just inside, and they began clapping as soon as he walked in. Hans came over and gave him several slaps on the back while Walt actually hugged him. The jubilation continued for some time before settling down, but Walt and Hans were in no mood to return to work.

"Jack, you old son of a gun. I don't know how you did it, but I want to hear all the details over a drink at O'Malley's."

"Walt, it's only two thirty. Isn't that a little early to belly up?"

"Nonsense. You pulled off the Michigan Avenue miracle, and we want to celebrate. We don't have much activity on Friday afternoon anyway, and Ana can call us if there's an emergency. We'll stay an hour or two and knock off early. Tell Juanita you'll be home in time for dinner."

"You talked me into it," said Jack. "I don't get to see you guys outside of work enough, anyway. It'll be good to catch up."

"Bullshit," said Offerman. "We're not going to catch up. We want to hear your story of conquest. Every goddamn detail." He chuckled as he grabbed his briefcase. "I'd give my left nut to see the look on that bitch Gerry Rourke's face when old man Simmons canceled that P.O."

Chapter Nine

"Hey, it's the gang from SPS!" The well-rehearsed smile spread across Tommy's face as he walked out from behind the bar to greet his new guests. Friday was always his busiest day of the week, and he saw dollar signs when the SPS people visited en masse.

Tommy pointed over at two bar tables that Jack and Walt pushed together to accommodate the whole group. After settling in, Walt ordered up several pitchers of beer and tequila shots for everyone. After downing their second shot, the conversation flowed freely, and the backslapping began.

"You ol' sonofabitch," said Walt as he playfully punched Jack in the arm. "You saved our asses today, my friend. I thought Simmons was history."

"Me too," added Hans. "Thought old man Simmons was letting the little head do the thinking for the big head. We were already planning on who was getting laid off." For a moment, the table went quiet until Hans burst into laughter and everyone followed, everyone except Kristin Lassiter, who smiled uncomfortably.

"I just reminded Big Bob about everything this company did for him. How many times we bailed

105

his ass out of the fire. Pricing; jobs we pushed his way; Saturday deliveries… We played a big role in his success, and I wasn't going to let him forget it. I was confident he would see it my way. Incredibly confident, in fact."

"Fuckin' amazing, Jack. Heating Experts has seventy-nine branches throughout the Midwest, and no one except you could keep that miserable bastard in line." Walt raised his glass. "To Jack, he saved our asses again."

They all raised their glasses as Jim Witt said, "To Jack, he saved our Christmas bonuses. Way more important than our asses." Again, everyone laughed, including Kristin this time.

Jack tilted his head, tossed his third shot back, and grimaced. When he brought the glass back down, his eyes were drawn to the entrance of the bar. The doors were open to let the built-up heat escape into the cooler September afternoon air, but it was the old woman who walked in that caught his attention.

The sound of his coworker's chatter faded into dull background noise as he watched her lumber with effort past the bar. Somehow, Jack knew exactly where she was going to sit. His eyes followed her until she reached the farthest table at the very back of the building. Her coat was much too heavy for such a warm day, and based on its shoddy condition, he imagined she was homeless or mentally ill. She unwrapped the scarf from her head and stuck it in her pocket.

Tall bourbon. Neat.

He knew what she was going to drink before Tommy walked over and took her order. When he

106

returned a few minutes later and placed the beverage in front of her, she raised the glass to her lips, and with shaking hands, took a long swallow. After setting it down, she looked over at Jack, and their eyes locked. A shiver ran through him, and everything outside the woman momentarily disappeared. The sounds, smells and sights in the bar evaporated, and he only saw her.

She reached out a bony finger and pointed at him. The gesture was slightly aggressive. Then, she moved her hand deliberately down under the table and slightly arched her hips while spreading her legs. Slowly, she began rubbing her vagina.

Jack recoiled in disgust and turned away.

"... Jack? Hey, earth to Jack, are you still with us?"

"Huh?" Jack looked to his left just as Walt placed a hand on his shoulder, a sloppy drunk smile on his face.

"Drink up, buddy. You don't get to be the hero every day."

Jack looked back over at the woman, who turned away and nursed her drink. "Sure, Walt. Gotta enjoy my fifteen minutes of fame, right?"

Over the next hour and a half, Jack did his best to avoid looking at the old hag, but every time he glanced in her direction, she immediately caught his gaze. After the fourth round of drinks, the table had split up into smaller groups, focused in on the latest office gossip and a variety of juicy industry rumors. Walt kept trying to draw Jack into a debate about whether Bobby Simmons was screwing Gerry Rourke, but Jack was distracted and couldn't stop from watching the old woman as she slowly sipped her bourbon.

Finally, after the last game of pool and the drinks were finished, Jack's epic conquest was ready to move into the SPS Supply history books. A few more handshakes and slaps on the back before the celebration broke up, and the crew started to file out the door.

As the last two left at the table, Walt grabbed Jack by the shoulders and held him at arm's length. Walt always got emotional when he drank, and his eyes teared up. "Damn, that may go down as your finest hour." Pulling Jack close, Offerman wrapped him in a bear hug.

Jack smiled and returned the embrace, but his attention was elsewhere.

When Walt finally left, Jack stood up and steadied himself by grabbing the table. His head spun slightly before he regained his equilibrium. She kept staring at him as he walked towards her. Within six feet, he stopped. They continued looking at each other until Jack broke the ice.

"Do I know you?"

She reached into her pocket and pulled out a scrap of folded paper. She extended her bony arm and wiggled her hand, encouraging him to take it, which he did. Jack unfolded the paper slowly.

1233 Hardy Rd, Des Plaines

He looked up at her and frowned. "What is this?"

"The address," she answered.

"Whose address?"

She whipped her head around. "Just keep it, pissant. You'll need it."

108

Jack continued to look at her as he fingered the paper nervously. "What are you talking about? Who are you?"

"Pathetic coward. I knew you would swallow it. Just remember you owe now, so be on time. You *can't* be late."

While shaking his head, Jack backed away from her. His forehead creases deepened as he raised his eyebrows. "Okay, sorry to bother you."

She stood up and closed the space between them. "Listen, pissant, you need to be there on time, understand? You're messing with all of them." She stabbed her finger in his chest for emphasis.

"What the hell? Get away from me. You're crazy, lady."

"Just be there on time." She pushed past Jack and lumbered toward the door, mumbling under her breath. Jack looked over at Tommy as she left, but the bartender just shrugged and shook his head. When the woman was gone, Jack ambled over to the bar and pointed at an empty glass. Tommy grabbed the scotch bottle and filled it.

"Tommy, who is that creepy woman?"

The bartender shook his head again. "No idea, Jack. She's come in a few times now. Always sits at the same table and orders a tall bourbon, neat. She mostly looks out the window. You're the first one I ever heard her speak to."

Jack gulped down the scotch and stood up. "The homeless problem gets worse by the day. She's probably drinking sterno on the street. Sad."

"Aw, I think she's harmless. She doesn't make trouble, at least not that I'm aware of."

109

"Yeah, probably." Jack laid ten dollars on the bar. "See ya later, Tommy."

"Don't be a stranger, Jackie boy."

***

The train couldn't get to Arlington Heights fast enough. His buzz was slipping away, and Jack needed to eat to sober up. Except for the occasional scotch or glass of wine at dinner, he didn't really drink, so three shots of tequila and the parting shot of scotch would put him to bed early. The drive from the station to his house was only a few minutes, but Jack would assess his sobriety when he got there and call Juanita if necessary.

Somewhere between Jefferson Park and Norwood Park, he experienced the sensation of being squeezed. Jack struggled to breathe as something pushed him up against the outer wall of the car. With a start, he sat up and blinked as he tried to make sense of his surroundings. A large man, who was stuffed into the seat next to him, smiled widely.

"You were dreaming, my friend. Talking in your sleep."

Jack looked around as the brain fog from his nap cleared. The train wasn't crowded, and there were several empty rows of seats throughout the car.

Why would such a large person want to be in such a small space?

"I need company. Always have. I'm not good with alone time."

"What?" said Jack.

"I was answering the question you wanted to ask. I'm not in one of the empty benches because I like having conversations. Usually, I'm on an earlier train, and there are lots of people to talk to. Today, I was held up at work, so I'm late... By the way, my name is Tucker, Tucker Lutz, but everyone calls me Tuck." He stuck out a sweaty, chubby hand.

Tentatively, Jack completed the handshake. "I'm Jack Clausen... So, how did you know what I was thinking?"

"I'm not sure. I rarely connect with someone telepathically."

"*Telepathically?* Are you a mind reader? ...Wait, you're about to tell me you're a... Damn, I can't quite recall."

"I'm a professional clairvoyant. That's what you were searching for."

Jack rubbed his eyes. "Probably not, but that's interesting. Do you..."

Lutz held up his hand. "It's happening again. You're going to ask me if I talk to dead people, and I'm going to tell you that defines the role of a medium. Then I'll explain how I work for corporations."

Jack's head tilted slightly. "Have we met before? I ran into someone else I thought I knew today..."

The steady *thumpity thump* of the train continued as they left Edison Park.

"Meeting you now doesn't feel quite right to me, like it's out of sequence. Too soon." Lutz looked off like he was trying to remember. "Jack, there's something very intriguing about you. Your resonance is fluctuating in a very unusual way."

"My *resonance*?"

"Your frequency… Damn it, I swear we already talked about this. On occasion, I can see a person's aura, especially if their frequency is off the 7.83 Hz Schuman standard, and yours is way off. Much lower than it should be."

Jack shook his head and smiled. "I have no idea what you're talking about, but with the day I've had, nothing surprises me."

"Next stop, Park Ridge," yelled the conductor from the front of the car.

"That's me," said Lutz as he began the arduous process of lifting his bulk off the seat. Panting and huffing, he reached into his wallet and pulled out a business card. His name was embossed in black lettering along with the word *Clairvoyant* in larger bold letters. On the bottom of the card was an email address and phone number. "Here, take my card. Something very powerful drew me to you today. I realize I didn't take the late train because of work. No, I needed to meet you, even though this feels very wrong."

"What? I—I have no idea what you're talking about."

"I know, it sounds absurd, but if you ever find yourself in a situation you can't understand, give me a call, okay?"

Jack grabbed the card and stuck it in his pocket. "Ah, yeah, sure."

"I've only experienced a frequency fluctuating like yours a few times in the past. It's often a sign that a cosmic or psychic event is coming. Something significant."

Jack could sense real concern in the clairvoyant's voice, and for a moment, he felt a pang of anxiety.

But this guy is just a fraudster, right?

"Sure, I'll keep your card and call you if I need to."

Lutz nodded, turned, and walked toward the exit as the train slowed. He looked back at Jack one more time before he debarked to the platform.

***

"I'm so proud of you," said Juanita as she leaned over and brushed his cheek with a kiss. "I know this whole Simmons thing was really bothering you, but I never lost faith you would figure it out."

Jack smiled as he finished chewing his last bite of pozole. Juanita's pozole was another favorite, and the way she prepared it made every bite pure heaven. The combination of herbs and spices resulted from generations of experimenting that could be traced all the way back to her great grandparents in Villa Nueva.

"It was a big win for sure, and it takes a load off my shoulders. I told Walt how weird the whole thing was. I was so confident, almost to the point of knowing it would work out. Very strange."

He glanced over as Bryson rose from the table. "Where are *you* going?"

"I'm finished eating, I have to get ready."

"Ready for what?" asked Jack suspiciously.

Bryson shuffled his feet nervously and looked away. "Ah, Bjorn is having a kind of get together tonight. Everyone is going."

"I see." Juanita sat down beside Jack. "And who is 'everyone'?" she asked.

Bryson shrugged. "Just some people from school. You know; Sean, Artis, Vaughn and a few others."

"And girls?"

"Ah, yeah, Dad, some girls are coming."

"Are Bjorn's parents going to be home?" Jack held up his hand before Bryson could answer. "Because if you tell me they are, I'm going to call them."

Bryson sighed. "Okay, they're gone for the weekend, but they know he's having a party. And his sister will be home; she's a junior in college."

Jack looked over at Juanita, who just shrugged and shook her head. "Okay, you can go, but you'll be back at midnight, or I'll be in the car at twelve-o-one."

"How about one…"

"I said midnight, and I'm still going to get your butt up at five thirty tomorrow, got it?"

"Sure, Dad, yeah." Bryson's expression feigned annoyance, but his body language betrayed him.

"Wait a minute. I'm not done. As always, I reserve the right to test you for drugs and alcohol. I take it you're going there with Tommy?"

Bryson nodded.

"If he does any drinking, you better think long and hard about calling me to come pick you up."

"There's no booze there, Dad. I swear."

Jack smiled. "You have a good time, but if you mess with me on this and break the bond of trust, you'll be in a world of hurt you never bargained for."

114

The words seemed to affect Leighton more than Bryson as his younger son's eyes widened for a moment. Jack couldn't resist the opportunity to pound home the point. "Oh yes, Leighton, the same rules are going to apply to you when you're sixteen." The eyes widened even more.

"What about me, Daddy? Am I in trouble too?" RosaMarie looked up at him with genuine concern. As always, she was too adorable for words. "Not you, princess. You're special." That made her smile, and she went back to eating her cookies.

Bryson was almost out of the room when Juanita yelled. "You remember what your father said because you'll think his punishment is weak compared to mine. Don't you mess with an angry Latina."

"Uh, absolutely, mom. I'm reading you loud and clear," said Bryson weakly.

Leighton and RosaMarie asked to be excused, which left Jack and his wife to clear the plates and load the dishwasher.

"I had a strange experience on the train today," he said while rinsing a bowl.

"Oh, do tell. My days on call are so boring I want to scream sometimes."

He set the bowl down and walked over, wrapping his arms around her from behind. "Just think, another six years and RosaMarie will be in middle school, and you can go back to work full time."

She slapped his arm lightly. "How did you coerce me into this deal again? Why am I the stay-at-home?"

"I got you drunk, and you agreed."

"I knew there was treachery involved." She placed her hands over his and squeezed.

He let her go and went back to the table to grab more plates. "So, I'm on the train going home, and I dozed off—you know how I get when I drink in the afternoon—and suddenly, I wake up feeling someone pushing me against the window. I look over and it's this huge guy all sweaty and smiling at me."

"What did you do?"

"I'm trying to clear the cobwebs, and he's introducing himself. He says he's a medium, no, wait, he said he's a *clairvoyant*."

"A person who sees the future?"

Jack nodded. "Yeah, I guess so. Anyway, he tells me there's something wrong with my frequency resonance. It's way out of whack, which I guess means something big is going to happen to me."

Juanita stopped loading and leaned on the counter. "Your resonance? That sounds pretty weird, Jack."

"Yeah, it was very odd." He hesitated a moment, but at the last second decided not to tell her about his encounter with the old woman at the bar.

With the last of the dishes put away, Jack retreated to his den to catch up on social media and do a bit of browsing on Amazon. He knew he would crash early from the effects of the alcohol earlier in the day, but between reading headline news and deleting his endless emails, he managed to amuse himself for a couple hours.

When the clock hit 8:30, he got up and went to his wife's office, where she was busy paying bills. "Nita, how about we go out for ice cream?"

Checking the wall clock, she replied, "Jack, it's 8:30. That's RosaMarie's weekend bedtime. I don't want to be loading the kids up on junk at this hour."

"Aw, c'mon, I know you could go for a big scoop of mint chocolate chip." The ice cream flavor came out in a singsong voice.

She smiled ever so slightly. "Okay, go get it and bring me back some."

He shook his head. "I can't. I was drinking earlier. Don't want to take the chance with the kids in the car."

She sighed and laid down her pen. "Nooooo," she whined. "I'm tired and want to get ready for bed soon.

"On the way back, we can pass by Bjorn's house where the party is."

Juanita smiled, stood up, and grabbed her keys. "Get the kids. Ice cream for everyone."

Chapter Ten

"Bryson... Bryson, wake up." Jack's oldest child moaned and waved his father away.

"C'mon, sport, the fish are biting. If you want to go, you've got to get up." He smiled and gave Bryson a small shove. Despite the challenges of raising a teenager, his first-born was a good kid.

Last night, the door opened at 11:55, and Bryson beat the curfew by five minutes. The 9 p.m. ice cream reconnaissance mission proved to be a big success for RosaMarie and Leighton but yielded nothing to their inquisitive parents. Much to Juanita's chagrin, Jack had her park down the street, and he quietly walked up the alley until he was behind the fence at the Swenson house. When he looked through the slats, he saw nothing but a bunch of kids dancing, laughing and drinking sodas. Jack left feeling embarrassed and a little ashamed, and Juanita rubbed it in and made it even worse as they rode home.

Doing their best to not wake the others, father and son ate a quick breakfast and snuck out the back door. Gathering the gear from the garage, they were on the road just as the sun peaked up from the east. Their early rise meant they would secure the best spot in the hidden cove Bryson found.

They were set up and had bait in the water just as morning established itself, and the new day officially began.

"Bryson! You got one!" They hadn't cast for ten minutes before Bryson's pole bent in the water, and the high-pitched whir of the line giving way signaled he hooked a big one. Taught well by his father, the younger Clausen let the monster fish take the line and run, wearing himself out in the process.

Jack coached from the bank, careful to let his son own the moment. "Easy... Slowly. He's just catching his breath. Get ready for a second run." No sooner did the words leave Jack's mouth, the fish took off again.

It was almost five minutes later before Bryson finally lifted his catch out of the water.

"Whoa!" said Jack. "He's got to be ten pounds at least."

"Can you believe it, Dad? Isn't he a beauty?" And for at least the next minute, Jack got to see his little boy again. All the layers of armor the emerging man wore to protect the inner child were stripped away. He watched and reveled in his son's excitement, and in that instant, the hands of time moved backward.

Several hours later, father and son finished creating another great memory in a long list of great memories Jack enjoyed with his kids. The cove in Busse Lake was isolated and remote, and they had it all to themselves. The fish bit early and often, and between them, Jack and Bryson hauled in enough bass for a fresh fish dinner tonight.

Jack leaned back in his fishing chair with his hat pulled down over his eyes, enjoying the gentle September breeze that blew across the water. He wasn't dozing, but the peacefulness of the moment felt similar to meditation.

A nearby rustling through the bushes startled him. A couple of middle-aged men came through with their poles swinging wildly and gear clattering. One of them turned around suddenly, and his tackle box sprung open, dumping lures, hooks, string and assorted tools on the ground.

"Aw, shit," he muttered as his friend looked back and threw his hands up in the air.

"Goddamn it, Marty, can you get any clumsier?" As irony would have it, Marty's friend lost his balance and stumbled into a shallow, craggy depression, whipsawing the shaft of his rod into the water. Jack rolled his eyes. If the fish weren't already scared away by the commotion, they certainly were now. He poked Bryson in the ribs.

"C'mon, sport, let's get going."

Bryson checked his watch. "We don't need to leave for another fifteen minutes."

"Amateurs always ruin the fishing, son. They won't catch anything, and now, neither will we. Let's pack up.

Bryson nodded, and they reeled in their lines. After folding the chairs and closing the gearboxes, they started the trek back to the SUV.

"Hey," said one of the squatters, "hope we're not running you off."

"No," said Jack as he smiled. "We were getting ready to leave, anyway. The fishing is good here; hope you catch a bunch."

"Okay, thanks." The man waved as he reached into his cooler and took out a beer.

They passed the second man, the one named Marty, who was still near the bushes gathering the contents that spilled from his tackle box. Jack and Bryson waved as they left, but just as they passed him, Jack heard, "Don't be late. Whatever you do, you can't be late, don'cha know."

Jack went rigid, and every muscle in his body seized. He turned and looked toward Marty, who sat on the ground, his dirty sleeveless t-shirt pulled up over his belly. Bryson kept walking, but Jack turned back and went over to the man.

"Excuse me, what did you just say?"

The fisherman looked up with a puzzled expression on his face. "What? I didn't say anything. I just waved."

"No, I heard you. You told me I can't be late. Why did you say that?"

Appearing slightly annoyed, the portly man stood up. "I didn't say anything... Is there a problem here, bud?"

Jack fought against a rising anger from a place he couldn't identify. He glanced around. The sun was still shining, but the landscape seemed duller, and the vibrant colors had faded. He turned back to face the stranger when he heard, "Hey, Dad, where are you?"

Jack shook his head and backed up with his hands outstretched and palms up. "Sorry, I must have misunderstood."

***

On the ride back to Arlington Heights, Jack had a sinking feeling beyond rational explanation. The early bright day continued to darken, although there wasn't a cloud in the sky. The air thickened, and his lungs grew heavier with each breath. Bryson was too wrapped up in his phone to notice, but Jack continued to struggle all the way home.

They made it to the baseball field with fifteen minutes to spare and joined Juanita and RosaMarie in the metal bleachers. Jack tried to control his breathing as he watched Leighton warming up. His middle child's pants were too long and his socks too short, but Jack made sure no one in the house ever made fun of him. Leighton was very proud of his uniform, and the day he joined the Arlington Cardinals, he instantly became a fan of the St. Louis major league team.

The umpire yelled, "Play ball!" and it didn't take long for Leighton to get in on the action. A short fly to center field sent him backpedaling, only to see the ball pop out of his mitt as he fell awkwardly and landed on his butt. A third inning at bat resulted in a strikeout. In other words, it was a typical Leighton performance.

By the fourth inning, RosaMarie complained of boredom, and with her mom's approval, she climbed down from the bleachers and went to play on the playground equipment, about a hundred feet away from the baseball diamond. Juanita and Jack had a good view of the play area, and they took turns watching Leighton while keeping an eye on RosaMarie.

In the fifth inning, Leighton came to bat. He quickly swung and missed twice. With an 0-2 count, Jack glanced over at his daughter as she was climbing on a jungle gym when he heard the crack of the bat. His head swiveled back in time to see Leighton running as the ball leaked through a hole between the shortstop and third baseman. Momentarily, the gloom abated, and Jack jumped to his feet, screaming along with the rest of the family as Leighton rounded first. The left fielder picked up the ball and threw it to second base just as Leighton arrived.

Safe!

"Yeah!" Jack hugged Juanita as they celebrated Leighton's first hit of the season, but a whisper in his ear caused him to stop and let go of his wife.

Where is RosaMarie?

She wasn't at the playground. Jack knew it before he looked. He bounded down the bleacher steps, and when he reached the playground equipment, he began yelling out her name, frantically looking in every direction. As he came closer to the jungle gym, he realized she wasn't in the area defined by the border edging and wood chips. The growing knot in his stomach accompanied the dryness in his mouth. The landscape grew darker.

Stay calm. You already know this turns out to be nothing...

"RosaMarie! ...RosaMarie!"

No reply.

A couple stood off to the side of the jungle gym as their son played. Jack approached and asked if they saw his daughter. He maintained a calm exterior, but he was terrified inside. The woman shook her head as the man picked up his son, and they both set out to help look for RosaMarie. Jack zigzagged through the playground in the kind of search mode that panicked parents assume when they're terrorized by thoughts of the worst.

No one remembered seeing her. *How the fuck can there be all these people here and no one noticed her?*

The next step was to widen the search to cover the whole park. He would give that exactly five minutes before calling 9-1-1. Things escalate quickly when you've lost a kid, but just as he reached the tennis courts, he heard a voice from behind.

"Excuse me. This one wouldn't be yours, would she?"

Of course...

Jack spun around so rapidly he almost lost his balance. An older woman stood smiling in a sympathetic way, her arm stretched out as she held RosaMarie's hand. Jack leaned down and grabbed his daughter, hugging her tight.

"Daddy, you're squishing me," said RosaMarie while giggling.

He looked up and said, "Thank you. I really appreciate it."

The woman nodded. "Oh, you're welcome. She just moved over to the volleyball court to play in the sand. She knew where you were, so I guess technically she really wasn't lost. I just saw you looking for her, and, well, my five-year-old-granddaughter hid inside a circular dress rack in a department store once, so I totally understand the feeling of helplessness."

Jack gently scolded RosaMarie on the way back to the bleachers, but when he got there, he realized Juanita and Bryson never knew RosaMarie was temporarily missing. Instead, they were completely focused on Leighton's baseball adventure.

"Everything alright?" asked Juanita, without looking at him.

Jack glanced down at RosaMarie, who would spend the rest of the game seated six inches from her dad. "Yes, honey. Everything is fine." And yet, the sinking sensation in Jack's stomach was still getting worse. The sky resumed its steady darkening but seemingly only for him.

"You missed it. The next batter hit a double, and Leighton scored. Isn't that amazing? ...Where were you?"

"Damn," Jack muttered, but he didn't want RosaMarie to think he was angry, so he kept smiling. "Uh, I had to go pee."

It would be ice cream and the video arcade for everyone after the game ended. Yet, even as his family celebrated, Jack noticed his ice cream lacked flavor, and playing the kids' favorite games at the arcade failed to generate his normal enthusiasm. By the time they got home, he thought he might be coming down with something.

***

It was late afternoon with the sun sinking in the west, but the landscape still lit up with just a hint of the color that signaled fall's arrival. Birds chirped, and the sound of kids playing in the neighborhood created the perfect suburban weekend. That is, for everyone except Jack, who hunkered down in his den trying to understand his gloom and crushing depression. He absently flipped through a magazine when he looked toward the door.

She's coming. Any minute she's coming, and it will start. But what? What will start?

"Daddy, do you have time to play with me?"

Jack stiffened. He couldn't shake the feeling something bad was going to happen, and like a coming storm, it kept growing closer.

"Sure, pumpkin. I promised, didn't I? And a promise is a promise."

When he walked into her room, he saw she already had the characters arranged in a way that set the stage for the adventure. As he looked at them, he was certain he had been here before in this same place and in this same situation. He experienced deja vu several times today, but nothing this strong.

He dropped to his knees and reached for Mickey, thought better of it, and picked up Donald Duck. "Whaaaaaa. I'm mad because Mickey gets all the attention!"

Still giggling, she picked up Mickey and replied, "Don't be mad, Donald, I'll be your friend."

It's coming.

For nearly thirty minutes, the game continued while the voice in his head kept talking, keeping in rhythm with the pounding of a crushing headache that popped up in the last few minutes.

It's coming.
It's coming.
It's coming.

The voice grew so loud and insistent that Jack had trouble concentrating. Just as the characters moved into the castle, the grandfather clock downstairs chimed, and simultaneously, the doorbell rang.

Three o'clock… It's here…

"Jack? Jack, are you up there?" Juanita called to him.

His skin burned, and his mouth was dry. Somehow, he forced himself to answer. "Yes, I'm with RosaMarie."

"Jamal is here. Could you come down and talk to him?"

Of course Jamal is here.

Jack looked over at RosaMarie, who said, "It's okay, Daddy. Go talk to Mr. Egebe. I'll have to finish without you." He watched her move Minnie Mouse next to a turtle.

Just like last time. What am I even talking about? Something is going to happen, but what is it?

Jack stood up and walked woodenly to the stairs.

I don't want to do this. Why am I doing it when I know it's all wrong?

As he reached the foyer, his wife and neighbor both turned to him and smiled.

"Hey, Jack," said Jamal as he waved. "Do you have a few minutes to show me that new mower?"

Jack smiled, and almost completely against his will, said, "Sure, follow me." Turning to Juanita, "We'll be in the garage. Just a couple minutes."

The sense of impending doom became so overwhelming Jack thought he might pass out. Almost as though he was a drone controlled remotely, he walked into the garage and over to his new self-propelled mower.

"That's a beauty, Jack. Craftsman, no less. That engine is a monster."

"Twenty horse and some special transmission." Jack recited the words like memorized lines from a play. "I think I could beat the BMW off the line for at least ten feet."

Jamal carefully inspected the machine, asking questions Jack somehow knew were coming in advance.

Don't ask me. Please, don't ask me…

"So, Jack," said Jamal, "I was hoping you might let me… I wondered if I could cut my grass with it today?"

"Today?"

No, no, for God's sake, not today.

"I don't know, Jamal. I had plans. I, uh…"

"C'mon, Jack, be a pal. Let me give it a spin. My lawn's a mess, and the old push mower won't start."

Jack nodded. He had no rational reason to deny Jamal a chance to ride his new mower, so like a robot carrying out a program, he started the engine and encouraged his friend to hop on. Once they arrived at the Egebe house, he turned the engine off and gave Jamal a quick five-minute lesson on how to operate the machine. By now, Jack was so nauseous he kept swallowing to avoid vomiting. The side panels of his vision blackened, and he wondered if he was going to faint.

"Hey, Jack, are you okay? If you're not feeling well, we can do this another time."

"No, I'm fine, Jamal. Here ya go." Jack tossed Egebe the keys.

With a wide grin, Jamal hopped onto the mower, started it, and began cutting his grass. Jack watched the somewhat ragged, circular path the mower cut into his neighbor's lawn as Jamal familiarized himself with the machine. Walking over to the porch, Jack took a seat, immersed in his own anguish as the dark, foreboding feeling deepened with each passing minute.

It's going to happen right now...

At that exact moment, Jack turned and saw Juanita running toward him as space/time ground to a complete halt, and the laws of physics no longer applied. His memory of this moment returned in a torrent as though a dam had burst. He did not belong to this time. The embodiment of his true life existed a little over a year and a half from now in an entirely different reality.

There was something about a pill and a small man. Without question, he knew RosaMarie had just been kidnapped, and she would die a horrible death at the hands of a child murderer today.

Jack was jarred back to full consciousness as the universe restarted, and he got to his feet so quickly, he knocked over Jamal's porch chair. Without slowing or even looking at her, he raced past Juanita. Existence was now a bubble, completely detached from the environment surrounding him. There was only one purpose.

The note. The goddamn note from the old lady. Where did I put it?

Jack burst through the front door and ran as fast as he could to the den. He grabbed his car keys and

129

picked up the folded piece of paper next to his wallet. Just before he left the house, he detoured into the garage and rummaged through his toolbox until he found a hammer. He had a concealed weapons permit but prayed he wouldn't need to use the gun in the glovebox.

By the time he reached the front door, Juanita was just coming in, and he nearly crashed into her.

"RosaMarie," she said. "She's gone... I..."

Jack only heard a garbled bunch of words. He slammed the door to the BMW and backed out of the driveway without looking and laid a thick layer of rubber on the street. As he turned off Maple onto Walnut, he verbally entered the address into his GPS.

1233 Hardy RD, Des Plaines.

"Twelve minutes to arrival at your destination," replied the soothing female voice.

The car lurched forward as he hit the accelerator hard. He tried to pick and choose his moments to speed carefully because he couldn't afford to get pulled over and waste time explaining the situation to the police.

Nine minutes. The phone rang.

In a voice quivering with tense emotion, Juanita said, "Jack, RosaMarie is..."

"I can't talk now, Juanita. I—I may know where she is. Just stay by the phone and wait for me to call."

"What? Please... please tell me..." He punched the *end call* button and turned off the phone.

Pounding on the steering wheel, he spontaneously burst into tears. With his heart beating so loud it rang in his ears, Jack couldn't

130

rationalize what was happening. Later, there might be time to contemplate how he came to be in this place and whether he had ever lived in the future at all. If he was wrong about all this, Juanita would never forgive him. Precious time was passing. Time he could have used to search for RosaMarie in the neighborhood.

Five minutes

Jack made the turn onto River Road at such speed that he almost lost control of the car. If there was a cop on the corner, he would certainly be stopped. He looked around frantically, but no cherries illuminated.

Two minutes

Oakwood to White to Courtland, Jack negotiated the residential neighborhood with no regard for safety. On Courtland, he drove a cyclist off the road into a patch of evergreens. Finally, he turned onto Hardy and slowed.

1157... 1169... 1183... 1201... 1221...

And there it was. 1233 Hardy Road. A nondescript small beige bungalow with added blue trim and peeling fascia. Jack jammed on the brakes and left the car in the middle of the road. He grabbed the hammer and ran toward the front of the house. The lock was engaged, so he kicked at the door, but it held steady. A large single pane window spanned the length of the living room, and he hurried over and shattered it with the hammer, oblivious to the shards of glass that embed themselves in his hand. After knocking the remaining pieces out of the frame, he stepped inside.

The house smelled like dead fish and castor oil, a sensory memory Jack would never forget. He looked down at his watch: 3:47.

"RosaMarie!" he yelled. There was no reply, but he heard some commotion from the rear of the house. With the hammer raised above his head, Jack walked through the living room, kicking away empty beer cans, pizza boxes and fast-food wrappers.

About a third of the way down the hall, a faint voice called out two words.

"Help me."

Jack would know RosaMarie's voice anywhere, but more than the words, the level of fear she conveyed simultaneously made him sick and enraged. He ran to the door where her voice came from, and without trying the knob, he kicked it with such force that it dislodged the hinges from the wood. Stepping inside the room, he stood panting for a moment while surveying the scene.

RosaMarie sat on the bed trembling. Her feet were bare, and her pink princess shirt hung off her neck, exposing her arms and torso. Bright red lipstick was smeared unevenly across her lips.

Jack's eyes shifted. Sitting next to her was a slender man with close-cropped black hair. He wore a white, soiled, short sleeve t-shirt, skinny jeans and Keds sneakers. A faded tattoo of John Wayne covered his right arm. His face appeared to have been ravaged by acne at some point, and his lips were cracked and bleeding. He cowered before getting off the bed and backing up against the nearest wall before sliding down into a sitting position.

"Nooooo," he moaned. "Nooooo, don't hurt me."

For a moment, Jack stared into the man's eyes. He looked past the gray-blue color and peered into the depths of the monster's soul and saw the black bilge that bubbled and flowed inside him.

Waving the hammer menacingly, Jack stalked his prey.

Chapter Eleven

The fury that enveloped him was so encompassing, Jack fought to draw in a breath. Only two things registered visually: a white floor lamp in the corner, and RosaMarie. His daughter whimpered and looked at him with such fright and terror in her eyes, Jack felt like his heart was being scorched with a red-hot branding iron. When the nightmares came, these were the images his mind would deliver.

"No, please, no." The slimeball recoiled and put his hands up farther over his head as his shaking intensified. In any other setting, Jack wouldn't have given the guy a second look. He radiated a tangible strangeness, but his outward appearance was rather ordinary. His stereotype of a pedophile was far different than the slender lump of sleaze that lay cowering in front of him.

The monster screamed when the first blow impacted with his shoulder. He tried to squirm away, but Jack blocked his escape and grabbed the collar of his t-shirt. A second blow landed on his back and a third on his leg. Pushing his weak hands out of the way, Jack dropped the hammer and punched the kidnapper in the face. He let out a shriek of pain and grabbed his nose. The next punch caught him in the ear, and he curled up in the fetal position as blow after blow rained down on him.

Blood covered both men, and it was impossible to tell if it came from Jack's knuckles or the other man's face. Despite his anger, Jack realized he couldn't inflict the punishment his inflamed emotions demanded with just his fists. He reached over and picked up the hammer.

He looked into the monster's eyes. "You son of a bitch. You took my daughter, you motherfucker. Now, I'm going to kill you." He aimed the hammer at the kidnapper's head.

"Please, I'm sorry, I'm so sorry. I—I had to do it. My son... I'm sick..." The voice sounded thin and high pitched for a man.

"Don't talk. Don't you say a word." Jack cocked the hammer higher for emphasis.

"Okay, okay." The freak sniveled as snot and spit converged in long, thick strings. "Please. Please kill me. My brain is sick. Their voices don't stop. I think I'm here, but I must not be. They promised... They fucking promised." He looked up at Jack. "How could you know?"

Jack snarled and looked at the pathetic figure with contempt so encompassing, he couldn't stop the compulsion to deliver the fatal blow. As the downward thrust began, the sound of RosaMarie's small voice reached his ears.

"Daddy, don't. Don't hurt him anymore."

Jack froze. His right arm quivered as he fought against the overwhelming urge for revenge. The next blow was aimed at the molester's head. At a minimum, the force would cause brain damage, and with any luck, a cerebral hemorrhage resulting in death. He gritted his teeth and fought against the urge to look over at RosaMarie. If he could let vengeance control his mind and body for just one second more.

Jack's eyes defied his brain's instructions, and he glanced over at his daughter. Her expression was something he never saw before. Past the trauma, confusion and terror, he realized she feared her own father.

The hammer dropped to his side as Jack staggered backwards. He took several deep gasps and brought his hand up to his chest. The kidnapper began to sob as a dark stain grew in the crotch of his pants as his bladder released.

RosaMarie got off the bed and came over to her father. He kneeled down to her level and looked into her eyes before pulling her close and hugging her so tight he had to relax his grip for fear of hurting her. He used his thumb to rub off the lipstick but only succeeded in smearing it more.

"There's a bathroom down the hall if you want to wash up..."

"You shut up." Jack pointed at the monster. "You just shut the fuck up."

He turned back to RosaMarie and held her at arm's length with both hands on her shoulders. "Did he... did he hurt you, RosaMarie?"

She shook her head. "No, he didn't hurt me, Daddy. But he—he scared me really bad. I—I shouldn't have walked down the wrong street, but I was looking for you and went the wrong way." She looked at the floor. "He made me get in the car, and I think he said some really bad words. I never even heard you, Mommy or Bryson say them before."

Then she looked back up, and her lower lip trembled. "Am I in trouble, Daddy?"

Jack tilted his head as he fought to fill his lungs with enough air to speak. "No, you aren't in trouble, princess. You're not in trouble at all.

***

The first phone call went to 9-1-1; the second to Juanita. The police arrived within five minutes, and Juanita pulled up ten minutes later. Jack turned RosaMarie over to his wife as he assisted the police in the apprehension of the kidnapper.

It turned out his name was Pauley Lattimores, if that even mattered. Oddly, he had no criminal record prior to this incident. The police explained it may have been the first time he was unable to control his impulses, or worse, the first time he got caught. As the uniformed officers led him out of the house, Lattimores stared at Jack with a look of complete bewilderment.

The detectives on the scene politely requested a debriefing, so Jack followed them to the station. He hugged RosaMarie a last time before sending her home with her mother. Juanita was a complete wreck, but RosaMarie just seemed confused as her undeveloped brain struggled to make sense out of the situation.

"Jack," said Juanita as she strapped RosaMarie into her car seat in the SUV, "how... how did you know?"

"Not now, Nita. I'll explain it all later."

Once he arrived at the police station, an escort led him into a conference room. This certainly couldn't be the same place they interrogated suspects because it was much too nice. The chairs were richly upholstered, and the wall hangings were pleasant and calming. After he settled in, two detectives came into the room. Before they began the questioning, one of them offered Jack a beverage, which he gratefully accepted. He was parched.

"Mr. Clausen, my name is Detective Luther Ferguson, and this is my partner Detective Anita Jones." Jack thought they made a strange pair. Ferguson was older, heavyset and balding, while Jones was a young, svelte African-American woman. He spoke with a thick New York accent while she had a long Texas drawl.

"I want you to know how sorry we are that your daughter had to endure this unpleasant experience. The good news is that based on what both of you told us, coupled with the preliminary report from the paramedics on the scene, we don't believe she suffered any sort of physical assault."

Jack breathed a sigh of relief and nodded. "Thank God."

"I'll tell you something, Mr. Clausen," said Jones. "If you hadn't got there when you did, I'm not sure this would have had such a happy ending."

Jack looked up. *"Happy ending?* You're kidding, right? My daughter is scared out of her wits. Every time she sees me, she'll relive it all over again."

"Yeah," said Ferguson, "but you and your family would have experienced trauma on an unthinkable level if you hadn't arrived when you did. These guys," the detective shook his head. "There's a sickness in them and a compulsion they can't control. Trust me. I've seen how it ends when it turns out the other way."

Jack didn't need to be reminded. Although his memory of the old reality remained hazy and was missing large chunks, he vividly recalled the image of RosaMarie's dead body. And now he knew who did it.

I should have killed the bastard.

"We're going to make sure we put him away for a long time. He won't be able to victimize another child. That's a very good thing, Mr. Clausen.

Jack nodded. "I'm glad. But I would really like to be with my daughter and my wife. Can I go home now?"

Jones took a slow sip of her coffee before setting the cup down and folding her arms. "Just a couple quick questions. I guess we're most curious about how you found him? How did you know where to go?"

Jack looked at her and hesitated. "I—I thought I saw a car leaving our street, right after my wife told me RosaMarie was gone," he said. "So, I got in my car right away and followed him."

Jones exchanged glances with Ferguson. "Interesting..." she said. "So, your wife must have realized your daughter was missing almost immediately after she walked out the door. Usually, for a child your daughter's age, it takes a parent at least ten minutes to discover they're gone.

139

Then, the family typically starts a local search in the neighborhood before considering the child might have been abducted."

"As you said, we were very lucky."

"Yeah..." said Ferguson slowly. "Lattimores smeared lipstick on RosaMarie and took her shirt off. If you had him in your direct line of sight, how could he have had time to do that?"

Jack picked up the water bottle and drained its contents. "Look, I was working on pure adrenaline. I lost him for a minute in traffic, but I stayed close enough to see him every time he turned... The lipstick? How the hell do I know how long that would take to put on?"

"Where did you first see his car?"

"Down the street a ways."

"Past Walnut?"

"Yes, on the other side of Walnut... Why are you interrogating me?"

Ferguson held out his raised hand and shook his head. "No, no, Mr. Clausen, don't get the wrong impression. These are questions the D.A. is going to ask us. We're just building our case."

Jack nodded. "Okay, but maybe tomorrow might be a better time. I'm quite upset, and my thinking isn't right."

Ferguson nodded as he slowly rose from his chair. "Just one more thing. Did you ever see Lattimores before today?"

"No," said Jack with more than a hint of irritation. "I don't hang around with child molesters, Detective Ferguson.

"I didn't mean to suggest you did, Mr. Clausen." He sighed. "I understand you had a terrible experience here today, but you need to keep telling yourself you probably saved your daughter's life. By the way, we won't reveal any personal information to the media, but they have a way of finding out the details of this sort of thing. I just want to warn you. Hopefully, your daughter's age should serve as a shield though... You good to drive?"

Jack nodded and got up from the table. Detective Jones did likewise and clapped him on the back as they all left the room together.

The drive home was a blur, and later, Jack wouldn't be able to recall even making it. He walked through the door and found his family sitting in the living room. RosaMarie was on the floor with her characters, seemingly unfazed by what happened. Leighton looked like he had processed the information and was ready to move on. Bryson appeared more affected, and Jack could tell his oldest son had been crying. Slumped in a chair next to the sofa, Juanita was still a mess. A balled-up handkerchief pressed up against her nose, and she looked up with swollen, red eyes.

After hugging each of his children tightly, Jack went over to his wife and dropped to his knees, taking her hands in his own.

"It's over, Nita. That guy won't get out of jail for a very long time. They assured me nothing happened to RosaMarie, at least physically. I understand this is bad, but we have to look at the good side. Everyone is safe."

She nodded, but the tears flowed yet again. "We came so close to losing her, Jack, and it's all my fault. I thought you were in the garage. She heard the mower start and said she wanted to see you and Jamal riding it. I didn't realize you drove it down to his house... I'm so stupid. We almost lost our child."

"But we didn't lose her," said Jack. "She's right here, safe with us."

Juanita stared into his eyes, and her expression was so serious he knew what was coming next. "How — how did you know? You never even let me tell you she was missing. She wasn't on our street, Jack. I looked everywhere before I started running toward you. RosaMarie said she turned a corner and got lost. At least ten minutes passed, probably more, before I ran to get you, but somehow, you knew."

"I don't know, exactly. It all happened so fast. She had to be on this street. I saw his car turn on Walnut, and it stayed in my memory for a reason I can't explain. I just guessed and caught up to him in traffic. It was all luck."

Without turning away from her game, RosaMarie said, "No, I got really lost, Daddy. I know our street. I just got lost, and that man said he would take me home."

"Thank God. Thank God, Jack," Juanita said quietly. He patted her on the arm and signaled for the boys that everything was alright. After calling in a pizza order, he retired to his den.

Jack saved the eighteen-year-old Dalmore single malt for a special occasion, and he couldn't think of a better time to crack it open. He poured a double, maybe even a triple for all he cared. His hand shook as he brought the glass up to his lips. The taste of the scotch triggered strong imagery, and he vaguely remembered that in the other reality, he was a full-on drunk.

More memories unexpectedly burst through his subconscious into the light of his conscious mind. The strange man called Torto at the train station; the ice cream shop and the yellow pill; the old woman who gave him the address of the freak, Lattimores. A year and a half of squalid, disjointed memories that followed the brutal death of RosaMarie. All of it wiped away and sanitized with the ingestion of a single yellow pill.

Was that life even real? Did RosaMarie really die? Is this life real? For a long moment, Jack wondered if he was losing his mind.

Yet, here he sat, drinking a scotch in his den. His family was safe and sitting together in the other room. Certainly, the events of the day would never be forgotten, but with time and new experiences, it would fade and never come close to affecting them in the way RosaMarie's death destroyed their family in the other reality.

I really must be losing my mind.

Jack tried to steady his shaking hand as he took another sip of scotch, letting it slowly drizzle down his throat. He reached into his pocket and pulled out the piece of paper. Crumpled into a ball, he opened it slowly.

1233 Hardy RD, Des Plaines.

He stared at it for several minutes. Tangible proof he was not hallucinating or imagining any of this. That strange little androgynous person at the station apparently had the ability to distort time, and the old hag was his messenger.

A pill. How in the fuck could a pill send me back in time? Who ARE these people?

At that moment, he recalled Torto's last words as he left the ice cream shop.

Broken man. Broken fam-i-ly. Torto help fix. Take pill, Jack. Then pay debt, don'cha know.

He took a much bigger drink of scotch. There was no one he could talk to about any of this. Even Juanita wouldn't possibly believe such a strange story. Yet, if the first part came true, and they gave him the chance to save RosaMarie, why would he doubt Torto's demand for repayment would be any less real?

Maybe he really was hallucinating, and there wasn't an alternate reality. The prospect that he imagined all of it was as frightening as the idea it might be real. He poured another, and just as he took a long swallow, he heard the doorbell ring.

"Jack, the pizza's here." Juanita called out in a voice that sounded exhausted.

As he walked down the steps, Jack heard the doorbell ring a second time. Using his phone, he checked the camera app. Jamal Egebe stood at the door.

"Jack, we've been worried sick... RosaMarie?"

"Jamal, I'm sorry. I should have called you. Everything is fine, but it just got so crazy. Losing a kid..."

Egebe wrung his hands and looked up at the sky. "Thank God. Carol and I were out looking for her for hours. You wouldn't answer your phone... What happened?"

Jack shrugged. "Man, I really am sorry. I found RosaMarie a few blocks over. I was so relieved and

144

out of my mind with worry, I might have been in shock. We had to get away from here, so we went over to Juanita's parents."

Egebe nodded. "Okay. I'm sure you're all still shook up, so I'm going to leave you alone." He gave a short wave and turned, walking down the steps until he reached the sidewalk. "You should have called me, Jack. That was a shit thing to do to us."

Jack nodded. Really, what could he say?

***

The following morning, Jack sat out on the patio with his laptop open. He searched the Examiner, an online and print newspaper that covered Chicago's northwest suburbs, until he found a blurb about the abduction in the section that covered Arlington Heights. As promised, the police withheld the name of RosaMarie and the family, primarily due to her age. Detective Ferguson was quoted as saying they received a 9-1-1 call from a "concerned citizen" who believed a white male suspect might have abducted a child. When they arrived at his address, the officers apprehended the perp and recovered the victim, who thankfully suffered no physical injury. The name of the accused would be released at a later time.

Jack did a more comprehensive search but discovered all the news feeds ran the same story. He hoped the cloak of secrecy would remain intact but wondered if that was even possible. There would be a trial, and he imagined some damn reporter would figure out what happened and track them down.

Chapter Twelve

In the old reality, the police recovered RosaMarie's body on Sunday, just a day after the abduction. After receiving a call from a detective with the Elgin Police Department, Jack left the house without telling Juanita and drove out to station headquarters. Accompanied by two forensic investigators, they took him to a wooded area just on the outskirts of town. A group of hikers discovered the body, and Jack recalled how one of them stood on the side of the road wailing, as though it was her own child. Even now, he remembered very little of that day, except the sight of a maimed and distorted version of RosaMarie lying in a shallow grave. That image was still fresh and vivid, as if it happened today.

Dredging up memories of the tragedy made this alternate Sunday seem even more eerie and strange, but the day proved to be mercifully uneventful. In fact, perhaps too uneventful. Detective Jones called, ostensibly to check on RosaMarie and the family, but in reality, she wanted to continue probing Jack about the location of Lattimores' car when he first saw it.

"So, you're sure you saw the car on your street, Mr. Clausen?"

"Yes, just past Walnut. I think I've answered the same question several times now."

"Yes, you have answered it several times, but… well, we had an eyewitness call in. They said they saw a little girl matching RosaMarie's description getting into a white sedan on Larson Street, which is almost three blocks away from where you claim you saw Lattimores' car. It's quite a discrepancy."

"I—I don't know about any of that," Jack said. "I saw what I saw. The car was on Maple, just the other side of Walnut. I had time to get in my car and follow. There's no more to it."

There was a pause on the other end. "What's strange is that when we questioned him, Lattimores also said he picked her up on Larson. He had no way of knowing a witness called in."

"Detective, where is this line of questioning going? I told you what I know. Am I under suspicion for something here?"

"Oh, God no, Mr. Clausen. We're going to file it away as an unexplained oddity, but either you're wrong, or both of them are wrong. It's possible that your mind, under great stress, became confused. You might remember it one way, even if that wasn't exactly how it happened. I'm just compelled to explore any aspect of the case that would raise a question, and your instant and almost prescient reaction to a rapidly unfolding chaotic situation is… unusual."

She quickly changed the subject back to the welfare of the family, suggesting they all attend counseling, but Jack still recognized the purpose of the call. There was a loose end in the case, and good cops hate loose ends.

At dinnertime, the family gathered together to share a meal. The practice dwindled as the boys got older, but Jack was determined to revive the evening ritual, especially now. He looked around the table at his three children talking with their mother, enjoying the simple closeness of family.

"Daddy?" Jack was lost in thought.

"Daddy!" RosaMarie's voice was more forceful than usual. It jarred him to attention.

"Yes, princess, I'm sorry. What is it?" The rest of the family continued talking, so they didn't hear the exchange.

"I feel different."

Jack laid down his fork. "What do you mean, sweetheart?"

"I don't know. I just feel different." Then, as though the thought passed like a wisp of smoke, she said, "Can I get a build-a-bear?"

He smiled, but something about her words made him uneasy. "Of course you can, princess."

***

Something pressed down, pinning him to the bed. It was heavy and kept pushing until he started gasping for breath. He didn't want to open his eyes, but it wanted him to. When he reached the point where he was suffocating, he looked up.

Scream. That was all he could think to do, but there was no sound, just that same deafening silence.

On Monday morning, Jack stumbled into the bathroom and looked in the mirror.

Rough night, buddy.

He showered, shaved and went down for breakfast. Getting back to a normal routine was cathartic, especially after a night of bizarre, disjointed dreams. Just outside the kitchen, he watched his family engaged in their early morning school and workday chaos. While the atmosphere seemed a bit more subdued than usual, Jack knew the comfort brought on by familiarity would ultimately lead to healing.

The trauma they experienced over the weekend lingered, but in the end, the family remained intact, and everyone was safe. With time, memories of the ordeal would fade, and he hoped they all would return to the good health and happiness they enjoyed before the incident.

"Hello, family," he said as he poured his coffee. After smothering two pancakes with syrup, he stood at the breakfast bar and started eating while periodically glancing at the clock to make sure he was on schedule. Canceling Boston turned out to be a blessing, considering what happened over the weekend. Instead of going out of state, he would travel downtown and meet with Hans and Walt to go over last month's sales recap. Jack much preferred being out in the field meeting with the branch managers and making sales calls, but the company was now big enough that bureaucracy set in.

"Dad, are you coming to my practice tonight?" said Leighton. "Coach Miller said to remind you it's your turn to help out."

Jack slapped his forehead as though it slipped his mind, but in reality, he had no idea he committed to help out with Leighton's team.

Starting today, he would have to study his calendar carefully. Plunged into this new reality, he had only a vague idea of his surroundings and responsibilities. Everything in his old world came to a grinding halt the day RosaMarie died, which meant he was in new, uncharted waters.

"Sorry, champ, I forgot all about that, but I promise I'll be there."

"Hey, Dad," said Bryson, "don't forget we have to go out driving this week. My instructor said I need to get behind the wheel every night to make sure I'm ready for the final driver's test. I want to get my license as soon as I get my certificate."

"Guys, c'mon, give it a break. I wasn't even supposed to be in town this week," said Jack as he hastily finished breakfast. Out of nowhere, he remembered his neglect of Bryson's driving. After RosaMarie died, the lessons stopped, and Bryson didn't get his license until he turned eighteen, and that was only because of Juanita's efforts.

He looked over and saw the disappointment on his son's face. "Don't worry, Mario Andretti, we'll get in some serious driving time."

"What about you, pumpkin?" he said to his daughter, who stared absently into space while slowly chewing a pancake. She looked over, and just for a moment, her expression hardened.

"I'm fine, Dad," she said and turned away. No one else noticed it, and the usual morning chatter continued, but Jack paused and looked at her carefully. Not that it was anything earth shattering, but this was the first time RosaMarie called him "Dad" and not "Daddy."

He gulped the rest of his coffee and kissed Juanita and RosaMarie before ruffling the boys' hair in the same way he remembered doing every morning. As he made his way out to the BMW, Jack wondered why he wasn't happier. The deep, dark hole of depression he remembered so vividly should be just that; a memory. Yet, with all there was to be thankful for, something indefinable and unsettling hung over him like a dark cloud.

As he pulled up to the train station and parked the car, Jack rubbed his temples and tried to recall more about his existence in the other reality. His memories of that future remained somewhat disjointed, and there were substantial gaps between them. For example, he couldn't remember who would win the Super Bowl this year. Somehow, he had an impression he lost his job and suffered another terrible tragedy that involved Bryson in a hospital, but the details were blurred. The fog that clouded his memory only served to confuse him even more and call his sanity further into question.

Jack boarded the train and traveled in a kind of disturbed haze. He wasn't sure if it was shock, psychosis or a full-blown delusion, but he found it hard to concentrate. This was another day that would be markedly different from what he remembered. Here he was, heading to work like a typical Monday, but he held on to the nebulous memory of the first Monday after RosaMarie died in the other reality. Drugged out and near comatose, he spent the next two weeks hoping the combination of alcohol and benzodiazepines would finish him off.

Once the train pulled into Ogilvie, Jack grabbed his briefcase and disembarked. His phone chimed just as the doors swished open, and he looked at the message from the Uber driver, who would meet him on Clinton Street in about three minutes. He picked up his pace to avoid being late. Ubers were ticketed if they pulled into the bus lane, but they also couldn't stop on Madison, so pickup and drop off had to be precise.

Weaving and dodging through the crowd, he checked his watch. Morning rush hour was typically a jungle, and he pushed his way past a woman in pumps and nearly knocked over a lawyer with a rolling briefcase. Reacting to the man's death stare with a classic commuter hand gesture, Jack left the platform and began walking briskly into the station when someone grabbed him from behind with such force it nearly jerked him from his feet. Even before he spun around, he knew who it was. The smell of stale cigarettes, body odor and bourbon invaded his nostrils long before he made eye contact.

The old woman from O'Malley's snarled and stuck out a bony forefinger she pressed into his chest. "It's time to pay up, pissant. You got what you wanted, so it's time to pay your debt."

Jack regarded her a moment and then slowly backed up. "Who the fuck *are* you people? Why are you stalking me? You need to leave me alone, or I'll call the police."

She smiled, which revealed a set of rotting teeth, stained deep yellow from her lifelong tobacco habit. Without seeming to move, she closed the distance. "Listen, pissant. You took the pill.

153

Nobody made you do it, but now you owe, and you *will* pay." She grabbed his hand, put something in it and closed his fingers around it.

"You have one day from right now," she said as she pointed to the large clock on an adjacent wall, which read 7:42. "Exactly one day to get it done, and don't you dare be late, or you'll fuck it up for all of them."

"A day to get what done?" Jack's voice sounded weak, and it quivered slightly.

She pointed at his hand. "It's in there." Then her eyes narrowed into slits, and she moved in so close Jack nearly became nauseous with her smell. "And I'll tell you something, pissant. You better do it because if you don't, you'll all pay holy hell. You do it, and be on time. Do you understand?"

Jack hesitantly shook his head.

"Good, now get on with it. You need a plan." Abruptly, she turned and began waddling away until she stopped suddenly and turned back, a broad smile plastered across her cracked lips. "You bought it, pissant. You bought all of it."

Fortunately, Jack was close to a bank of chairs, and he sat down as he watched her shuffle away before eventually leaving the building. He would be late to the office today. In fact, he might not even make it in, but honestly, who cared about that? The Uber driver was no doubt pissed off and probably left by now.

The phone rang, but Jack ignored it. For a seeming eternity, he looked at his shaking hand, terrified to open it. When the need to know his fate finally surpassed the fear of what that fate might be, his fingers slowly uncurled to reveal the crumpled note, which looked identical to the first one the old woman gave him in O'Malley's. Carefully, he unfolded it and smoothed the paper out on his leg. In the same cryptic cursive, it read:

Kill Edward Parmantier. 1695 W. Rose St, Glen Ellyn. Takes dog for a walk at 9:45 pm at the park on the corner of Glennon and Thistle. Do it then.

Jack's first instinct was to laugh at the absurdity of the demand. Instead, he raised his hands to his face and shook his head while stifling a scream. This couldn't be happening. Was he caught up in some kind of hellish delusional dream?

Call the doctor.

That was the logical next step. He pulled out his phone and scrolled through the contacts page until he came to Harry Seldon's entry and hovered over the call icon. Seldon would give him a referral to a psychiatrist. That's what he needed, right? Yet, how should he deal with the physical evidence in his hand? At home, he still had the note with Lattimores' address, and now he had this one. The old lady couldn't be a figment, unless…

Am I actually writing these notes to myself? Oh my God, I'm going insane.

He shoved the piece of paper in his pocket and remained motionless on the chair, absently watching the Great Hall thin out as he tried to control his breathing. His phone rang again; it was work. He glanced up at the clock: 9:26. He had been sitting in the same spot for almost two hours in a near catatonic daze. The phone buzzed again, and this time caught his attention.

"Walt, I'm sorry. I should have called in earlier. I'm under the weather today."

"… Ah, okay, sure, Jack. Totally understand, but we were getting worried. Anyway, after a kill like you had Friday, you deserve a day off. Hans and I can somehow figure out how to conduct a meeting without you." Walt laughed to cut through the awkwardness.

"I appreciate that. I'm sure I'll be better by tomorrow, and I'll see both of you on Friday."

"Don't worry, Jack. You get some rest. Hans has the whole thing power pointed, anyway. I'll make sure he forwards it to you. Nothing to get excited about. Sales are strong. We just have to get on top of some supply chain issues."

"Yeah, I'm seeing the same thing. I'll look at it tonight. Call me if anything important comes up in the meantime."

Once he put the phone back in his pocket, Jack started shivering. They were in the middle of an Indian summer, but he was very cold. He just couldn't wrap his mind around any of this. How should he respond? The shrink? The cops? Who would believe him? Even Juanita would attribute it to a breakdown or PTSD.

In a flash, a whole myriad of possibilities raced through his mind. Could he be in a coma in a hospital bed somewhere? Did he suffer a mental breakdown? Did the alcohol finally catch up with him and manifest itself in hallucinations? Jack continued to labor, recognizing he was on the verge of a panic attack.

Focus on positive outcomes. Control your breathing. Observe the feelings as an outsider. Slowly, he regained a semblance of calm.

Among his jumbled and confused thoughts was a single point of clarity. The only path to the truth, if there even was one, went through the old woman. Either in this reality or the other, he remembered Tommy telling him she stopped by the bar a few times before their first encounter. Jack gathered himself and opened the Uber app. Sure enough, the driver he stiffed gave him a zero, but that only reduced him to a 4.7. Fortunately, he got someone else to respond, and when she arrived, he was waiting at the curb. He gave the driver the address for O'Malley's and settled back, trying to calm his racing mind. Somehow, he had to find the old hag.

***

Tommy shook his head as he refilled Jack's glass. "I have no idea where she comes from," he said. "Like I told you before, she only started stopping by recently, maybe two weeks at the most. She must live close though because she always walks from that direction." He pointed out the window, west down Erie Street.

"I have to find her, Tommy." Jack raised his glass and took a drink. "It's really important." He reached into his pocket and pulled out a business card. "If you see her, will you tell her to call me on my cell?"

The bartender took the card and glanced at it. He squinted as he looked at Jack. "Okay, pal, but why would you want to talk to her? I'm pretty sure she's homeless."

Jack flashed Tommy a look the barman understood immediately. "Got it. Got it," he said while sticking up his hands. "No questions. If I see her, I'll give her your card."

"And if she comes in, try and find out where she hangs out, okay?"

"Sure thing. I'll do my best, and I'll call you if I learn anything useful."

Moving from the bar to one of the tables, Jack unfolded the note the old woman gave him at the station and stared at it.

Kill Edward Parmantier. 1695 W. Rose St, Glen Ellyn. Takes dog for walk at 9:45 p.m. at park on the corner of Glennon and Thistle. Do it then.

Trying to control the tremors in his hands, he gripped the phone and typed, *Edward Parmantier, Glen Ellyn* into the search engine. A whole litany of information came up, and Jack started scrolling through it. Piecing together different bits from a variety of sources, he learned Parmantier was 39, divorced, and had two kids. On Facebook, Jack found out he enjoyed boating, and his LinkedIn page touted his work as the chief mechanical engineer at Salkland Industries, an aerospace company.

Jack paid twenty-nine dollars to get a detailed report on Parmantier's background. After his contentious divorce, a domestic violence charge was later dropped by his ex-wife. Other than a couple traffic tickets, he had no criminal history. A list of relatives, friends and possibly exes was also included, as well as two lawsuits related to a traffic accident (not his fault) and theft of trade secrets (he settled).

The listed address was the same as the one on the note, which confirmed he had the right Edward Parmentier. Now, what to do with the information? If someone wanted this guy dead, Jack had to warn the authorities…

But how?

The cell phone ID systems were so sophisticated, it was virtually impossible to make an anonymous phone call.

For the next few hours, Jack nursed his scotch and ate a sandwich, hoping the woman might come in, but she never did. Finally, by late afternoon, he decided the effort was futile, so he paid his tab and said goodbye to Tommy. If he didn't leave soon, he would miss the train, and he would get the third degree from Juanita. Jack hadn't forgotten his commitment to Leighton either. While walking out to his Uber, he steadied himself and instantly regretted drinking during the day.

After arriving at Ogilvie, he looked up and realized he had about ten minutes before his train departed, so he took a seat and passed the time by watching some random cable TV news show on the giant screen monitor. The entire scope of the situation taxed the limits of his comprehension. Deep in thought, his eyes followed an attractive woman as she went over to a bank of public pay phones on the west wall.

Wait a minute. Public phones.

Ogilvie might be one of the last places in the city with pay phones, and in that moment, Jack realized he found his solution.

After recalling Edward Parmentier's personal information, he went over and picked up one of the phones, careful to keep his head down in case there was a camera watching. He pulled a dollar out of his wallet and slid it into the slot to get a dial tone. Carefully, he punched in the number, waiting for the recorded voice that asked him for another $2.75. After putting a five-dollar bill in the receptacle, he heard a series of clicks, and the phone on the opposite end started ringing. After the fifth ring:

"Hello?"

Jack hesitated, opened his mouth, but words escaped him.

"Hello? Is anyone there?" The voice sounded slightly annoyed.

"Are you... Are you Edward Parmentier?"

A pause. "Who is this?"

"Mr. Parmentier, I—I wanted to tell you that you may be in some sort of danger."

The pause was much longer this time. "Who the *hell* is this? What do you want? Listen, if you're pulling some sort of prank..."

"It's not a prank, and I might be totally wrong, but you need to be very careful because I think someone may be out to... They may be out to hurt you."

Silence. "Why would you say that?" Parmentier's voice became quiet and subdued. "Are you telling me someone is trying to kill me?"

"I don't know. I'm not even sure if this is real. But I wanted... No, I needed to warn you."

Jack hung up the phone. He had less than three minutes to board his train.

Chapter Thirteen

Jack looked out the window and stared at the colorless vegetation in the backyard. The sun was setting, which only deepened his sullen mood. Everything around him appeared to be out of sorts, almost as though the universe was ailing. With effort, he tried to clear his mind of the racing thoughts that always made the worst possible outcome seem likely.

"Can I be excused, Dad?" RosaMarie was the last to leave the table. Jack looked at her plate, and his facial muscles tightened.

"You didn't eat much, pumpkin. You haven't had an appetite for the last couple days, and Momma made one of your favorites, mac and cheese casserole... What's wrong?"

"Nothing, really. I just haven't been that hungry, but I'm sure tomorrow I will be."

"Hey, I'll tell you what," said Juanita. "How about I make your all-time favorite, shrimp scampi?"

"Goodie!" said RosaMarie as she pushed away from the table. Even though she seemed excited, Jack sensed an underlying lack of enthusiasm. No one else might have caught it, but he was finely tuned into his daughter. It came from a weird sixth sense some parents seem to have. For Jack, the insight only applied to RosaMarie. He watched as she climbed the stairs, and he waited until he heard her bedroom door close.

"I'm worried about her, Nita. Something is off," Jack said as he pushed the food on his plate around.

"She's been through a lot, Jack. We have to expect there will be some residual damage. We can help, but RosaMarie's going to have to work it out on her own. It's going to take time."

"I understand." He looked down and said softly, "Nita, I—I think I'm having some issues."

She reached out and took his hand. "Of course you are. What happened on Saturday isn't something that can be overcome easily, especially when it's so fresh. Everyone is focused on RosaMarie, but I haven't forgotten it was you who found her. That had to be horrible. I'm not sure how you made it to work today having to act like nothing was wrong."

"Actually, I..." For some reason, he choked up, and a single tear dropped onto his plate.

Juanita squeezed tighter. "Hey, Jack. What's going on? Tell me what's wrong."

He looked up and tried to fight back the tears. "I didn't go to work today. Something happened. Oh, Nita, I'm so fucked up. I can't talk to anyone. No one would believe me."

She took his other hand. "Look at me," she said. "There isn't anything we can't talk about with each other. You're hurting; I understand that. But it's going to be alright, Jack. The police psychologist

162

recommended counseling for all of us, and I think maybe she's right."

"When is RosaMarie scheduled?"

"Tomorrow at eight-ten before school starts. The psychologist wants to see her alone. She said it would make RosaMarie feel more comfortable. I'm good to take her since I don't have a showing until ten." She hung her head, and her long, curly raven hair fell over her face.

"Jack?"

"Yes?"

"I really need to know how you found that monster's house. When you left, you had such a sense of purpose. Please, tell me."

They didn't make eye contact, and Jack carefully considered how much he could share without convincing her that his mental illness was much worse than she might have suspected.

"I don't know for sure. This is going to sound crazy, but I picked out a car and followed it. Blind luck? Intuition? Something told me to follow that car."

Juanita looked up, and the motion parted her hair. After twenty-four years of marriage, he knew when she didn't believe him. This was one of those moments.

"Okay, Jack. I guess sometimes we have no choice but to believe in divine intervention and miracles. However you figured it out, thank God you did."

Jack nodded, but he still didn't look at her directly. "I have to get going, or we'll be late for Leighton's practice... How was RosaMarie today? I mean *really*, how was she?"

163

"I'm not sure," said Juanita as she got up from the table. "On the surface, everything seems alright, but just like you, I sense something else is going on inside her head."

***

RosaMarie didn't really want to go to Leighton's practice, but Jack insisted, and he made sure she was within his line of sight the entire time as he worked with the outfielders. After they returned home, he squeezed in a night driving lesson with Bryson before his day was finally finished. Slumped in his chair inside the den, Jack poured himself a scotch. Somehow, he had four drinks before exhaustion set in, and it was only then that he realized he was inebriated.

With all the kids finally in bed, he went into RosaMarie's room, walked quietly over to her, and kissed her forehead. She looked so innocent and peaceful, but Jack still had trouble accepting she was alive and well. Two days older in this reality, tomorrow would be the third. As he looked at her lying there, breathing slowly and rhythmically, he had no regrets. Perhaps the pill the strange humanoid provided put him into a permanent coma, but this seemed real, and he never wanted to go back to a place where RosaMarie didn't exist.

Just like yesterday, he would spend much of the night sitting on a folding chair in her room, dozing in and out of sleep, plagued by vivid, distorted dreams of the other reality. Each morning he woke up remembering a little more about his other life, especially the nightmares that focused on Bryson.

He cried out when he recalled how his son died and the suicide attempt that followed. No, he never wanted to return to that place. Death would be a much better option.

Jack finally left RosaMarie's room just before daybreak. As he lumbered toward the bathroom, he wondered if he would ever feel comfortable leaving her alone again. The raw wounds ran deep, and it would take many years for them to scar over, if they ever did.

After a hot shower and shave, he grabbed a pair of khakis and a button-down polo. Steph arranged for him to work with Jeff Franks in the Roselle facility today. Roselle consistently overperformed, and Franks was one of their best managers. Jack imagined he should have a relatively stress free day.

Tuesday was his turn to cook, so that meant soggy French toast and scrambled eggs. He had to hurry because Juanita was taking RosaMarie to school early to meet the psychologist. Breakfast duty also meant making sure everyone got out the door on time. The kids preferred their mom's cooking, but as Jack reminded them, beggars couldn't be choosers. Leighton and Bryson usually accepted their French toast squares and wrinkled their noses, but RosaMarie was always sympathetic and came to her father's defense.

But not today.

She came down the stairs looking disheveled, which was unusual. Leighton and Bryson required prodding, but Jack's daughter was almost always ready before breakfast. Every child has certain characteristics that define their individuality and

165

delight their parents, and punctuality was one of RosaMarie's. So, when she appeared in her nightshirt with her hair in a curly, tangled mess, Jack was taken aback.

"Are you alright, pumpkin?"

She shook her head. "I'm fine, Dad. Can I just get breakfast?"

Jack continued to eye her as he fixed her French toast. He watched curiously as she slathered on the butter and doused the wedges in syrup. Again, out of character. RosaMarie always used butter sparingly and measured out her syrup, using the precise same amount every time. Exactly one-quarter cup.

She cut a piece, and with one chew, scowled. "This tastes terrible. Maybe you should get a cookbook, Dad." The boys chuckled, but Jack found the comment rather odd.

"Well, princess, as I told the boys, beggars can't be choosers."

Juanita came down a bit later, dressed smartly in business attire that made her look professional with just a hint of sexuality. She kissed Jack, grabbed her coffee, and chewed carefully on a piece of bare French toast so as not to smudge her makeup. Ten minutes later, the boys left for the bus stop. Jack cleared the plates as Juanita grabbed a light jacket.

He looked up at the clock: 7:47. All morning, he watched the numbers turn with dread, but the old hag's deadline passed, and his family was still intact. There was no Cinderella effect, and he didn't suddenly wake up back in the horrible old reality. Nothing bad happened to any of them.

A hallucination or coincidence. It passed. Maybe I'm losing my mind, but everything is going to be okay.

"Hey, sweetheart," he said to RosaMarie, "you better finish up, or you're going to be late."

With an elbow on the table, she rested her head in her hand. "I don't want to go to school today."

Jack stopped and set the utensils in the sink. "Since when? You love school. What about Mrs. Crimmins? She'll be lonely without you."

"I don't want to go there anymore. It's a waste of time. And I don't want to talk to a 'cologist'."

Jack nodded. "I see. You know, RosaMarie, sometimes it helps to talk to someone about the things that are bothering you. That's what a counselor does; they make you feel better."

"I'm not going to tell her anything, and I don't want to go to school anymore."

"...Well, I'm sorry, princess, but you have to go to school. Kindergarten is big stuff. Give the counselor a chance... Now, c'mon, go get ready."

"No."

Jack turned and regarded her for a moment. In hindsight, he supposed he should have expected it at some point, but RosaMarie never openly defied him before. He remembered the first time Bryson and Leighton rebelled, but this was far more disappointing. Still, no matter how she might be acting out, Jack had to remind himself they were only three days past a horrific and traumatic experience.

Juanita walked over and stooped down so she was at eye level with her daughter. "You listen here, young lady. Get off that chair, go upstairs, get dressed, wash your face and brush your teeth. We're late. You have ten minutes."

RosaMarie must have sensed her mother's resolve because she huffed and grunted but got up and climbed the stairs, stomping her feet as loudly as possible.

"I hate you both," she said, loud enough for her parents to hear.

They looked at each other, and the hurt was evident.

"What was that all about?" Juanita asked.

Jack just shrugged. "Growing up, I guess?"

A few minutes later, Juanita yelled upstairs, "You have five minutes."

Nearly ten minutes later, RosaMarie came down in a black shirt and a pair of jeans. Her hair was combed but parted differently. The change was dramatic enough that Jack stopped rinsing the dishes and gave her a long look of disapproval.

RosaMarie glared at him as she walked by, but Juanita's ringing phone saved them from an unwelcome confrontation. After overhearing the first few sentences, Jack realized it was her work, and before she hung up, he knew he would be driving his daughter to school today.

"Jack, I'm sorry. The client needs to meet us at the house at nine."

He waved her off and smiled. "See you tonight. Love you."

After a brief kiss, Jack wiped his hands, grabbed his briefcase and jacket, and ushered his daughter out the door. She moved slowly, obviously to annoy him, so he pointed to the car and waited until she walked over and got in.

"I hate this stupid car seat. No one else in school has to be in one. Why can't I at least have a booster seat?

"Maybe next year, RosaMarie, you'll be big enough to get a booster."

"That stinks."

He turned around and looked into the back seat. She creased her forehead and squinted at him. "Why are you in such a bad mood?" he asked.

She looked away but said nothing.

"RosaMarie, if there's something bothering you, please tell me. Is it about that man who took you Saturday?"

She remained quiet until he pulled up in the u-shaped drop-off driveway at her elementary school. After getting out, she closed the door but leaned in through the open window. "Daddy, is Mr. Egebe a bad man?"

He frowned and tilted his head. "No, of course not. Why would you ask such a thing?"

"If he hadn't come over that day, I wouldn't have been stolen."

"Mr. Egebe had nothing to do with it, RosaMarie. He just wanted to see my new mower. After he realized you were missing, he felt terrible about it."

She considered his answer. "I guess so. But he should have stayed at home. Bad man... Very bad man." She looked at him, and her eyes conveyed an underlying anger.

"Look, you're late. Can we talk about this later? Remember, you're to go to your room, and Mrs. Crimmins will take you to meet the counselor."

She nodded, and Jack watched as she walked up the stairs and disappeared inside the building. He continued staring at the front doors for some time.

***

Jack drove out to the freeway with his mind fractured into rotating stills, almost like a picture carousel on a website. Between RosaMarie and questioning his sanity, there was little time to think about work. He continued to glance at the digital clock on the dash as he entered the on-ramp to I-90. Once again, he was way late, and just as he sped up, he hit traffic.

Missed work yesterday, and now I'm late. Perfect. I wonder who will call Walt first to rat me out? ...You know what? Fuck it. RosaMarie is alive, and I'm worried about being late to work? Screw them all.

The majority of the trip was smooth, and by the time he reached Irving Park Road, Jack had the radio cranked up as he sang along to an old Van Halen tune. For the first time since he woke up in this new past, he allowed himself to enjoy a sliver of optimism. He thought of all the positives besides the big one. He had a year and a half to live over again, but this time with a healthy, happy and complete family.

Instead of self-destructive behavior, he would focus on getting it right by strengthening the relationships with his wife and children. In the other reality, they never understood what he was going through, but with another chance at happiness, they would never need to understand.

With every day that passed, he imagined the memory of his old life would fade.

Jack arrived at the branch and pulled into the parking lot. Wholesalers didn't deal with the public, so the reception areas were usually small and sparsely furnished. When he walked inside the building, he found the branch manager and his staff huddled together. They looked over at him with expressions of concern.

Something is wrong.

"Jeff, how are you?" said Jack while forcing a smile. Jeff Franks' worried look did not change.

"Jack, we have, uh, kind of a problem," Franks said with obvious awkwardness.

"Problem? Okay, it's Tuesday, why shouldn't there be problems. What is it?"

Teri Flannerty, the receptionist, said, "There's somebody here to see you, Jack, and she's very insistent and — disruptive. Claims she knows you. I wasn't sure what I should do with her."

"What company is she with?"

"See," said Mark Lantz, the lead salesperson, "that's the thing. She's not a customer or an industry person. It's like…"

"Where is she?" Jack looked back down the hall before turning to Franks.

"She's in my office. It's the only place I could put her where she couldn't run off the customers with her foul language."

Jack tilted his head before nodding. "Okay, I'll check it out." He walked down the short hallway to Franks' office. His conscious mind wouldn't allow him to register what his subconscious already knew before he turned the knob on the door.

Stale cigarettes, body odor and bourbon.

She sat in the chair the customers and vendors used when they met with Franks, so her back faced Jack, but he instantly recognized her. The dirty wool coat and her trademark faded red babushka announced the old woman's presence.

Without turning, she hissed in a voice loud enough for everyone in the office to hear, "You pissant. You didn't pay your debt, and now you're all fucked. They did their end, and you welched. I knew it. You were supposed to be on time. I told them you were nothing but a pissant."

In stunned silence, Jack walked around Frank's desk and sat down so she was directly across from him. In the light of the fluorescents, the lines in her face looked even deeper, and the snarl on her lips was wider. She reached into her pocket and took out a pack of her unfiltered cigarettes. With shaking hands, she snapped a Bick lighter, lit up, and puffed deeply.

"What is it you want?" he said in a measured tone. He fought to control his breathing, and his heart pounded in his ears.

She took another puff on her cigarette and blew smoke in his direction. "What do I *want*? I don't want anything from you now," she said as spittle flew from her lips. The words were hardly out of her mouth before she went into a deep, productive coughing spasm. Emphysema at least, he figured, but it could be something much worse.

"But I know what *you* want," she said as she smiled and flashed her filthy teeth. Her legs widened, and she put a hand to her exposed crotch.

"Come on, pissant, I know you want to hit it again."

Jack fought the urge to retch. He knew everyone in the office was listening as the drama unfolded. "I need you to get out of here," he said in a low voice that went dry and caught. "Get the fuck out of here, and leave me alone."

She leaned in and stared. He could hear the wheezing as she breathed. "I'm here to tell you that you made your bed, pissant." Then, she straightened up a bit and looked around the office. "Nice place. A lot better than the street for sure."

"What is it you want?" Jack said again through clenched teeth. "Stop tormenting me, or I'll..."

"...Or you'll what?" She paused a moment. "I'll leave, but I want a hundred bucks, and give it to me fast. Otherwise, I'll tell everyone here what you did."

Jack hastily reached into his wallet and pulled out a fifty and three twenties and threw them at her. "Here. Now get the hell out of here, and don't let me see you ever again."

She leaned over and picked up the bills, and after stuffing the money somewhere inside her layers of clothing, she locked onto him with narrowed eyes and again pointed her finger.

"I'm here to give you a warning. You broke the deal, and now you're going to pay. You don't want to see me again? It won't matter because they're all going to pay because of you, pissant. You remember. It's all your fault. "

She threw her lit cigarette butt at him, and he frantically brushed it off his chest while pushing the chair backward so hard it slammed into the wall behind him. He stubbed the butt out with his foot, and when he looked up, she was already shuffling down the hallway. Unfortunately, she wasn't leaving without inflicting further damage.

"Your boss is a no good, lying motherfucker!" she screamed. "Yeah, that's right. He's a lying sex pervert and a rapist. He fucked me and liked it." She walked out the front door, leaving the people inside the lobby and hallway to observe the fracas in shocked and stunned silence.

Jack's face was flush and crimson as he followed her out. His eyes turned to the ground, but he could sense his coworkers and the customers in the lobby staring through him as he struggled with the intense embarrassment.

Jeff Franks gently gripped his shoulder. "Jesus, Jack, what the hell was that all about? Should I—should I call the police?"

Without looking up, Jack shook his head slightly and then left the building. By the time he reached his car, he was in a full-fledged meltdown, and he fought against the walls closing in from all sides. For several minutes he sat in the parking lot, certain he was having a heart attack.

Chapter Fourteen

Jack continued to hyperventilate as he reached the freeway. After leaving the Roselle facility, his phone blew up with calls from the main office. With such high drama, he knew Franks would call Walt or Hans immediately after he left. Ordinarily, he would have filed it away and repaid his branch manager at a later date, but today, Jack had no stomach for office politics.

The situation with the old lady was growing worse, and he was struggling with how to handle it. His encounter with her at O'Malley's was bad enough, but she had grown increasingly belligerent, and now she was threatening his job. Confronting him at the train station was one thing, but showing up at his workplace crossed the line.

He wondered how she was able to learn so much about him. No one outside his family and a few coworkers knew his daily schedule. One of them must be providing her with a copy of his calendar.

Who could it be?

The most likely suspects were Tad Newsome or Rob Williams. Both were aggressive regional managers who would salivate at the prospect of bringing him down. They may laugh at his bad jokes and congratulate him on his success in public, but Jack knew they both would shiv him in a heartbeat if the opportunity presented itself.

Bastards. It had to be Williams. He was at the party Friday and saw me talking to the old hag. His hands tightened on the steering wheel.

How could he possibly return to the branch today or ever for that matter? He thought about driving downtown and going to the office, but there was no way he could make up an excuse that sounded plausible. Worse, he wondered what would happen if it escalated further? What if she showed up at the Michigan Avenue office when Walt and Hans were there?

The phone rang again, and he almost turned it off before checking the caller ID. It was Juanita.

"Jack, can you meet me at RosaMarie's school at three-thirty?" After being married this long, he judged the seriousness of the situation by the tone in his wife's voice. In this case, she appeared moderately concerned.

He struggled to change his focus. "Ah, yeah, sure. What's the problem?"

"I don't know, actually. The psychologist who saw RosaMarie today asked us to come in after school let out. She sounded pleasant enough, but there was something in her voice..."

Jack sighed. "Great. Just great," he muttered.

"Is there something wrong? You sound stressed out."

"Oh, it's nothing," he said. "Just typical work stuff… I'll figure it out." His phone started beeping, signaling another call. No doubt it was the office again.

"Okay," she said cautiously. "I hope your day gets better. On the good news side, the showing went well. I think my clients are going to make an offer tomorrow."

"That's wonderful, hon," he replied, but there was no enthusiasm in his voice.

"Alright, Jack, I'm going to go. Try and cheer up, and I'll see you at the school this afternoon."

Jack stepped on the gas and abruptly turned the car around. The old woman could no longer be categorized as a mild annoyance. Showing up at his workplace and causing a scene made her a stalker, so the problem must be dealt with. If only he knew where she hung out. If only…

Without warning, his mind opened a back door into the old reality. Even before the encounter with Torto, he remembered meeting her at O'Malley's, where she gave him the very first warning.

"Remember, you can't get out of it. You must be there and pay your debt, you pissant."

Memories of the nightmares also returned. How she climbed on top and rode him while Torto and the others bit and sucked his flesh. Jack frowned in disgust as he drove on with a vague recollection of a house in the dream. A bizarre, surreal environment filled with grotesque and macabre scenes of debased debauchery.

Back in Roselle, he turned the car into the parking lot, took a deep breath, and walked with purpose back into the branch's lobby. Avoiding the earlier drama would just make the gossip wheels turn more rapidly. The best choice was to project swagger and confidence. Fortunately, the courtesy area was empty except for the receptionist at the counter. She looked up with a sense of alarm.

"My God, Jack, are you okay?"

"Yeah, I'm fine, Teri," he said. "I'm having a problem with that woman. She saw me at a restaurant, and for some reason, became obsessed. I have the police involved, and I'm in the process of getting a restraining order. Hopefully, that ends it."

She nodded. "I totally get it. I was involved with an obsessive boyfriend. These whackos can make your life hell."

Jack was grateful for her understanding. There was nothing like commiserating with someone over shared experiences, even if they were negative. Still, his situation wasn't ordinary stalking. He waited while Teri called Franks, who came to the lobby and greeted Jack with concern that seemed real, at least on the surface. After relaying the same information he gave to Teri, Jack swiftly moved the conversation back to the business at hand, and there was no more discussion of the matter for the balance of the day.

On the way home, he dialed Walt to further extinguish the brush fire before it got out of control.

"Look, Walt, you understand office gossip. Someone gets a traffic ticket, and by the time the blather machine is done, he's murdered his wife. I'm having a bit of trouble with a homeless person. Clearly, her mind isn't right. I'm talking to the police, and it'll be taken care of."

"It wouldn't happen to be that bag lady you were talking to at O'Malley's on Friday, would it?"

Jack hesitated. "As a matter of fact, it is her. I was hoping it would resolve itself on its own, but it hasn't, so I'm going to let the cops take care of it."

"Wow, what a damn nightmare," said Offerman tentatively. He paused to give Jack an opportunity to provide a more detailed explanation but continued when the silence grew uncomfortable. "We just get concerned when our ace is out of action. You missed yesterday and now this. Are you sure everything is alright, Jack? If I can help…"

"No worries. It's all good. Tell Hans he can come in off the ledge." Jack laughed, and Offerman did as well, but the tension wasn't released.

"Let me know if you need anything, Jack. I mean it. Anything."

"Sure thing, Walt, but it's under control." Jack wasn't fooled by the insincere show of support. Offerman would go to the ends of the earth for you, at least as long as you were producing.

***

By the end of the day, Jack had done a reasonably good job of fielding phone calls from his subordinates and tamping down the reaction to the earlier confrontation. He imagined that a week from now it would be in the rearview mirror, and the office gossip machine would move onto the next drama event.

Now, for the time being, he turned his attention to the meeting with the psychologist at the school in less than an hour. Jack noted that Juanita never mentioned if RosaMarie would participate, so he imagined Bryson would be watching her at home.

He pulled into the parking lot around 3:15, and when he walked into the conference room, Juanita was already there along with the counselor, school principal and RosaMarie's kindergarten teacher. Brief eye contact with Juanita confirmed this was going to be a serious meeting. The vibe was tense.

"Mr. Clausen, thank you for coming. I'm Jane Gowdy, the principal here at Westlake Elementary. You already know RosaMarie's teacher, Pam Crimmins." She gestured in that direction. "And this is Dr. Mary Whitfield, the counselor who is working with RosaMarie." After introductions and greetings, the psychologist pulled out what appeared to be a questionnaire from her folder.

"Mr. and Mrs. Clausen, I want to tell you how much I enjoyed meeting RosaMarie today. She is a bright, attentive five-year-old, and she obviously comes from a loving home."

Juanita smiled, but Jack remained stoic. "Dr. Whitfield, I get the sense a 'but' is coming," he said.

"Please," said the psychologist, "call me Mary."

Jack nodded. "Then by all means, call us Jack and Juanita."

Mary Whitfield's smile widened. "Of course." She looked down at the evaluation form for a moment. "I suspect I know the answer to this question, but I have to ask. Prior to her abduction, did RosaMarie ever speak of hearing voices?"

Jack looked over at Juanita, who shook her head slightly. "No, of course not," he said. "Are you telling me she's hearing voices?"

"I'm not sure, exactly. Our conversation got off to a great start. She talked about both of you,

180

school, her brothers and the things she enjoyed doing. All pretty pedestrian stuff. However, when I gradually shifted to the abduction, her mood and demeanor darkened considerably."

"Well, wouldn't that make sense? I mean, I can't imagine a more traumatic event for a five-year-old child."

"Actually, it's all about degrees of darkness," she said as she rifled through her notes. "The police report says the kidnapper's name is Pauley Lattimores. RosaMarie told me some of the things he said to her. Some of the things he said he was going to do to her."

"My God," said Juanita as she brought a balled fist up to her mouth.

"Don't be alarmed, Juanita. As we all know, this outcome could have been much worse. That said, words can have a lasting impact on a child, especially when they're delivered by someone who frightens them."

"I knew it. I should have killed the bastard," muttered Jack.

Dr. Whitfield said nothing, but her back stiffened ever so slightly, and her jaw clenched.

"What exactly did he say to her?"

"Frankly, it's better if I don't tell you, Mr. Clauson," she said while addressing him formally once again. "Suffice to say it was the kind of language a child should never hear. There were threats that terrified her, but she doesn't want to tell either of you about that, at least right now. Still, I'm pretty sure we can undo the damage, but that's not what bothers me." She paused and took a sip from her coffee cup. "It's the direction our talk

181

went that disturbs me more than what Lattimores said."

"I'm not following you," said Juanita.

"Has she ever mentioned the Identicals?"

"Who? Excuse me?"

"According to RosaMarie, they are beings of some kind. Short, slick, bald and roundish. Your daughter believes these creatures are communicating with her. She says they started talking to her on Saturday right after the abduction."

Jack froze. *Could it be? No... It can't possibly be them. Please, God, not them...*

"And what are they saying to her?" asked Juanita.

"I want you to listen to this part of the interview." Whitfield reached into her pocket and pulled out a small digital recorder. After cueing up the clip, she pressed play.

Identicals? My, RosaMarie, you have a vivid imagination. Who are these people?

They're not people... I'm not sure what they are. But they talk to me now. They tell me things. They're probably things I'm not supposed to know, but now I do know them.

What "things," RosaMarie? What do they tell you?

Bad things. Very, very bad things. Things I would never do because I know I would get in trouble, but they want me to do them.

So, tell me what these things are. It would be just between you and me.

There was a long pause with only the sounds of shuffling on the recording. And then: *They would like to gut you and leave your insides to bake in the sun while the buzzards eat them.*

182

She reached over and pressed stop. Juanita gasped and nearly fell out of her chair. Jack immediately went over to comfort his wife and looked back at the psychologist with a mixture of confusion and fear. He opened his mouth to speak several times but couldn't find the words. Finally, when Juanita recovered, he went back to his own seat.

"What does this mean, and how serious is it?" he asked.

"I don't know yet. Hallucinations associated with severe childhood trauma are not uncommon. It's often a byproduct of pediatric PTSD. The key is to deal with it early on, which we are doing. At this point, I'm not concerned RosaMarie is a threat to any of the other children, but it is something we're going to have to watch for."

"That's impossible," blurted out Juanita. "She would never..."

The doctor nodded at RosaMarie's teacher. "Mrs. Clauson, I know how difficult this is," said Pam Crimmins as she opened a folded sheet of drawing paper. "Art is RosaMarie's favorite subject, and before the incident, all of her drawings looked like this."

She pushed a large piece of construction paper forward. It was covered with flowers and butterflies bursting with vivid colors. A large, rainbow spanned the length of the paper. In the center was a crude rendition of a small girl with red, curly hair and a huge smile. An arrow pointed to the girl with a single word printed in red crayon above it.

"Me."

Juanita dabbed at her eyes and smiled at Jack while the teacher pulled out another paper of similar size and constitution.

"This is the drawing she made today." Crimmins' smile faded as the corners of her mouth turned down.

Drawn almost exclusively in mono black, the first impression conveyed nothing more than the scribbling of an infant. Yet, as Jack drew closer, he could see more detail. Small people running and screaming as even smaller people chased them. Those who were running had blood, depicted in red crayon, leaking from their bodies. Those chasing had blood leaking from their mouths. In the corner of the drawing, there was one word: *Identicals.*

Once she grasped the scope of the drawing, Juanita fell apart. She cried openly, and it took several minutes of consoling from the teachers and the doctor before she gained some measure of composure, shrinking into her seat and staring blankly at the floor.

Jack turned toward Dr. Whitfield. "What do we do now?"

Pensively, Whitfield chose her words. "I want her to undergo a full set of labs to rule out any underlying physiological issues. Assuming everything is okay, I'd like to start seeing her twice a week, and I might start her on Duloxetine, which is an antidepressant."

"An antidepressant? No—no way," said Juanita as she looked up with alarm. "RosaMarie is only five. We're not putting her on a damn antidepressant."

Dr. Whitfield leaned in and made eye contact. "Look, Juanita, as a mother, I understand. I have a nine-year-old, and I wouldn't want to put him on any unnecessary medication. Trust me, I wouldn't recommend it if I didn't think it was necessary... There's also something else."

"What? What more could there possibly be?" said Juanita.

"RosaMarie hinted at self-harm. She didn't threaten anything specifically, but she said the Identicals told her this morning that someone in her family was going to die soon, probably her."

"This is crazy talk," said Jack. "RosaMarie is a happy, well-adjusted little girl. I'm going home right now to talk to her about this nonsense."

The psychologist shook her head. "You can't. She was adamant that I tell neither of you any of this. If you destroy the bond of trust I'm building, she might shut down, and then we'll have no way of knowing what's going on in her mind."

After a few moments weighing Whitfield's words, Jack nodded while Juanita continued to weep. The doctor did her best to assure them this was a common manifestation of horrific childhood trauma, and in most cases, the long-term outcome was good.

"What do we do if she brings it up?" said Jack while everyone stood up as the meeting drew to a close.

"Mostly listen," said Dr. Whitfield. "If you believe there is any chance of danger or self-harm, call me immediately." She handed Jack her business card. "Don't change how you interact with her. Children are very perceptive, and most of all, reinforce to her that you love her no matter what."

***

When Jack got home, he walked into a scene out of a typical Clausen family day. Leighton was in the living room on the big screen playing Grand Theft Auto, Bryson was on his cell phone with his fingers flying across the keyboard, and RosaMarie sat on the floor singing, hunched over the coffee table while drawing on a large piece of paper.

Both parents did their best to avoid treating her differently, but Jack couldn't resist the temptation to look over his daughter's shoulder to see what she was drawing. At first glance, it seemed pretty much in character with her other happy, colorful renditions. There were two large, red flowers in the middle of the picture, with an orange fish to one side and her version of a frog to the other. The sun was shining, and the sky was blue with a single fluffy cloud floating by. Nothing to be alarmed about, at least until he looked at the far-right corner.

There, RosaMarie had drawn a small, odd-looking character. Due to her age and lack of skill, Jack couldn't tell what or who it was supposed to be, but the outline was in black, the eyebrows slanted down, and it had two, large fangs out front.

"Wow, that's a really nice picture, princess."

"Thanks, Dad," she replied.

"I love the flowers, and what a great frog. He paused and watched her smile. It felt good to see her smile. "I'm trying to figure out who that is in the corner there."

Instantly, the smile disappeared. She grabbed a black crayon and scribbled over the figure until it was blotted out.

"Whoa, I didn't say I didn't like him. I was just wondering who he was?" She turned towards Jack with her face drawn into a frown and her eyes smoldering. "It's none of your business," she said curtly.

Stunned, Jack took a step back. Ordinarily, he would have responded by sending her to her room or putting her in time out, but he remembered Dr. Whitfield's words.

"Okay, RosaMarie, I'm sorry I asked," he said while holding up his hands. She went back to her drawing and started humming a different and more melancholy tune.

Chapter Fifteen

Thankfully, the rest of the week passed quickly, remarkable only in its complete lack of turmoil and chaos. Leighton was enjoying video games and sports, Bryson continued to pester Jack about driving, and RosaMarie wasn't raising any concerns at home or in school. Her physical and bloodwork came back negative, so Dr. Whitfield decided therapy was the best way to get to the root of the child's strange behavior. A second session went better, so the antidepressants were put on hold.

Jack spent Wednesday and Thursday traveling to the branches, and each time he pulled up to the building, a knot formed in the pit of his stomach. Fortunately, the old woman stayed away, and he prayed that she was gone for good.

On Friday, he traveled downtown for his weekly with Walt and Hans, but to avoid tempting fate, he drove instead of taking the train. As an extra precaution, he turned down the invitation to join the crew for their Friday afternoon happy hour gathering at O'Malley's, falsely claiming he had to make it home to see Leighton's school play.

By Friday night, he finally allowed himself to relax. Sitting in his den with a scotch, he sipped slowly while absently watching an old NCIS episode on one of the streaming channels. That the balance of the week lacked any drama was a true blessing, and he leaned back and closed his eyes for a moment. Relaxation was a state of mind Jack had lost completely over the last year and a half, or the last week, depending on which reality he referenced.

He was drifting into a state of semi-sleep when a voice in the doorway startled him.

"Dad, can I ask you a question?"

Jack opened his eyes and looked over at his daughter. "Hi, RosaMarie. Isn't it past your bedtime?"

"I need to ask you something."

He pushed his chair forward, sat up and rubbed the sleep out of his eyes. "This sounds serious."

She continued to stand in the doorway, unwilling to commit to coming inside the room. "Is Mr. Egebe a bad man?"

Jack paused. "RosaMarie, we had this discussion. Of course he's not a bad man. Jamal Egebe is a very good man."

"If he didn't come over, you would have stayed and played with me, and I wouldn't have gone outside and got stolen."

Jack got up, walked over to RosaMarie and crouched down so he was at eye level. "Once and for all, you can't blame Mr. Egebe or anyone else for what happened. The only one responsible was that bad man who took you. Do you understand?"

She continued to stare at him. Her expression did not waver. Finally, she spoke slowly and deliberately. "Some people think different."

Jack stood up and regarded her carefully. "Who thinks differently?"

"It doesn't matter who." In an instant, her expression changed, and her eyes lit up. "Can we play characters tomorrow?"

"Ah, yes, of course, pumpkin," he replied, "but tell me who it is that thinks differently about Mr. Egebe?"

RosaMarie tilted her head and frowned. "What are you talking about?"

"Mr. Egebe. You said…"

"Oh yeah, Egebe. I have a play date with Katie, Tanya and Jahala Egebe at Jahala's house tomorrow. Can we do characters after that?"

Jack leaned to one side and scratched his head. "Uh, sure. I should be finished with my yard work by then… And RosaMarie?"

"Yes, Daddy?"

"No more talk about Mr. Egebe being a bad man, okay? He was very worried about you."

"Sure, Dad." She nodded slightly and smiled before walking away, leaving Jack completely confused. Her animus toward Jamal Egebe seemed genuine for a moment but then disappeared. He made a note to mention it to Dr. Whitfield.

Later, after brushing his teeth, he joined Juanita in bed, lying on his back with his hands laced together behind his head. He glanced over, but she was engrossed in a romance novel on her Kindle.

"Okay, what is it?" Juanita put the device on her nightstand and looked at him.

"Huh? What do you mean?" he said while unlacing his hands and sitting up.

"You've sighed three times since you came to bed. I've been with you long enough to know that means something is troubling you."

"No, I'm fine. It's just that…

"Just what?" she repeated.

"I don't know," he said. "I'm still worried about RosaMarie. She seems alright on the outside, but I sense she's really struggling emotionally far more than I'd hoped."

Juanita paused and looked away. "Well, maybe we're having trouble understanding just how deeply this affected her. She was kidnapped, Jack. Part of me is still in shock and can't accept it either. For a five-year-old…"

He nodded, but his expression was blank.

"Look, Dr. Whitfield said this is going to take time. RosaMarie is working through some serious trauma, and she isn't mature enough to process it quickly. We have to remain patient."

"You're right. It's just that something is different, and I can't put my finger on it." Turning to her directly, he continued, "She asked me tonight if Jamal was a bad man because if he hadn't stopped by, Lattimores couldn't have kidnapped her. That's the second time she's brought that up."

"I don't think it's that odd. She's trying to decide who the heroes and villains are. Until this Lattimores creep showed up, everyone was a hero. Now she knows better. As I said, she's trying to process all of it."

"Yeah, but when I told her the only person responsible was Lattimores, she said others disagree. I tried to find out what that meant, but she changed the subject. That's disturbing as hell."

191

Juanita nodded. "I imagine there's more going on with her than we can comprehend. The terror she must have felt..." Her head drooped, and Jack could sense her sadness.

Now, it was his turn to reassure her. "Keep remembering what you just told me, and keep reminding yourself how blessed we are that we have her here safe and sound." Jack's mind immediately conjured up images of the other reality when he first saw RosaMarie in the shallow grave. No matter how emotionally messed up she might be right now, nothing could compare to the horror of looking at her dead corpse.

Juanita gently lowered her hand onto his arm. "Are you ever going to tell me the truth about how you knew where Lattimores took RosaMarie?"

"I did tell you. It was blind luck." He rolled over and put his arm around his wife. "Turn out the light, Nita. I need you tonight."

***

Jack woke and looked outside at a beautiful fall September day. The sun was shining, and he could hear birds singing in the background. He reached out for Juanita, but she was already up, so he glanced at the clock.

Nine-thirty. Holy shit.

"Hey, sleepy head." Jack stumbled into the living room to find his wife standing near the door with her arm around her daughter.

"Hi, Dad. We're going to the Egebe's house for my playdate. I'll be back in..." RosaMarie looked at her mother. "How long?"

"Two hours."

"Two hours," she repeated.

"Good, good," he replied. "Leighton... He's got a game... When does he have to be there?"

"Relax," said Juanita. "The game doesn't start until two. That gives you time to drive with Bryson while I'm gone, and then you can play with RosaMarie before we have to leave." She rolled her eyes and whispered, "I got the better part of this deal."

Jack shook his head and smiled. He watched as his daughter and his wife went out the front door hand in hand. A memory suddenly spiked, and he pictured Juanita walking out that same door, leaving him with a vow never to return, which sent him deeper into the bottle. This reality may be strange and confusing, but he would gladly live out his days here as opposed to returning to that nightmare.

Just as the door closed, Bryson came bounding down the stairs, jingling the car keys to Juanita's SUV. "Ready to risk your life?" he said with a mischievous smile.

His father groaned and nodded. Looking up over the railing, he yelled, "Leighton, I'm going driving with Bryson. You don't leave or let anyone in. Is that understood?"

"Sure, dad," came the reply from above with just a hint of annoyance. Leighton was old enough to stay by himself for short periods, but considering RosaMarie's abduction, Jack was tempted to tighten the reins on him, but he knew it wouldn't be right.

Once inside the car, Jack buckled up and placed his feet firmly on the floorboards as though he was bracing for a collision. Whether it was now or in the other reality, he worked the invisible brakes often as his son's questionable judgement placed them in harm's way on at least a half dozen occasions. Bryson was particularly challenged when making double lane turns, and he occasionally drifted across the dividing line. One of these drifts almost ended in a wreck, and Jack recalled the screech of tires and the long honk that followed.

Fortunately, Bryson's driving improved quite a bit over the last month, so about an hour into the lesson when a VW suddenly changed lanes without signaling, Bryson deftly moved into the double yellow median divider and braked, creating enough space between the two vehicles to avoid an accident.

Once his heart crawled up from his stomach to its proper anatomical position, Jack swallowed hard and breathed a sigh of relief. He looked over at Bryson and said, "Son, I think you're ready to get your license."

Bryson glanced over and grinned widely. This was another one of those moments, father and son connecting on a level that went beyond words. Jack was keenly aware these memories were few, so he leaned over and playfully cuffed his son's shoulder, and the chapter was complete.

Just as he pulled his hand back, the phone rang.

"Hello, Nita, Bryson just saved our lives. I think he's ready for his drivers test."

"Jack... Jack, get back here right away. It's Jamal."

"What happened?" Bryson looked over, but Jack motioned for him to pay attention to the road.

"What happened?" he repeated.

"He fell. Everyone is guessing he had one foot on an extension ladder and the other on a side ledge while he was trying to clear the gutters. Somehow, the ladder gave way, and he hit his head on the brick ledge and then the air conditioner. Jack, it's serious. He was knocked out, and he's still unconscious."

Jack lowered the phone for a moment and calmly told Bryson to pull over.

"My God," he put the phone back up to his ear. "Who found him?"

"Huzaifa heard a loud bang against the outside wall of his bedroom... And, there's something else." Jack gave her time, but Juanita didn't continue.

"What, Nita? What else?"

"RosaMarie was standing next to Jamal when Huzaifa found him."

He ran his hand through his hair. "What was she doing there?"

"I don't know. The girls were playing a ring toss game, but I guess RosaMarie left. She must have walked around to the side of the house because that's where she was standing when Huzaifa got there."

"What did she say about it?"

"Nothing when we were there, thank God. But when we got home... When we got home, she told me Mr. Egebe was a bad man and deserved it."

Jack's hand covered his mouth, and he shook his head slowly. "She didn't say anything while you were there?"

"No. I immediately took her home." Her voice cracked as she spoke. "Jack, do you think she…"

"Of course not. I…" His voice faltered. "We're going to come home. I need to check on Jamal, and we need to talk to RosaMarie."

"Yes. And I'm going to call Dr. Whitfield right away."

Jack changed places with Bryson and drove as quickly as he could, giving his son the short version of Egebe's accident while avoiding any mention of RosaMarie. As he walked inside, he saw Juanita sitting with their daughter in the living room. RosaMarie had her hands folded in her lap, staring out into space while Juanita was reading. They both looked relieved when they saw Jack and Bryson.

Juanita forced a smile, but RosaMarie remained stoic. Jack took a seat in the recliner across from her and gave Bryson a signal to leave the room.

Once settled in, he leaned forward and studied her for a moment. She seemed particularly small and fragile. "Mommy told me a terrible thing happened at the Egebe's. Want to talk about it?"

RosaMarie shook her head and continued to look at her shoes.

"Okay, that's fine. I'm just glad you were close by. Mr. Egebe would be in much worse shape if you hadn't found him when you did." He paused, but RosaMarie didn't reply.

"You didn't see how he fell, did you, RosaMarie?"

She looked up at him, and her expression hardened. "Mr. Egebe is a bad man."

"RosaMarie, stop it. We talked about this."

"He's a bad man, and I'm glad he got hurt. Lots of people are glad he got hurt!"

"RosaMarie!" Juanita dropped the Kindle and turned toward her daughter with a look of horror. "You apologize for saying that right now!"

Jack watched RosaMarie while signaling to Juanita to stop talking.

"Who told you that Mr. Egebe should get hurt?

RosaMarie spoke through gritted teeth. "There are a lot of people…" She paused, locked her fingers together and turned them inside out before blurting, "The Identicals told me."

After exchanging worried glances with Juanita, Jack said, "Who are the Identicals?"

Her brow furrowed, and the corners of her mouth turned down. "You already know who they are, Dad. Why are you asking me?"

"Who do you think told us about the Identicals, RosaMarie?" asked Juanita.

RosaMarie snapped her head around. "I *knew* that damn Whitfield wouldn't keep a secret, but that's not what I'm talking about. You don't know about them like I do… but Dad does."

Jack straightened up and tried to process. "Watch your language, young lady." He glanced at his wife and caught her surprised and troubled expression. Then, looking back at his daughter, he said, "I've never heard of any Identicals, RosaMarie. Why don't you tell us about them?"

She sighed and shook her head while getting up from the couch. "Please. Identicals are like us, only different. You know about them. You've known about them for a long time, Dad. They're mad at you because you cheated them."

A chill started slowly in the small of Jack's back and began spreading throughout his body. By the time it reached his extremities, he was trembling.

"What are you talking about?" he said in a dry, raspy voice.

"Don't act stupid. You know." RosaMarie stood up and started walking toward the staircase.

Juanita moved quickly and blocked her path. "Did you push Mr. Egebe off that ladder?"

RosaMarie looked over and smiled sweetly. "He put the ladder on the rocks, and it was wobbling, Mommy. Then, it just fell over..." She kept smiling as she walked around her mother until she reached the stairs. Slowly, with one hand on the railing, she turned her head back towards her parents.

"Mr. Egebe isn't the only bad person. You all should have been there to keep that bad man from stealing me, but you didn't care, did you?"

"RosaMarie, that isn't true. Come back here!"

Jack heard small footsteps running up the stairs, and the bedroom door slammed shut, leaving him in stunned silence.

"Oh my God. She pushed Jamal off the ladder, Jack. She did it."

Jack walked over and sat next to his wife, placing his arm around her. "She didn't admit to anything, Nita. She just said..."

Juanita pulled away. Her eyes were red, but there were no tears, just puffiness and blotches of red. "She did it, Jack. I'm her mother; I know. We have to get her into Dr. Whitfield tomorrow."

Jack nodded. "Okay, but we can't say anything to anyone about this, *especially* Dr. Whitfield."

***

After Juanita called the next morning, Mary Whitfield scheduled a special session with RosaMarie that lasted nearly two hours. Once she returned to class, Jack and his wife arrived without their daughter's knowledge to talk to the psychologist.

"I'm afraid RosaMarie isn't improving as I had hoped." The doctor appeared troubled and wrung her hands as she spoke. "In fact, I believe her condition is getting worse. She's grown hostile towards me and accused me of betraying her confidence. Today, she called me some rather vile names and threatened me. Listen to this." She pushed an icon on her phone.

You're a bitch, Whitfield. A bitch and a bad person. Just like Egebe. Identicals hate bad people like you, and now, you're going to get yours!

Jack stared at the phone without speaking. The voice sounded like RosaMarie's, but the words? No, it couldn't be possible. "That—that isn't RosaMarie. She's—she's only five…"

"It is, Jack. It's RosaMarie's voice." Juanita spoke in a whisper.

"According to her teacher, Mrs. Crimmins, RosaMarie is also becoming more aggressive in class. She ripped another student's dress today, pushed a boy down on the playground and called another student 'a fat whore' and threatened to hurt her.

"Your daughter's mental health seems to be deteriorating rapidly." The doctor stared down at her notes. "I'm curious as to why you requested an unscheduled meeting? Did something happen at home?"

Jack exchanged a worried glance with Juanita. "No, not exactly. I guess it was just a series of things that were out of character, similar to what's happening in class."

"Who is 'Mr. Egebe', and why does RosaMarie claim he's such a bad man?"

No one spoke until Jack finally said, "He's a neighbor. He fell off a ladder this weekend, and he's in a coma. RosaMarie doesn't like him because I was with him when she was abducted."

"I see..." Dr. Whitfield scribbled on her notepad.

"Doctor, what are we going to do about this? We're really starting to worry," asked Juanita.

"I understand, and I share your concern. I'm going to give you two scripts. Let's see if they help. One is an antidepressant, and the other is a sedative. I don't want you to become alarmed. These are common drugs that have a history of helping children like RosaMarie who are struggling."

"What is it, doctor? What does RosaMarie have?"

"I'm entering a diagnosis of pediatric post-traumatic stress disorder accompanied by depression. You probably heard of PTSD and its association with military personnel who have seen combat. However, anyone who has experienced a traumatic event can develop the disease. It's often accompanied by depression, and together, they

200

play havoc with the person's mental health and well-being."

"But she's just a child," said Juanita as she sagged down into her chair. Jack remembered that profile; that look. It came from the old reality. "What can we do to help her?" she asked quietly.

"Honestly, Juanita, I'm not quite sure yet. This has become very serious in a short time. Besides the PTSD and depression, there is something else that's bothering me. RosaMarie brought up these Identicals again. I've indulged the fantasy because I thought her mind may have manifested it as a way to work through the trauma, but now I'm not so sure. Today, the delusion seemed more like a hallucination."

Jack exhaled a long, exhausted breath.

"What's worse, she believes you're deeply involved with them, Jack. She keeps mentioning some sort of debt you didn't repay, and now the Identicals are angry. RosaMarie talks in riddles, and much of it is hard to follow, but that's the gist of it, and I don't like where it's taking her.

"Continue to give her love and support, but don't push her," said Whitfield as she extended her hand and passed the prescriptions to Juanita. "There is one more thing. We have to monitor RosaMarie's tendencies closely. I don't want to cause undue alarm, but she can't be allowed to endanger the other children. If we're unable to get this resolved soon, you will have to make other arrangements for her schooling."

"*Other arrangements?* What does that even mean?" Juanita took a step back.

"There are places more suited to handle unstable, disruptive children. They offer extremely humane treatment, and the staff is well qualified. I'm still hopeful we won't get to that point, but RosaMarie's teacher is very concerned, and the school has significant liability."

"I don't give a damn about the school's liability. You're a doctor, so do your fucking job and figure out what's wrong with my daughter..."

"Juanita!" Jack took his wife by the elbow and led her toward the door. "I'm sorry, Doctor," he said as they left the room. He didn't let Juanita go until they reached the car.

Chapter Sixteen

For several days, Jack and Juanita barely spoke. She continued to insist they go to the authorities and tell them what they knew about Jamal Egebe's accident. Jack resisted fiercely, contending that RosaMarie's life would be forever altered over something she might not even have done. After all, Jack argued, RosaMarie never explicitly said she pushed Jamal.

In the end, Juanita relented, but that all changed when she received a phone call from Carol Egebe.

"Jack, Jamal regained consciousness, but Carol says he has a—deficiency. He can't control the left side of his body, and he can barely speak. But..." She dropped her head and brought her hand up to her forehead.

"But what?" said Jack impatiently. He was already late for work and couldn't afford to keep skipping out on his responsibilities. Walt brought it up at last Friday's meeting. The reference was casual and blanketed in a joke, but the intent was clear. Apparently, a few of the managers complained he forgot to sign off on their bonuses, and when money is involved, even the timid speak up.

"She said Jamal keeps saying, 'RosaMarie' over and over. I sensed her anger, and she told me the police started an investigation. Carol has always been so passive, and she's never spoken to me like that before. She knows, Jack."

"Fucking great," he said while gritting his teeth. "Just what I need right now." He swung his head around. "Where is RosaMarie?"

"I dropped her off early at school. She has an appointment with Dr. Whitfield before class."

Jack grabbed his briefcase and headed for the front door. "I'm late again... I'll be working out of the Carol Stream store today. Can we have at least one day of peace?"

"Sure, Jack," Juanita yelled after him. "Let's pretend none of this is happening."

"Well, if you just had watched her that day..." He regretted the words before they left his mouth. Without turning back to witness her reaction, he left and slammed the door.

The unresolved conflict made the ride to Carol Stream seem longer than usual, and even when he arrived at the facility, Jack was distracted. The usual enthusiasm and fire was missing, and the employees sensed it.

In a fiercely competitive industry, sales could stagnate in a week or two, and that was not lost on Walt and Hans. They had a business to run and were losing patience, and Jack knew he could only stay preoccupied with RosaMarie for so long. Whether he was in a new reality, a simulation or a delusion, he needed to get his act together soon.

"... And that's the problem with the inventory... Jack? *Jack?*"

"Wha? Oh, sorry, Barry. What were you saying?"

Barry Steiner looked at Jack awkwardly. "The inventory. We need to keep eight by one pipe covering in stock, or we won't sell any half by one without it. I don't care what that damn program says about turns and eliminating slow moving inventory. If we don't have all the sizes, the customers will go somewhere else... Jack?"

"Uh, yeah, sorry... Look, I understand your point, but you know Walt is big on the Kitner software. It's the most sophisticated AI for inventory and distribution..."

"Yeah, we've heard that for a year, but its lack of flexibility is costing us business... Are you even listening?"

Jack jerked his head up and drew in a deep breath. "Okay, Barry, give me a list of all the items the system is closing out, and I'll look them over. If you want me to go to battle with Walt, you have to give me a detailed explanation of why you need them. Stories like you just told me about the pipe insulation are exactly what I'm looking for. Be as specific as you can."

"You got it. I'll get to work on it tomorrow, and I'll have it ready for you before your meeting downtown on Friday," said Steiner.

Jack rose from the conference table and gathered his reports. He usually worked at the branches until four o'clock, but at 2:30, he was ready to call it a day. "Just watch those margins, Barry. You're running razor thin."

"It's freakin' Airco. They keep bombing the prices." Steiner seemed to realize he just broke a cardinal rule of sales. The boss doesn't want excuses. "Don't worry, Jack, we'll figure out some way to get the margins up." The branch manager followed him to the door and out into the parking lot. When he reached his car, Jack looked over his shoulder.

"Is there anything else, Barry?"

"No, I—Is everything alright with you, Jack? You seemed preoccupied, and to be honest, you look a bit ragged. We're all concerned."

Jack smiled. "I'm fine. A little tired maybe, but nothing more. We have a lot going on at corporate, and I'm putting in a ton of hours." He looked up and saw the worry flash across Steiner's face. "But it's all good, I promise. You're going to be very happy when you hear about the new bonus program I'm working on."

"Great, Jack. That is exciting, but take care of yourself, okay?"

Jack nodded, shook Steiner's hand and got into his BMW. He watched as the manager walked back to the building, and he smiled and waved one last time before starting the engine. Mercifully, he was able to get away without having to answer any more questions about his health and appearance.

For an instant, Jack considered stopping at a bar on the way home just to unwind. He turned off his phone as a kind of Pavlov's dog response. These days, when the phone rang, something bad usually followed.

The thoughts that kept running through his brain were increasingly disjointed. He had no way of understanding what was happening to him. Every time he started accepting this new reality, the old one would rear its ugly head and remind him he was a transplant, a misplaced person contaminating a different timeline.

If he stopped at a bar to drown his troubles, he knew it would end badly. No question, the best plan was to go straight home, especially after the cruel words he said to Juanita earlier that morning. Plus, the drinking was becoming a problem again, so he listened to left-brain and pointed the car toward Maple Street. Just as he completed the thought, right-brain butted in and reminded him of a fresh bottle of scotch waiting patiently at home, anyway.

A little after 3:30, he pulled into the driveway. The boys were probably walking home from school about now, and he imagined RosaMarie was with Juanita grocery shopping, so no one was home. The silence inside the house was eerie and uncomfortable. Jack had grown accustomed to the controlled chaos environment that surrounded him every day.

He walked into the kitchen to get some orange juice when he saw the note on the refrigerator:

Dr. Whitfield called. RosaMarie was out of control and attacked another child. I'm going to the school. They're holding her there. Tried to call you. Please come quickly.

Jack grabbed his keys, dashed out to the car and made the short trip in a fog of worry and fear. As he walked toward the conference room, the walls of the elementary school seemed to grow progressively narrower. The first glance at Dr. Whitfield and Juanita conveyed the seriousness of the situation.

"Mr. Clausen, please have a seat." Whitfield's demeanor was all business. The compassion she displayed in their previous meetings was missing. In that moment, Jack realized she had changed sides. "RosaMarie is in the arts and crafts room with Pam Crimmins, so your wife and I have had a chance to talk for a while. I'll summarize what I told her.

"It's clear to me RosaMarie is dealing with several significant issues that make her a threat to herself and the other children. This afternoon, she attacked another child and tried to gouge her eyes out. Mrs. Crimmins had trouble getting her to break off the assault, and it took two teachers to restrain her."

"Dear God," said Jack. "Is the other child alright?"

Whitfield nodded. "She's traumatized but physically okay. However, there are gouge marks all over her face and bruises on her arms and chest." She showed Jack a picture on her cell phone. The poor girl's face was covered with scratches, and her eyes were swollen as if someone punched them.

Jack looked at Juanita. "Not RosaMarie. There is no way RosaMarie did that."

"For God's sake, stop denying what's happening, Jack," Juanita replied without looking at him. "She did it. RosaMarie attacked that little girl."

"As I said, your daughter has some serious issues, Mr. Clausen. I'm afraid there isn't any quick fix for this."

"Why won't anyone understand that a damn child abuser kidnapped her?" he said. "Who knows what he told her? She just needs more time."

"She needs far more than time. RosaMarie is slipping into a deep psychosis, and she requires treatment from doctors far more qualified than I am in dealing with illnesses like this."

"What are you suggesting?"

"I want your permission to send RosaMarie away to a facility in Chicago where she can receive the care she needs."

Juanita shook her head, and her expression hardened. "I told her no, Jack. Not that. We'll do anything, but not that."

"Out of the question," he said. "There is absolutely no way I'll agree to putting her in a mental institution."

"Please, Mr. and Mrs. Clausen, be reasonable. Modern mental health hospitals have nothing in common with the places you're thinking of. They are extremely comfortable and accommodating. Most importantly, RosaMarie will get the treatment she desperately needs. I want to avoid a tragedy."

Jack's breathing quickened, and his jaw muscles worked. "The only tragedy would be if you put my daughter in an institution." He paused as his voice started cracking. "Look, Dr. Whitfield, you don't understand. If you insist on committing RosaMarie, it will destroy my family."

"I'm sorry, Mr. Clausen. I truly am. However, RosaMarie's mental health is declining rapidly. Her anger continues to rise, and I'm really afraid that if we don't intervene, someone will get hurt."

"I will fight you on this."

Whitfield's jaw tightened. "I hope you don't. Believe me, this is the last thing I wanted to have to do, but I will get CPS to go to court for an involuntary commitment if I have to." She got up from her seat. "You two have a lot to talk about, and I'm sure RosaMarie is ready to leave by now. Please make sure she is taking her medication until this is resolved."

They made the drive home in silence. RosaMarie refused to make eye contact and wouldn't respond to anything said to her, no matter how gently the words were spoken. When they walked inside the house, she immediately went to her room and shut the door, showing no interest in eating or interacting with the family. Juanita took a plate to her room and left it inside, but several hours later, the food was still untouched.

***

Jack spent the rest of the night in a haze of anger, doubt and self-pity. As he poured another scotch, he wondered how his new life had gone so wrong so quickly. Perhaps he only succeeded in swapping one hellish reality for another.

Just as he took the first swallow from his fourth drink, he heard the sound of shattering glass and a commotion coming from the other end of the house. Wobbling on legs unsteady from the effects of the alcohol, he stumbled out of the den. What he saw as he approached the living room made him pause as he tried to make sense of the scene playing out in front of him.

"RosaMarie! Put that… stop that."

Juanita stood at one end of the room, jabbering insensibly while leaning over with her arms outstretched. The boys were standing behind her, stuck in a rigid pose with their eyes locked on their sister and their mouths hanging open.

Slowly, confusion gave way to shock, and Jack felt sluggish, almost like swimming in molasses. He tried to comprehend the visual, but his brain glitched and wouldn't process the information his optic nerves provided. Someone, or something, stood near the fireplace next to the cracked and broken coffee table. It resembled RosaMarie, but it wasn't her. The entity's facial features were distorted somehow, and the thing, whatever it was, looked much, much older than his daughter. Many decades older, in fact. Maybe centuries older.

It held a jagged shard of glass in its hand, and the point was pressed against its other arm, pushing hard enough to draw blood near the wrist. In the dim light in the living room, he saw an outline behind it, which passed through it, and finally stood out in front. It flickered like a hologram while changing size and shape. Jack tilted his head to the side and frowned, but a flash of light illuminated the creature completely for a moment, and he knew.

While hideous boils and lesions created a mask that amplified the hate behind the deep snarl, he recognized the shape of its face and body. The small stature and rounded shoulders; the evenly cut pointed teeth and facial features spaced too far apart. He was looking at Torto, but not the version he encountered in the other reality. The animus and enmity drifted up from the slick layer of sweat that

211

covered its body. Jack could smell it, a stench unlike anything he had ever experienced before.

"Why, Daddy? Why you not pay what you owe?" RosaMarie spoke with the same dialect and inflections as Torto.

"Jack? Jack, what's going on here? Why is she talking that way?" Juanita backed up, still keeping her arms extended to keep the boys behind her.

"RosaMarie," said Jack, "put the glass down, princess. Please, put the glass down."

"Torto make fair deal, Daddy. You want girl back. He do his part, but you not do yours. Now… now you not right up. Nothing right, don'cha know."

Jack held out his hand and started slowly walking toward his daughter. He stopped twice as he saw her press the sharp edge deeper into her wrist.

"RosaMarie, put down the glass and let's talk about this."

"No, Daddy," said RosaMarie. "Jack say what he did. Jack say he not pay debt."

"Okay, okay. I'm sorry I let you down, and I'm sorry I didn't—I didn't pay my debt." Jack noticed the pressure on her wrist lessened slightly. A little more of RosaMarie emerged as the apparition of Torto faded a bit.

"I'll do what he wants, RosaMarie. I'll find him and do what he wants. Just drop the piece of glass. Please…"

She hesitated, and her expression softened. The next words were in her own voice. "Do you mean it, Daddy? Do you really mean it?"

"Yes, I'll make it right, RosaMarie. Just drop the glass." While they were talking, he continued to inch forward until he believed he was close enough to grab her arm.

"Jack not lie to Torto. Jack tell truth this time, right?"

Jack stiffened. This voice *was* Torto's. Instinctively, he lunged and grabbed RosaMarie. She realized his intent just before his fingers touched her, and she tried to draw the piece of glass across her wrist.

Juanita screamed as she saw the first drop of blood drip off of RosaMarie's arm and land on the tile with a small splash. Jack forced the shard out of her hand and flung it across the room before wrapping his arms around her. She kicked, screamed and struggled like a trapped animal until exhaustion set in, and she finally went limp in his arms. He held her close for a long time as Juanita ran and got a gauze bandage that she wrapped tightly around the superficial wound on RosaMarie's wrist.

In shock, and increasingly aware of her surroundings, RosaMarie started crying in deep, agonizing sobs. Juanita tried to provide comfort, but the fear and terror had grown deep roots. After sending the boys upstairs, the two of them spent the next several hours watching over their daughter as she sat wrapped in her mother's arms while sullenly staring at cartoons on the TV. She refused to eat anything but eventually started yawning and nodded off.

Juanita handed RosaMarie to Jack, who gently carried her up to her room, carefully laying her on the bed. Juanita followed and pulled the covers up, and they both stood at her bedside, watching as she stared at the ceiling with a vacant, expressionless look on her face.

Afraid to leave her alone, Jack pulled up a chair and sat down while Juanita went to tend to the boys. He watched his daughter blink periodically, but she still wasn't talking. The silence grew in volume until it became ear shattering, interrupted only by the foreboding and sinister periodic hooting of a barn owl in the distance.

There was no way to know just how much time passed before RosaMarie closed her eyes and rolled over. Soon thereafter, her rhythmic and deep breathing suggested she was finally sleeping. Jack stood up slowly and tiptoed to the door, but just as he left the room, the damn doorbell rang.

He tried to listen but couldn't make out what was being said downstairs. However, Juanita's volume and inflections suggested the visit was confrontational. Just as he stepped out to go join her, he heard a soft voice from behind.

"Daddy, what's happening to me?" RosaMarie looked at him as the tears flowed down her cheeks in two distinct lines.

"You'll be fine, pumpkin," he said while walking back and reaching down to hug her. "You're having a rough time right now, but everything will be fine."

"But—but I don't know why I say and do things I don't want to do," she said. "I see them, but nobody else does. They tell me things, Daddy. They tell me to be bad."

"Who do you see, and what do they tell you, princess?"

She paused. "Identicals. Torto. They're all named Torto. They say you cheated them, Daddy. They say I have to do bad things to make up for it."

Jack sat back down in the chair. He grabbed one hand with the other because they were both shaking.

"I know Torto, RosaMarie. Tell me what he wants."

"He wants you to give him what you owe him, Daddy." She paused and wiped the tears from her cheeks. "What is it you owe him?"

Jack ran his hands down the length of his thighs as he thought of ways to answer her simple question. "It's a misunderstanding, RosaMarie. I'll talk to Torto tomorrow and get this all worked out. The Identicals won't bother you anymore."

She nodded and lay back down on her bed. "Okay, Daddy. I'm tired now. I think I'm going to go to sleep."

Jack leaned over and kissed her forehead.

***

Leighton was outside playing, and Bryson left earlier with some friends, so Jack retreated to the den and poured himself a double. It was just past dinnertime, and he hadn't eaten, so a bracer would have to do. He closed his eyes and tried to make sense of it all.

Torto. I'll find that little bastard and kill him. I swear.

Juanita came into the den and stood silently. Before she spoke, Jack noticed how tired she looked. Her eyes had darkened, and they seemed to have sunk deeper into their sockets. The light was dimming quickly just like before.

"Hitting the bottle again, Jack?" she asked curtly.

"In case you haven't noticed, it's been pretty tense around here. I'm trying to take a little of the edge off... Who were you talking to downstairs?"

"Detective Ferguson. He wants to interview RosaMarie. I told him she was under the weather, but that won't hold him off for long. Apparently, Jamal is regaining some limited ability to communicate, and he becomes very agitated when they bring up the accident and mention RosaMarie. I'm sure they'll talk to Dr. Whitfield about how she attacked that little girl today."

"Don't worry, they won't find out anything. Whitfield has to honor patient confidentiality, and Jamal... Jamal may never fully recover."

"Look, Jack, she almost admitted it..."

"But she *didn't* admit it, Juanita." Jack snapped at her and slammed his glass down.

She raised her eyebrows. "I heard you talking to RosaMarie. This isn't the first time she's brought up these Identicals or whatever they're called. She also keeps talking about some debt you owe. And who is this Torto person? What's going on, Jack? When she held that sharp glass to her wrist, it didn't even look like RosaMarie. I need to know what's happening to my daughter."

He took another long swallow of scotch before answering. "There's nothing to tell," he said flatly.

"You heard the doctor say she's delusional. I'm playing along because I'm hoping if I can persuade her that I've settled my debt with this imaginary Torto character, I can put an end to all of this."

Juanita took a step back and turned toward the door. Over her shoulder, she said, "Something is very wrong with RosaMarie. We both know it. I think you know much more than you're letting on, Jack. If anything happens to our daughter because of something you've done or are hiding from me, I swear to God…"

Without looking up, he said, "Get the hell out of here, Juanita.

A half bottle of scotch later, Jack sat sprawled in his chair looking at pictures of his family that sat off to the side of his desk. He lifted his glass and took a sloppy slug and studied their smiling faces. When the camera caught those moments, they were all happy, and each photo radiated its own natural warmth. As he reached for one of the pictures, something fell off the side of his desk. Almost tipping over as he leaned down, he picked up the business card with a name on the front so bold it caught his attention.

Tucker Lutz, Clairvoyant

Jack rifled it through his fingers like it was a playing card. He remembered what Lutz told him when they met on the train: *I know, it sounds absurd, but if you ever find yourself in a situation you can't understand, give me a call, okay?*

For several minutes, Jack held his cell phone. The number was punched in, but he hesitated to hit the call button. Finally, after another long drink, he summoned up the nerve. The phone barely completed a single ring before it made a connection.

"Hello, Jack. What can I do for you?"

Chapter Seventeen

"I know, Walt, I know. I just need one more day. It's a family situation."

"No, I don't think you do know, Jack. You're missing work almost every day, and even when you're here, you're not here. You look like you haven't slept in weeks, and the employees are starting to talk. Why don't you tell me what's going on? I mean, *really* going on."

Jack pursed his lips and grimaced. The last thing he wanted was to bring Walt and Hans into his nightmare.

"It's RosaMarie."

"...Geez, Jack, why didn't you say something? Is she sick?"

"Not exactly, but she is going through some mental health challenges. We're working through it. Honestly, Walt, I—I really don't enjoy talking about it."

"Alright; I understand. I only wish you had told me sooner. Jesus Christ, I always say family comes first. Okay, take the day off and try to get whatever it is resolved. We need you with your head on straight. Stay in close contact on this. We've got Atlanta coming online in a month, and I can't afford to have you any less than a hundred percent."

"Thanks, Walt. I'm sorry. I'll get my act together."

"Just focus on your kid, and give my best to Juanita."

Jack hung up just as he turned into the driveway of a modest Tudor Revival in Berwyn. He glanced at the card to make sure he had the address right. The yard was neat, and the house kept up, but the grass grew over the concrete path all the way up to the porch. The absence of bushes, yard decorations and other frills gave the appearance of a rental unit.

The door opened before he reached the landing.

"Hello, Jack, please come on in." Tucker Lutz was dressed in a pair of sweatpants and a t-shirt that read, "This is not here."

Once inside, Lutz motioned him into the living room. The interior of the house reflected the same level of neatness and austerity as the outside. Jack took a seat on the sofa as Lutz flopped into an old recliner opposite the coffee table. He made no offer of refreshment.

Each waited for the other to speak until Lutz motioned for Jack to talk first.

"I—I really don't know where to begin. You told me I should contact you if I found myself in a situation I couldn't understand. Well, I'm involved in something so bizarre I'm wondering if I'm losing my mind."

Lutz nodded. "Okay. Why don't you start by telling me what's happening."

Jack cleared his throat. "Ah, my daughter is having a breakdown of sorts. She's the sweetest five-year-old on the face of the planet, but lately, she has become violent."

"In what way?"

"Last night, she broke our coffee table and held a sharp piece of glass against her wrist. If I hadn't grabbed her, I think she would have cut herself on purpose."

Lutz nodded and rubbed his chin. "Is she under the care of a mental health professional?"

"Yes, but that's not what it's about. There's more to it than that."

"What does that mean, exactly?"

Jack took a deep breath. "Her counselor played us a disturbing recording. RosaMarie, that's my daughter's name, used language we never heard before, and she expressed incredibly dark feelings in some recent drawings. Her art was always bright and cheery, but these pictures were sinister. And…"

"And what, Jack."

"She may have pushed our neighbor off a ladder."

Lutz sat back in his chair, waiting a moment while he collected his thoughts. "Usually, that kind of sudden change in behavior is caused by a traumatic event. Did RosaMarie recently experience anything that might have triggered her?"

"Yes… She was abducted."

"…Oh, my lord. I can't imagine the trauma your family is going through, Jack. I'm so sorry."

"Thank you. Mercifully, she didn't suffer any physical abuse that we know of. In fact, she was only with the monster for a few minutes before she was rescued."

"Thank God. And how was she rescued so quickly? Who found her?"

"Well, actually, I'm the one who rescued her. I saw the car that abducted her and I followed it."

Lutz moved forward in his chair. "I'm getting a coke. You want one? I have bottled water too."

"Sure, water sounds good. My throat is actually kind of dry."

With some difficulty, Lutz used his stubby arms to push himself up off the chair. Jack heard him rifling around in the kitchen before he returned with the bottled water, coke and a worn spiral notebook. He handed the water to Jack and took his seat.

"I believe everything you told me, except the last part about seeing the car the creep was in. That's bullshit."

"Now wait a minute..."

"No, if you aren't up front with me, I can't help you. You're here because you know this isn't a mental health problem. It's much deeper and more complicated than that. Your resonance, it's... You did rescue her, but you're not being straight about how you knew where to go."

"Uh..." Jack ran his hand through his hair several times. "Look, if I told you that part, you'd never believe me. You'll think I'm crazy, and..." Jack lowered his head. "Maybe I am crazy."

Tuck took a long swig of his coke, draining nearly half the bottle. His face contorted for several seconds, but Jack didn't realize he was calling up a belch until Lutz opened his mouth and the deep sound bellowed out.

"Uh, sorry." He wiped his mouth with the back of his hand. "Was it the Identicals, Jack? Were they the ones that told you how to rescue RosaMarie?"

A hot flash raced through Jack's body as Lutz's revelation caught him off guard. He stuttered and stammered before saying, "I don't understand…"

"You're marked, Jack. I knew it the instant I saw you on the train. I've seen it before in different places. You might say I'm drawn to it like a homing pigeon. I was on the train that day we met because my 'spidey sense' told me someone had been touched by them."

"How much do you know?"

"About your situation? Not a lot, but I do have some insight into the Identicals. I also sense you're not from here. I mean, not from this reality. You're from another time or another dimension, perhaps. Those who have taken up with Identicals have a distinctly different aura, and they resonate at a much lower frequency."

Jack wasn't sure how to react now that he knew there was someone who shared his terrible secret. In one sense, he felt relieved, but in another, he was more terrified than ever. "That's preposterous," he blurted out.

"Look, Jack, if you want to pretend, then let's shut this down, and we'll go our separate ways. I've heard the story several times, and it never varies. It starts with an overwhelming personal tragedy. An old woman approaches the person most affected by the death, and they're warned to be on time. Next, an Identical makes an offer to undo the damage but expects payment in return. A yellow pill is provided, and when taken, the victim is thrust into the new reality just in time to save their loved one from the impending catastrophe. Do I have it about right?"

Lutz paused and drained the rest of his coke.

"But then the payment terms are revealed," Jack said quietly.

"Indeed, Jack. And the terms are typically harsh... Were you supposed to kill someone?"

"...Yes, but I couldn't do it, and now... and now everything is falling apart."

"Of the cases I'm aware of, four victims repaid the debt and two did not."

Jack leaned forward; his eyes were wide. "And what happened to the ones who didn't repay? Tell me, Lutz, what happened?"

"Nothing. Nothing happened to either of them."

"Seriously?"

Lutz shrugged. "As far as I know. And yet, I admit it's all very strange. In both instances, the victims suddenly stopped talking to me. I tried to contact them repeatedly, but they claimed they never met me before, and frankly, I believe they were sincere."

"How can you explain that?"

"I can't. Everything about these Identicals and the warping of reality defies logic. I can speculate, but that's all it would be. Look, Jack, these are extraordinarily powerful beings. I have no idea where they come from or what their purpose is. I suspect they are very, very old. Yet, my sensitivity toward them is heightening. With every encounter, I get closer to an answer."

Jack sighed and his shoulders sagged. "Well, what should I do?

"Besides confirming you haven't lost your mind, I'm afraid I can't be of much help. That said, I do have a developing theory. Everything with the Identicals is interrelated. One act affects another. It's like a cascading effect. It's quite possible the person who abducted your daughter was trying to repay his debt. Go talk to him. Start there."

Jack's head snapped up. "*What?* Are you out of your mind? There's no way I'm going to see that pervert, Lattimores.

Lutz leaned forward and raised his eyebrows. "Lattimores? Not *Pauley* Lattimores?"

"Yes... Does that name mean something to you?

"Jack, Pauley Lattimores is one of the two people who defied the Identicals. I found him in Indiana about a month ago. He refused to pay his debt and was desperate to escape the horrors the Identicals were inflicting on his family. I tried to help him, but at one point he just shut down and told me he couldn't remember ever meeting me. We lost touch after that. But now you say he's here?"

"Yes, he's here. The bastard kidnapped my daughter. Why would he deny knowing you? He must have been faking it for some reason."

"No, I don't think so." Lutz shifted uncomfortably in the chair. "It's almost as though I remembered something that no longer existed for him. Like he was living in a second new reality. The same sequence played out with the first victim who defied the Identicals... Jack, you need to talk to him."

"I—I can't handle any more of this... Lattimores? No, I can't do it. I just can't..."

Lutz pointed his finger and stabbed at the air. "You listen to me. Your aura is pitch black, and your frequency is resonating at .8 Hertz. That's much too low, almost to the point of nonexistence. If nothing changes, I fear something terrible is going to happen to you. Talking to Lattimores might help. Anyway, do you have a better idea?"

Their eyes remained locked before Jack finally nodded. "Could you introduce me to the others who took the pill?"

"I'm afraid not," said Lutz. "None of them want anything to do with the Identicals or the events that followed. In fact, they desperately want to forget the whole thing. No one wants to relive killing another innocent human being."

Again, Lutz struggled to get up. Once he was stabilized, he reached out to shake Jack's hand. "You have my card. Call me if you need me."

Jack's hands moved to his forehead. "What am I supposed to do? My family is falling apart because of this, but I can't kill someone. I just can't."

"Start with Lattimores. If by some chance you learn where the Identicals live… nest, for God's sake, please let me know. I sense they are shielded telepathically, but I would relish an opportunity to meet them in person."

Before he could reply, Jack's cell phone rang. "Excuse me."

Lutz nodded and went to the kitchen to discard his empty Coke bottle.

"Get home right now," said Juanita in a panicked voice. "Please, Jack, you need to be here."

A surge of adrenaline shot through his body as he left the house, barely remembering to wave back

226

at Lutz, who had just returned to the living room and stood in front of the picture window with a confused look on his face.

"What? What is it?"

"Dr. Whitfield... She's—she's dead!"

Jack's knees buckled, and the blood rushed to his head. "*Dead?* You can't be serious. How?"

"Principal Gowdy called. One of the children went in for a session and found her slumped over her desk." Juanita gasped as she talked, seemingly on the verge of hyperventilating.

"Nita, slow down. What happened?" By now, Jack was in his car and heading for the freeway.

"The child found her with a pair of scissors sticking out of her neck. Apparently, someone stabbed her from behind."

For an instant, Jack thought he might faint. The car swerved, and he slapped himself in the face, which jarred him back into the moment. "RosaMarie. Where was she?"

"In class, but she was the last appointment before the other child found Dr. Whitfield."

Jack fingered the steering wheel nervously. "Are there security cameras in the room?"

"I'm not sure, but they have them in the hallways... Jack... Could she? Could she have?"

"Damn it, Juanita, RosaMarie didn't push Jamal off the ladder or stab Mary Whitfield. There's got to be another explanation. Go to the school and get her out of there before she's detained. We need to talk to her before the police do."

"I'm already on my way. They're letting the children leave while the inquiry is ongoing. They're going to figure it out. Fingerprints and DNA on the scissors." Jack heard the phone drop and crying in the distance. "My God, what is happening to us?" The voice was faint and small.

Jack stepped on the accelerator. It was only a matter of time before the police investigation led them to RosaMarie. He had no doubt the principal and her teacher would tell the detectives about his daughter's strange and aggressive behavior.

The drive was interminable, and by the time he entered the house, he noticed the air had grown thicker and even heavier than usual, like after a hard rain in high humidity. The colors inside appeared washed out, casting a monochrome tint over everything he looked at. As he moved around, it was like watching an old movie, more as an observer instead of a participant.

Something was horribly out of place. No, many things were out of place. He noticed a family portrait was missing from the wall next to the grandfather clock. The couch was positioned differently, and the chair had been reupholstered. A decorating magazine lay on the end table, but this morning, he swore a dry floral arrangement sat in that exact spot.

Why did Juanita change everything, or did she? Hold on a minute…

Something about all of it was familiar, but Jack couldn't quite place the when or where. He walked down the hallway to the dining room, looking for the kids and his wife. As he reached the kitchen, he looked over to the family room where Leighton played video games on an Xbox.

Xbox? Doesn't Leighton have a Playstation?

He heard a car backing out of the garage and looked just in time to see Bryson leaving in his Miata... But wait, Bryson was still on a permit, and they didn't have a Miata...

Oh my God. Yes, we did.

He swung his head back around as Juanita came into the kitchen from the bathroom. She looked gaunt and sickly thin. No one could have lost that much weight in a day. With a look of utter contempt, she dismissed him and walked over to check on something in the oven.

She turned back and said, "Jack, why are you staring? You look like you've seen a ghost."

"Juanita, where is RosaMarie?"

She raised her head and extended a bony arm with her finger pointed at him, like the grim reaper selecting its next victim. "You think you're fuckin' funny, Jack? It's almost five o'clock. Why don't you have another drink?"

"I'm serious. Where is RosaMarie?"

"You bastard. Why would you torment me? ...She's dead, Jack, just like yesterday." Juanita walked away while muttering, "Goddamned drunk."

Ordinarily, her words would have cut him like so many sharp razor blades, but his attention was focused elsewhere. Everything around him was the same... but different. The same... but different. The same... At that instant, he realized he was back in his old reality, a year and a half from now. The house was exactly as he left it, and RosaMarie was dead all over again.

Jack staggered and swooned, gasping for breath as he made his way over to the couch. His field of vision narrowed while the gray color thickened until it blacked out everything. A sudden, blinding flash caused him to cry out as he brought his hands up to cover his eyes. He sat completely still, refusing to move for fear of finding he lost his sight.

"Jack! Jack, are you alright?"

He heard Juanita's voice, and when he opened his eyes, he saw her standing over him with RosaMarie just off to the side.

"Are you sick, Dad?" his daughter asked. "Mom said you fainted."

"No... I'm fine. Something strange happened. It seemed like I was back..." He sat up, and that's when he noticed the pounding in his head. "I'm okay, I just have a crushing headache."

"I'm sorry, Jack. I know you should rest, but we have to talk."

He nodded as he massaged his temples.

"Wait a minute. I'll be right back. Juanita left the room, and he could hear the icemaker running.

"I'm sorry, Daddy," whispered RosaMarie, "but you knew what was going to happen, didn't you?"

"No, I... What are you talking about?"

"You're being dumb again, Dad. Don't do that. It only gets worse if you play dumb."

Who was this person? She looked like a version of his daughter manipulated in photo software. A darkness shaded her face, casting her in such a way that she appeared to have dermatitis or some other epidermal disease. Her once smooth and flawless skin tone now had the texture of gravel, and deep, dark circles rimmed her eyes. Gone were the beautiful flowing red locks, replaced by a dull auburn, tangled in the same kind of knots as the old woman.

"Can you tell me what you're talking about?" he asked.

"If you won't say it out loud, then everyone will suffer."

Juanita returned with an ice pack that Jack gratefully accepted and held up to his forehead. When she settled in next to him on the couch, she turned to RosaMarie.

"Was Dr. Whitfield alright when you left her office?"

RosaMarie shrugged. "You asked me that before. I don't know." She lowered her head so her stringy hair covered her face.

"RosaMarie, do you know about what happened to Dr. Whitfield?" Juanita's tone was friendly but firm.

Another shrug. "No, I told you that too. Why do you keep asking me?"

"Well, I'm sure this will be hard for you to understand, but you won't be seeing Dr. Whitfield anymore. She—she passed away at school today."

"Does that mean died? Oh…" RosaMarie's face remained shrouded by her hair.

Juanita arched her eyebrows. "That's it? 'Oh'? You're not surprised, sad or sorry?"

A third shrug. "I guess so."

Juanita looked at Jack with incredulity before continuing. "She was your counselor. You saw her several times in recent days, and now she's dead, and you feel nothing?"

RosaMarie threw her head back and the hair parted. Her eyes smoldered, and she spoke through clenched teeth. "Whitfield was a lying bitch. She was a bad person. I told her things, and she promised to keep it a secret, but she told you. I'm glad she's dead."

Juanita jumped out of the chair like she had been pushed. Covering the short distance, she grabbed her daughter by the shoulders and shook her violently. "Don't you *ever* say you're glad someone is dead. Who *are* you? Who the *fuck* are you?"

When RosaMarie smiled, Juanita impulsively reached back and slapped her across the face. In an instant, she realized what she had done and backed away in horror. RosaMarie looked at her mother with shock and surprise, and finally, it triggered a response. A long wail came from deep inside, and she collapsed on the floor in a fetal ball.

"Mommy hates me," she cried out over and over again.

Jack was too stunned to react, and he sat gawking at them both. Juanita rarely even raised her voice to any of the children and never to RosaMarie.

"My God, I hit her. I hit her," she moaned. Without saying another word, Juanita ran to their bedroom and slammed the door, leaving him to process the shock of the moment. He looked over at RosaMarie, who still whimpered on the floor.

Gently, he reached down and stroked her tangled hair, struggling to keep a shred of his sanity intact.

What have I done? My God, what have I done?

At the time, he thought it was all a cruel joke by some freakish dolt who just wanted an ice cream.

Maybe if my brain wasn't so rotted by alcohol, I would have walked away. If he had just let me step in front of the train, I wouldn't have been alive to take the damn pill. But this...

For the first time, he wondered if his family wouldn't have been better off if he let RosaMarie rest in peace.

Chapter Eighteen

As Jack sat next to RosaMarie while hugging her tightly, she looked up at him, her eyes blinking in a way that conveyed her confusion and fear. He listened to her steady heartbeat as his own continued to break into ever-smaller pieces with each passing second.

"Why are they doing this to me, Daddy? Why won't they leave me alone?"

He leaned over and took her small hand into his own, gently caressing her tiny fingers with his thumb. "It's my fault, princess, but I'm going to fix it."

"Do you promise? Do you really promise to fix it this time?"

"Yes, I promise, and remember, a promise is a promise. Now, why don't you go upstairs and take a nap?" He softly kissed her forehead. Her skin chafed his lips, and she felt feverish, like she was burning up.

Later, after the boys came home from school, Jack told them about Mary Whitfield's apparent murder. A dark blanket of dread smoldered and crept through the house until it extended into every crack, crevice and cranny. Around five, Juanita finally came out of the bedroom and put a pan of frozen lasagna in the oven. An hour later, the four of them sat down for dinner without RosaMarie, who didn't have an appetite and remained upstairs in her bedroom. Conversation was sparse and forced, and the tension palpable. Jack felt especially concerned for Juanita, who looked like she might be on the verge of a nervous breakdown. He tried several times to draw her out, but she continued staring off as though he wasn't there.

After dinner, Jack retreated to his den and filled his glass to the brim. The liquid warmed him as it traveled down his throat, and the effects of the alcohol were almost instantaneous. Just as he took his first swallow from the second glass, the landline rang. After the fourth chime, Juanita walked into his office.

"Are you going to get that, or are you already too drunk? I'm not answering it, Jack."

He nodded, reached over, and picked up the phone. No introduction was necessary; caller ID announced who it was.

"Mr. Clausen, this is Detective Ferguson. I'm calling to check on RosaMarie."

Jack took another swallow of scotch. "She's fine, all things considered, Detective, but I appreciate your concern. Thank you for calling."

"Of course... I assume you've heard about the death of Mary Whitfield at RosaMarie's school?"

"Yes, I have. It's a terrible tragedy."

"I was wondering, would you mind if Detective Jones and I came to your house tomorrow mid-morning, say around nine? We reviewed the security tapes in the hallway outside Dr. Whitfield's office, and, well, they raise some questions. We really need to talk to RosaMarie. The sooner the better."

"Why her? Are you interviewing all the other children?" The ever-present knot in Jack's stomach cinched up, and the throbbing in his head resumed.

"I'd rather not go into that tonight, Mr. Clausen. We'll talk about it tomorrow. Please make sure RosaMarie is available. It's very important."

Jack stared at the phone for several minutes after he hung up. He knew what Ferguson and Jones were coming for tomorrow morning. They would ask RosaMarie a slew of questions because they suspected she killed Mary Whitfield and pushed Jamal Egebe off the ladder. In fact, they would have arrested her by now, but her age protected her.

How could anyone wrap their minds around the idea of a five-year-old stabbing an adult woman in the neck? After they finished with their questions, a social worker would arrive shortly thereafter, and they would take RosaMarie to some facility for observation. For all he knew, she might never return home again.

The booze flowed freely as Jack drank heavily into the night, trying to make sense of it all. He thought about confessing everything to Juanita, but he knew it wouldn't help. In the other reality, when he was sloshed, conversations with her never went well. Instead, he decided to stay quiet and finish off the bottle alone.

Somewhere between the third and fourth drink from a second bottle, Jack sensed someone was very close and pressing into him. Hot breath on his neck. He recognized the reeking smell of stale tobacco, and he rubbed his eyes and grunted.

Somehow, he found himself lying on the leather couch set in the middle of his den. Something pressed down on him like an anvil on his chest. A pelvis ground against his lower extremities, trying to arouse him. Jack fought the effects of the alcohol and strained to sit up but to no avail.

He turned his head to see out, but long, stringy, gray hair hung down and covered his eyes. When he reached up and pushed it away, he found the old woman's face was only inches from his own. She smiled. Each breath was ragged and labored, and every time she exhaled, Jack smelled her sickness. He wiggled to get out from underneath her, but somehow, she kept him pinned.

"I told you, you pissant. I told you something really bad would happen if you didn't pay your debt." She began coughing, and the intensity of the odor overwhelmed him.

"What do you want? Let me up... Let me up, goddamn it... Owwwww!" Something sharp dug into his left leg and then again in his right. Jack squirmed to get away, but she held him fast, and there was another intense puncture in his abdomen.

Identicals. He recognized the sensation. They were biting and sucking on him again.

He looked past the old woman down the length of his naked body and saw the creatures with their teeth bared and sunk into his flesh. *Identicals.* All of them looked exactly the same, as though they were clones of Torto. Perhaps, as RosaMarie claimed, they all *were* Torto.

In the same instant, they all looked at Jack as one. Their eyes were blazing with lust, and they hissed and snarled before burying their teeth back into the various regions of his body.

"Owwww... Shit, stop it..." Jack begged and tried desperately to free himself as a sense of panic enveloped him. The more he fought, the harder the old woman pushed down. As the pressure from the Identicals sharp teeth continued to dig into his flesh, Jack's mind shut down, and he stopped struggling.

The old woman leaned over him so her lips touched his ear. She licked it slowly, and then whispered, "They own you now, you stupid pissant. When you agreed, you gave them your soul. It's gonna get a lot worse for you. A *lot* worse... You have a lovely family, pissant." Her laugh started small but morphed into a loud cackle until the wheezing and deep rattle of phlegm sent her into another coughing spasm.

Jack thrashed about while muttering, "No, please, no. Leave my family alone. Please, leave us alone."

"You didn't pay your debt, but now you'll pay, pissant!" she screeched.

"No, fuck you!" Jack somehow got his hands under her body, and with all the strength he could muster, he pushed her off the couch. With a look of surprise, she tumbled to the floor in an awkward, sprawling position. He violently kicked his legs out in an exaggerated butterfly stroke motion, which shook off the Identicals.

The struggle was intense, and he tried to get to his feet, but there must have been poison or a numbing agent in the Identicals' bite because no matter how hard he tried, he couldn't sit up.

Summoning all the effort he could channel, Jack closed his eyes and grunted with exertion.

Concentrate. Concentrate. Concentrate…

The day was bleak and cold, and he was standing outside as mists of rain soaked his face. Gray clouds floated overhead and gave the landscape a colorless appearance. He looked to his left at the street sign on the corner. *62nd and Union Hills*. He knew where he was. The peeling paint and smell that seeped out was like an infection oozing pus. The house came straight from the dream he had in his old life.

Jack started up to the porch, but his foot seemed to get stuck on each step, almost like he was anchored by a fast-drying glue. By the time he reached the landing, he could only dislodge his legs by pulling them up with his hands. Carefully, he reached down and twisted the door handle, but some unseen force yanked it open, and a powerful gust of bitterly cold wind pushed him inside.

Just as before, a woman sat in the corner of the filthy kitchen. The same creature sucked at her bosom, except now it looked older, and the blood-red veins covered most of its skin. It disengaged from its mother and faced him. With deep-set, emerald eyes flashing, it could barely contain its rage. Just as Jack turned to leave the room, it let forth a tortured howl that shook him to his core.

He turned back around in time to see the creature writhing while reaching desperately behind itself in a futile attempt to extract a knife plunged deep between its shoulder blades. Jack looked over at the woman, who stumbled as she tried to get to her feet. Her eyes pleaded for a rescue Jack could not provide.

He moved into the living room and encountered more of the bizarre. A woman with hooves where her hands and feet were supposed to be; a gnome and a person the size of a sumo wrestler attempting to have sex in an impossible position on a waterbed; a sow with lipstick and diamonds draped around its neck. At the far end of the room, Torto sat as before, surrounded by the other Identicals and the old woman.

"Torto not happy, Jack. Jack make deal with Torto, and Torto do his part, don'cha know.

"I can't kill someone," Jack replied. "I—I *can't* kill someone." He dropped to his knees and clasped his hands as though he was praying. "Please… Please leave my family alone."

The Identicals shook their heads in synchronous concert. "No. Jack make deal then break it. Now, he pay. Too bad. Jack buy Torto ice cream, don'cha know. Torto like Jack, but now…"

"No… no, please. Please don't hurt my family. Leave RosaMarie alone. Please!"

Jack sat up with a start and looked around. "What the fuck?" For several seconds, he thrashed about in a panic that came from fear and confusion. The old woman and the Identicals had disappeared, if they were ever there in the first place. He took a deep breath and rubbed his eyes.

A dream. Nothing more than a dream, except…

He was still dressed in the same clothes from yesterday, but when he unbuttoned his shirt, he saw the perfectly round reddish-purple bruises where the Identicals' feasted on his torso.

240

Another alcohol induced nightmare? I'm slipping back into exactly who I was before.

By now, Jack was awake enough to recognize the odd sense of stillness in the house. He got to his feet and turned on his desk lamp. The digital clock read 4:16 a.m. He glanced up at the clock on the wall, which displayed the same time, but the sweeping second hand wasn't moving.

The stagnant air pushed in on him with such intense pressure it almost felt solid, and the monochrome landscape appeared more washed out than ever before. He slowly buttoned his shirt and ran his fingers through his hair. Maybe a splash of water would help with the horrible headache, and anyway, he needed to brush his teeth to get the taste of garbage out of his mouth. With effort, he staggered out of the den and walked toward the bathroom, but he noticed lights on in the boys' bedrooms.

That's odd. What would they be doing up at this time of night?

Jack changed directions and headed for the stairs, following the nightlights spaced at a distance to ensure a nightwalker wouldn't inadvertently collide with something unseen. At the top of the landing, he decided to go into Bryson's room first. His son lay on his side sleeping peacefully, but almost instantly, Jack knew something was wrong.

He plunged into the surreal state of a woken dream. His feet moved, but he didn't want to approach. Brain circuits began to disconnect and screamed at him to turn around, but he couldn't stop moving. One sluggish step at a time, he

241

continued forward until his legs brushed up against the edge of the bed.

Something is wrong. His head. What is that on his head?

Jack brought his fist up to his mouth and bit down hard on his knuckle. All the air seemed to be sucked from his lungs as he looked at the misshapen skull, crushed in as though someone took a full swing with a baseball bat while Bryson slept. The black sheets and pillowcase hid much of the blood, but a large wet stain covered whatever rock band was on the front of his son's white t-shirt.

"Juanita." It came from his throat as a quiet croak. Jack grabbed Bryson by the shoulders and turned him over onto his back, instantly recoiling at the sight of the caved in forehead, with the right eye purged from its socket, lying where the cheek was supposed to be. On autopilot, he found the strength to check for a pulse, found none, and then collapsed to the floor. Briefly, he considered CPR, but there was no mouth to breathe into.

Leighton.

As much as his mind wanted to shut down completely, something forced Jack to his feet. He remembered now. This feeling, the same one he had when he first saw RosaMarie's lifeless body, bloody and brutalized. The image and accompanying despair enveloped him completely, and from that moment forward, he could never remember one without the other. Now, he would have another horrible memory to store away forever.

Before he walked in, Jack knew what he would find in Leighton's room. His younger son was apparently struck twice in the head. The first blow must have been glancing, because it left a large, bluish lump but only a small amount of blood on his forehead. Did he put his hands up to deflect the blunt force? Somehow, Leighton was able to get out of bed, and he made it halfway across the room before he took the second strike to the back of his head. This one impacted the base of the skull, which seemed to have dislodged the atlanto-occipital joint. Leighton's neck looked oddly stretched, as though the skin that bridged his head and shoulders was all that kept the two structures attached.

There was no reason to check for a pulse. Leighton's eyes were glassy, empty and lifeless. The essence of his younger son had left his earthly vessel. Jack walked over, picked up Leighton's body, and hugged him close, rocking back and forth as he wept. How long he stayed there gently cradling his middle child he didn't know, but at some point, the cruel reality started creeping through his shock and despair.

RosaMarie had murdered her brothers.

In a state of confusion, he laid Leighton down, walked out into the hallway and turned towards RosaMarie's bedroom. Just before he entered, he heard a voice from down below.

"Jack... Jack, help me... Please help me." Juanita sounded small and pitiful.

Without thinking, he bounded down the stairs two at a time. Reaching the lower level, he followed the dim light towards his own bedroom, encountering Leighton's baseball bat up against the doorway, covered in blood. He waited outside for several seconds while wondering what to do next. Impulsively, he shoved the door open and entered the room, crouching on his haunches with his arms spread wide.

At first sight, he encountered the incomprehensible. Juanita lay prone on the floor just outside the foot of the bed with RosaMarie sitting on her back. With one hand, she pulled hard on a tangle of her mother's hair, forcing her head to bend unnaturally at the neck. In her other, she held a kitchen knife, the red-handled one from the cutlery cabinet designed specifically to cut meat. The knife pressed against Juanita's throat. Jack could see two distinct circles of fresh blood on her nightgown just below her breasts.

She stabbed Juanita. RosaMarie stabbed her mother.

There could be no understanding or comprehension of what he saw in front of him, so Jack stood motionless, searching for words. RosaMarie's eyes were lifeless, as dead as when he saw her in the morgue, except now, they projected a kind of terrifying malevolence he felt on a guttural level. They stared at each other for a very long time.

"I warned you, Daddy. They told you to be on time, but you didn't listen. You should have paid your debt. You should have admitted you're a piece of shit welcher."

"RosaMarie, my God, what have you done? Oh, Lord, no..." He raised his arms and took a step. "Please, put the knife down, and let your mother go."

"I—I can't, Daddy. Identicals know everything, and they'll eat me if I don't do what they say. Besides, Torto says you deserve it. You deserve all of it." She snarled and then let loose with a raucous chortle so loud it cut through the thick air and shook the house.

Jack took another step forward, but her head snapped up, and the look of loathing grew deeper. "Don't come any closer, or I'll slit her throat. I stabbed that bitch Whitfield in the neck, and I killed Bryson and Leighton. You think I couldn't kill Mommy?" The knife pressed tighter against Juanita's jugular.

"Jack... Don't let me die," croaked Juanita. "She's already stabbed me twice. I—I'm bleeding out."

"RosaMarie, listen to me. Put the knife down this instant."

"Come closer and I'll cut her bad. I mean it."

Jack crouched down and took an aggressive posture. "RosaMarie, this is the last time I'm going to tell you to put the knife down."

Her expression softened. Tears welled up, and the corners of her mouth turned down. "Would you hurt me, Daddy? Really? I—love you. Why is this happening to me?"

In that instant, he saw his child. This was the real RosaMarie, with a look of pain and confusion on her face so unnerving, Jack slowly stood back up. "RosaMarie... Princess. Please give me the knife. We can get this all worked out."

The pressure on Juanita's neck lessened, and RosaMarie started crying. Without thinking, Jack seized on her momentary lapse and lunged.

245

Reaching out, he grabbed the hand that held the knife and pulled it back while using his momentum to push her off Juanita. The impact sent RosaMarie's tiny body skittering across the tile floor, and in the process, the knife was knocked out of her hand.

Jack scrambled over and grabbed the weapon. Once it was secure, he looked over at RosaMarie, who was rubbing her head and trying to recover from the hard blow. "Just sit there and don't move. I need to help Mommy."

As confusion gave way to understanding, RosaMarie pointed at her mother as a smile slowly spread across her lips, revealing her missing front tooth. She began giggling until the volume and intensity grew into a deep, guttural laugh. "Too late, Daddy. Look!" Jack followed her outstretched arm and finger.

Juanita was on her knees, coughing up blood and sputtering. He crawled over and spun her around. Both of her hands were pressed against her neck, but they couldn't stop the blood from pulsing out between her fingers.

"I told you, Daddy. You should have paid your debt, don'cha know. You should have paid your fucking debt, pissant."

Chapter Nineteen

The sight of his wife clutching her throat, gasping and choking with her eyes wide in terror while blood poured from the gaping wound in her neck, pushed Jack over the divide between sanity and insanity. A low growl came from deep in his gut, and he bent over and ran toward RosaMarie at full speed, launching himself like a missile. There was virtually no resistance during the impact, and the weight of his body slammed her up against the nearest wall. Jack brought his hands up to his daughter's neck, and he began to choke her with ill intent.

RosaMarie's face changed from red to purple, and her lips and eyes swelled. Between sputtering and gasping for breath, she tried to say something, but Jack couldn't make it out. He felt a slight pressure on his arm, and when he looked down, he saw her tiny fingers trying desperately to grab onto his forearm. The pitiful sight triggered something deep inside, and just for a moment, the familiar melting began. He lessened the pressure on her neck.

"Daddy, I can't breathe. Please... stop hurting me," she managed to rasp out in a small, helpless voice.

Her words sliced through the fog of shock and outrage, and Jack let go and stood up. He screamed and backed away. The room started spinning, and consciousness faded. His breathing was labored, and he felt chest pains.

For some time, he stood panting, trying to make sense out of an utterly senseless situation. The grandfather clock showed 5:26. Ferguson and Jones would arrive in three and a half hours.

Before he did anything, he would figure out what to do with RosaMarie.

With all meaning and purpose stripped from his life, Jack grabbed her shoulders and lifted her up. "Leave me alone," she squealed and resisted, kicking her feet and punching at him.

RosaMarie's strength was surprising, and restraining her proved unusually challenging. Jack held her arms tight and dragged her toward the rear of the house. Inside the detached garage, near the back of the building, a workshop housed his tools and a few basic shop machines. He pulled her outside and muffled her screams with his hand as she continued to kick and claw at him.

When they reached the workshop, he opened the door and literally threw her inside before snapping the padlock shut. RosaMarie beat on the door and screamed profanities and demanded to be released.

"Listen to me," he said. "I'm leaving for a while. I'm going to lock you in here until I get back. Do you understand me?"

The beating stopped abruptly, and soft sobbing followed shortly thereafter. "Don't leave me, Daddy. I'm afraid."

For just a moment, Jack hesitated and reached for the key. Just as quickly, the thought of Bryson and Leighton, with their skulls crushed, flashed across his mind, and the feeling passed.

"You stay in here until I get back. It won't be long."

She inhaled deeply and let forth a loud wail. "Don't let them kill me. Don't let the Identicals kill me. They said I had to do it, or they would come to get me. Daddy, I don't want them to eat me alive."

"You'll be fine, RosaMarie. I promise the Identicals won't hurt you anymore."

She began yelling again. "You're a motherfucker who doesn't keep his promises. You're gonna die, you pissant."

Jack heard her screaming as he walked away, but when he closed the overhead door to the garage, the sound was muffled and barely audible. Hopefully, Ferguson and Jones would leave without looking in the backyard, but it was a chance he would have to take.

***

Jack pulled out onto Maple with a strange sense of calm that took complete control of his body. Serenity washed over him in waves and brought an intense focus and alertness. He picked up his phone and used the assistant to find the number for the county jail. Several automated transfers later, he got connected to an operator in the inmate locator department.

"I need to speak to an inmate. His name is Pauley Lattimores."

"I'm sorry, sir, but inmate telephone contact must be initiated by the inmate, and you must be on the approved list."

"This is an emergency. A matter of life and death. I *must* speak to Pauley Lattimores.

"Sir, emergency contact has to be initiated by the inmate's attorney."

Jack took several deep breaths. "Look, his son suffered a horrific injury and may not survive. I am a family friend. I need to talk to him."

The operator sighed. "… Okay, what is your name, sir, and is this the right number to reach you at?"

"Jack Clausen, and yes, this is the number. Tell him it's urgent."

"I'll pass the information on, Mr. Clausen. It will be up to Mr. Lattimores to respond."

The phone disconnected, and Jack cursed and threw it on the passenger's seat. He looked at his watch, knowing the last thing he needed was to be stopped for speeding by some Arlington cop. Fortuitously, he found an open spot next to the handicapped parking at the station. Just as he shut down the engine and opened the door, his phone rang.

"This is the Cook County Sheriff's office. You have a collect call from inmate seven-three-four-seven-seven at the Cook County jail. Press one to accept or two to reject." His finger hovered over the keypad for a moment before he pressed the "one" key.

Heavy breathing on the other end of the line. "Clausen. What is it you want? I damn well know it isn't about my kid."

Jack dispensed with formalities. "You took the Identicals' pill to save your son, but you didn't pay your debt, did you? That's why you had to kill my daughter, isn't it? You had to pay them back, and the second debt was much bigger than the first."

He heard shuffling and the noise of other prisoners in the background. "They're gonna cut off this call quick, Clausen. I get it now; I understand why you showed up so soon. You took the pill to save your daughter, didn't you? But I bet you didn't follow through and pay your debt either. You're right; I welched and paid a horrible price. Now it gets worse for you, Clausen. Much worse. I'll bet your life is falling apart."

"Tell me about these Identicals. What are they?"

"Identicals? How the fuck should I know? Why do you think I kidnapped your daughter? You're not the first one they came to with this hellish deal, and you're not the first one who reneged. I could have gotten away with a simple murder of some rich asshole, but I couldn't do it. To stop the horror they inflicted on my family, I had to... I had to do what I did to your daughter. The other thing they made me do was even worse."

"What can I do to stop this?"

"I don't know." Lattimores' breathing was fast and deep, and his words were clipped. "My debt overlapped into yours, and it fucked everything up for me. I guess that's how it works. All of the lives they've spoiled are somehow connected. None of it is random."

"What does that mean, 'connected'? Jack clutched the phone to his ear tightly.

251

"You fucked up my life to save your own ass, Clausen. You pulled me into your goddamned reality, and instead of walking away free and clear, now I'm in prison for the rest of my life. My son may have lived, but he hates me.... Fuck you Claus..."

Click

Six minutes before the 7:15 departed. The train would be packed already, but Jack didn't care if he threw someone off. There was no way it left without him. Not today.

On most days, the farthest car from the engine was the least crowded, but even it was filled to capacity. The temperature was much colder than usual for late September, and the sky looked ominous, which motivated those usually driving to work to take the train.

The passengers pressed against the aisles, displaying their passive aggression by refusing to move aside as Jack tried to get by. Fortunately, he found one open hand rung, and he pushed in between a large man, who was sweating underneath his thick European cut trench coat, and a lithe woman who smelled of sweet-scented body soap. The man scowled, but the woman just turned away and inched over.

Jack looked down at his rumpled clothing and imagined he must look like a bum from 35th and Federal or a drunk who just rolled out of bed. Actually, the latter wasn't too far from the truth. A streak of dried blood stained his shirt, and he pulled his suit jacket over to cover it. The man pressed up on one side may have been sweating, but Jack could only imagine what *he* smelled like. Body odor mixed with stale alcohol.

His phone buzzed, and he looked down and saw it was Walt Offerman. This could be "the call." They would want him to come downtown, where they would deliver more bad news. Leave of absence? Layoff? Firing? As if Jack cared at this point. He ignored the call.

In the end, it all worked out worse than the other world. RosaMarie lived, but everyone else died, and my life is even more horrible than before.

By the time they passed Park Ridge, he found himself surrounded on all four sides. Rain started to fall, and at Norwood Park, another group of travelers boarded. They tried to keep from getting the other passengers wet, but the closing of umbrellas and shaking of coats inevitably transferred some moisture, adding to an already miserable ride in the packed car.

Jack eyed a particular passenger from this new group. She had a different look about her. Raven hair peppered with gray, and a stubborn cowlick near the uneven part, confirmed what the dark circles under her eyes suggested. She hadn't been sleeping. Her jeans had wear wrinkles across the waist, and one of the lapels of her jacket remained tucked under. No question she was focused on something else besides appearance.

The woman's effort to get to the rear of the car was aggressive and sometimes bordered on minor assault. When she reached the spot where Jack stood, she pushed the heavyset man out of the way and grabbed the open rung. Overcoming his surprise, the stocky passenger inched back and stared down at the disheveled wretch, but the menacing look she gave him made him think better of starting a confrontation. He moved slowly to the front of the car, jostling other passengers and getting his new Brunello Cucinelli trench coat wet in the process.

With the space cleared, the unkempt woman turned her focus to Jack. The distinct smell of a dog's dirty, wet hair drifted off her body, and he wrinkled his nose in disgust.

They pulled away from Norwood, and even though he faced away from her, he felt her inching closer until they were pressed up hard against each other.

Fresh booze. She's been drinking heavily and recently.

Jack could feel her proximity. With his own high state of shock and mental instability, he was in no mood for games. Fixing for confrontation, he turned, but a hand reached out and shoved him hard in the back.

"Don't turn around, Jack Clauson. Keep looking away from me." He felt something sharp and straight poking him in the back. In the moment, when a thousand possibilities passed through his mind, Jack hoped, no, *prayed,* it was a knife. Whatever reason this person had for threatening him, she had no clue just how little he cared about his own life right now.

"Who are you, and what do you want?" The woman on the other side, who he now faced directly, thought he was talking to her. She pulled back slightly as her eyebrows drew together, and she turned away.

"It doesn't matter who I am," Even in a whisper, the voice from behind sounded harsh and agitated. "It only matters that I have to pay my debt. They... they said I have to kill you... I'm sorry, Jack. So, sorry."

"Identicals. You took the pill," Jack replied. As the words left his mouth, he turned suddenly to face the threat, making sure to keep in direct contact so the knife remained hidden.

"Do it," said Jack, as they stared at each other from no more than four inches away. "You will be doing me a great favor."

"Torto? You know him too? Is that what they're called, Identicals?" The pressure on the knife eased just a bit. Jack reached down and grabbed the woman's hand, pushing the tip of the weapon back into his stomach.

"Yes, I took the yellow pill. My daughter was alive again, and for a short time, my life was happy. But I never knew that my part of the bargain was to kill someone. After I refused, everything fell apart. I—I just left my family. My wife and two boys are—they're dead, and my daughter killed them."

"My God..."

"So please," said Jack as his voice cracked, and two solitary tears rolled down his cheeks, "kill me. I want to die. Maybe you can save your own family. I don't know. Please... just do it."

The knife tore through the fabric of his shirt as the hand holding it trembled. The sting from the blade piercing his flesh caused Jack to gasp, and he involuntarily sought to cover the wound.

Inexplicably, the pressure relaxed before disappearing completely. Jack was confused as he looked down at the growing red spot on his blue shirt and then back up to the woman still holding the knife.

He leaned over and whispered. "Don't stop. Finish it."

"I can't." The knife dropped unnoticed to the floor of the train. "I can't, Jack. God forgive me, I can't." Her voice was coarse and ragged, and now her own eyes welled up.

"You don't understand. They'll destroy your family if you don't do it. The one you saved will be the worst. You'll experience indescribable horror."

The conductor yelled out, "End of the line!" as they slowed on their arrival to Ogilvie.

"My name is Sonia... Sonia Williamson," she said. "Maybe... maybe we could fight this thing together?"

Jack shook his head. "It wouldn't work. You have no idea how complex all of it is. Identicals have abilities we can't comprehend. Please, pick up the knife and kill me. I won't make a sound."

"No. I—I won't have blood on my hands. I just can't..."

"Then you're a fool." Jack pursed his lips and looked away as the passengers gathered their things and began to depart. "I'm sorry, that's all I have. You're a fool."

Williamson nodded. Her eyes were bloodshot and watery. "I feel like this is hell, Jack, and I'm not sure if I'm even really alive anymore. What are these Identicals?"

"Who knows? But a friend seems to think they are very old, and they've been among us for a long time."

He nodded and placed a sympathetic hand on her shoulder as she slumped down into one of the vacant seats. Just before stepping out onto the platform, he turned and looked back at her piteous image a last time. She had so much more to learn, and all of it was bad.

With a brisk pace, he headed past the newsstands and baggage claim area, making his way toward the entrance of the building. Several people stared, looking at the fresh bloodstain on his shirt, so he reached down and buttoned his jacket just as he arrived in the Great Hall.

The bustle of activity was typical for a weekday, as merchants, commuters, retailers and traders went about their business. But Jack's shabby attire and messy appearance set him apart. Like a stray wolf who tries to enter an established pack, those around him sensed he didn't belong, and his incongruity attracted attention.

A security person stood off in a corner out of the main thoroughfare, and sure enough, she eyed him as he moved forward. There was no doubt there wouldn't be time to loiter for long.

Born from utter desperation, two hastily conceived plans continued to evolve. He was in the process of executing the first, although there was no rational reason to believe it would succeed. The second plan was far simpler. He would walk back to the platform and throw himself onto the tracks in front of an oncoming train. That way, at least everything would come full circle.

He sipped at an expensive latte while glancing at his phone log. Three more calls from the office, and at the end of the list, a phone call from Ferguson. The detectives must have visited the house by now, and when no one answered, they tried to contact a family member. Without an immediate response, they wouldn't wait long before getting a search warrant, unless they heard RosaMarie inside the workshop. If that was the case, a judge was probably in the process of preparing Jack's arrest warrant.

Unfortunately, the coffee didn't provide enough cover to satisfy the security agent's suspicions, and with each sip, Jack became more self-conscious. Slowly and deliberately, she started walking in his direction while continuing to stare him down, as he looked around with a sense of desperation. He spotted a men's store across the aisle.

The salesperson's face tightened a bit as he walked in, but Jack ignored the snub and went over to the coat rack.

"Can I help you, sir? The clerk kept a distance, and the smile on his pursed, thin lips was pretentious and barely hid his distaste.

Jack acted like he was browsing, keeping his eye on the door. "I need a fall jacket. It's cold out, and I forgot mine."

"Of course. What did you have in mind?" Glancing over toward the concourse, Jack saw the security person approaching, albeit at a slower pace.

He reached up and grabbed the first jacket he saw in a medium size. "I'll take this one."

The clerk's eyes lit up. "My, what an excellent choice. You, ah, did see the price tag?"

"Yes, yes, please ring it up."

"Of course, sir." The clerk walked over to the register as the security guard stopped outside the store and watched the transaction. Jack didn't want to, but he used a credit card. He had no choice. The jacket was $900, and he didn't carry that much cash.

After instructing the clerk to pull off the tags, he put the jacket on, which dramatically changed his appearance. Genuine Italian leather will do that. It not only covered his rumpled and stained sport coat, but he didn't have to worry about the bloodstain on his shirt showing through.

Once he left the store, Jack started toward the platform. Increasingly convinced plan A wasn't going to work, with dull determination, he calculated where he would need to be positioned so the next incoming train wouldn't have time to stop when he stepped in front of it. His phone rang again: Ferguson calling for the third time. Jack hit ignore and crossed from the station to the platform.

From behind, a familiar voice said, "So, you're going to throw yourself in front of a train again, pissant?"

Chapter Twenty

Jack froze for a moment and then turned around slowly. The old woman stood behind him with a lit cigarette in her mouth, drawing looks of incredulity from the passing travelers. Seeing the smug look on her face and that condescending half smile, Jack struggled to control his rage.

"Either kill me, or let me go back to my life in the other world. I never thought it would be possible, but this reality is so much worse."

"It's all your fault. I told you not to be late, pissant. All high and mighty thinking you're a somebody. Well, now you know you're a nobody. Just a loser like all the rest of them. You didn't pay your debt. They *always* make you pay your debt."

Jack shuffled his feet and moved closer. His eyebrows arched, and he extended his hand. "Please. My family is dead, and my daughter is a monster. Help me. Take me to Torto."

She spat out a piece of tobacco, and her eyes narrowed. "Pathetic. You're a pathetic pissant." Without warning, she turned abruptly and started walking back into the terminal. Jack hesitated but followed at a distance, still under the watchful eye of the security person.

The old woman kept a steady pace as she passed through the Great Hall and finally reached the revolving doors leading out to Canal Street. Jack caught up to her at the corner, and he raised a hand to hail a taxi, but she reached up and batted it down.

"The bus, pissant. I take the bus when I'm here. Blue line. I don't ride in no goddamn cabs or cars." The bus stop was about twenty feet from the courtesy area, and she moved toward it while muttering under her breath.

Once onboard, she flashed a pass to the driver, but Jack had to dig into his pocket for the two-dollar fare. As the bus pulled out into traffic, she found a seat near the emergency exit and motioned for him to sit next to her. In such close proximity, he fought against the urge to gag.

They sat in silence for several minutes as the diesel engine puffed smoke, and the bus rocked from side to side on worn shocks. The driver wasn't a veteran, and his shifting was jerky, which caused the passengers to sway forward and back every time he changed gears. When Jack looked over, he saw the old woman had actually cracked a grin.

"You like riding the bus?" he asked.

The smile disappeared. "I get away from it when I ride. For just a minute, I get away."

"Get away? From what?

She jerked her head, and the snarl returned. "After all this, you have to ask? Are you that dumb, pissant?"

"Identicals?"

"Shhhhhh…" She tapped her finger to her lips multiple times. "You don't talk about that. You know what they can do." She snapped her fingers. "Like that, pissant. Like that and you don't exist no more."

"What is it they want? Just tell me. My family… My poor family… They're all dead."

"Don't blubber to me, pissant. I told you to be on time. I told you to pay your debt. You're the one who fucked it up. You got what you deserve."

Jack pulled back and eyed her for a moment. "Listen to me, you dried up old cunt. I've had about enough of your abuse. You don't seem to understand; I don't give a shit what happens to me now. They're all dead. I saw my sons with their heads bashed in by my daughter. I saw her slit her own mother's throat. So don't you *ever* talk to me that way again."

Instead of cowering, she thrust her face into his. "You want me to take you to them? Then you better keep your goddamn trap shut… And I'll call you any goddamn thing I want… *Pissant!*"

While she wouldn't back down, Jack's willingness to defend himself seemed to give the old hag some sense of respect. For the remainder of the ride, she left him be and looked out the window or played with the buttons on her fraying wool coat.

They transferred twice, and the ride took almost an hour with stops and traffic. Jack was sure they could have cut twenty minutes off the trip if they had taken a cab, but he knew he was traveling with a strange mind, and he didn't want to do anything else that might set her off.

At 63rd and Ashland, they got off the bus, and she began walking north. Jack realized they were in West Englewood, one of the toughest neighborhoods in Chicago. Once a year, he traveled with the salesperson who covered this area, and he was always happy when the day ended. The hag kept up a surprisingly swift pace, and she turned onto 62nd and headed west. Up in the distance, Jack spotted the next street sign: *Union Hills Drive*. For a moment, it triggered a brief flashback.

He knew beyond any doubt that Union Hills was their destination. So, when they turned the corner onto the street with four houses surrounded by several empty lots, he didn't need to be told where they were headed. Jack remembered the drab white color and large shards of paint peeling away, revealing the rotted plywood beneath. The roof was missing shingles, and the window frames were warped and twisted in a way that permanently sealed them shut. Several tendrils of mold climbed up the outer wall, like demonic tentacles reaching out from the underworld.

This was the same house from his nightmares.

The old woman reached the front porch when she turned back toward Jack. "Well, are you comin' in or not?"

He walked slowly up the cracked concrete steps, and when she opened the door and went inside, he grabbed it and followed.

The experience of entering the building was either real or it wasn't, but Jack would never know for sure. In hindsight, he decided this place existed within a space of its own. Whether an alternate universe, a different dimension, or something beyond his comprehension, this was not his reality. Like a finger thrust in a glass of water, it pushed whatever surrounded it out of the way. The house served only as a facade to hide the existence of this spatial cavity from the physical world that surrounded it.

Inside the kitchen, the filthy woman from the dreams sat in a corner, making eye contact with him as the child/beast suckled on her breast. As expected, it turned and hissed, and Jack was more repulsed by its appearance than he remembered. Maggots crawled out of its mouth as it continued to snarl, and the red veins that ran through its head, torso, legs and arms grew thick and pulsed as the color flushed and deepened. The woman reached out her hand, and the despair in her hollowed eyes was pitiful.

"You're not from here either," she whispered. "Help me, please…"

Jack took a quick step toward her when he felt a strong pull on his arm. He looked down to see the boney hand of the old woman exerting a sure grip. "Not for you, pissant," she said in a voice that was almost gentle. "That's not the road you want to take."

She led him through the doorway into the dining room, where a man in a hood lay on his stomach, his hands and feet chained and locked to the legs of a solid, thick wooden table. The dominatrix reared up and brought a nine-tail whip down on his back. The man howled in pain as a spray of blood coated his skin and everything surrounding him. She pulled the whip off him slowly and then turned her masked eyes toward

Jack. Extending her forefinger, she gestured for him to come closer, but the old woman strengthened her grip and pulled him forward.

Off to his left in one of the bedrooms, he saw the decaying, gray body from the dreams, only this time, the skin was peeled back to reveal the twisted muscles, tendons and fat it shrouded. As he passed, the living corpse sat up and reached out with both arms while moaning and muttering. Jack listened closely and could barely make out what it was saying.

"Help me. Help me. I didn't mean it. Decay… I have decayed for so long, I don't know… Is it 1956 yet?"

Jack's mouth dropped, and he pulled away from the hag. "For God's sake, what the hell is this place?"

"You wanted to play the big shot, pissant. Make it all better, so here you are. Whatsa matter? You thinkin' maybe you should have stepped out in front of that train after all?"

From the other bedroom, a shrill scream sent Jack reeling backwards. No words could explain the depths of despair and terror conveyed by the second scream that followed, but there was something else… A low-pitched growl, but not the sound of an earthly animal. Jack didn't want to look, but something compelled him.

The beast, and there was really no other way to describe it, stood on its haunches. Its teeth looked like rusted iron, and they thrust in and out from the area usually occupied by eye sockets in land animals. The epidermis was gray and scaly, yet its head was distinctly human. The creature was a biped, and when its gaze found Jack, he sensed it was sentient. A long moaning growl came deep from its guts before it sunk its teeth into the flesh of a woman who couldn't have been over thirty-five. The emaciated appearance, red streaked track marks and hollow eyes left no doubt she was a junkie.

"There you go, pissant," said the old woman. "Now we're more in your world. How much booze you drinking these days? You're real close to having that one become your permanent best friend."

She pulled him forward as they continued walking toward the living room. Seven Identicals stood up against the drapes that covered the large dirty window behind them. Since they all looked so similar, Jack had to assume it was Torto who was sitting on a wood stool in the middle of the group. The climb up to reach the round seat couldn't have been easy, and his feet dangled to the sides without touching the floor.

Just as he remembered from his dreams, the Identicals wore matching attire. The fabric was a kind of canvas fashioned into a seamless shirt. Long tails extended down past their waists, so he couldn't see how they fastened their trousers, but he noticed there was no fly sewn into the front panel. They appeared to be androgynous, but the biological gender, and even species for that matter, remained a mystery.

"Jack, (once again sounding like 'Jick') make Torto sad. Jack agree to deal, but don't do his part, don'cha know." Torto shook his head. "Bad, very bad. Don't be on time and everything..." Torto seemed to struggle for the words. "Jack make it all go bad. Much work to fix. Now Jack here. Why?"

"My family. All of them are dead, and RosaMarie... RosaMarie has become a killer. My pain is much worse than it was before. I can't live with this." Involuntarily, Jack began sobbing and dropped to his knees. "Please, please help me. I'm losing my mind, and I can't even tell what is real anymore. I can't live another minute knowing what I've done. Please, send me back to the old reality or have someone kill me."

"So," said Torto while raising a hairless eyebrow. "Jack want one more chance." He looked over at the other Identicals individually. Their expressions changed, and they started moving their mouths in a way that should have been anatomically impossible. Jack imagined they were communicating, most likely telepathically.

Finally, Torto turned back. "Torto say okay. Jack get second chance, but deal now different. Jack owe Torto *two* deals, right?"

"If you want me to kill someone... I—I don't know if I can. Anyway, you already sent someone to kill me. Please, just finish the job. I..."

"Torto think Jack not do deal, so Jack not needed. But if Jack *do* deal, maybe Torto change mind, and he live." Torto's brow furrowed, and simultaneously, the brows of the other Identicals furrowed at the exact same moment.

"Alright, alright," said Jack as he extended his arms. "Two deals and you give me a second chance. I'll do it and pay my debt. Who... who is it you want me to kill?"

Torto pointed to the old woman. "Woman tell Jack. Woman tell *all* the deals."

Jack nodded. "Fine then, I understand. Now, please, send me back, and let me start over. *Please...*

Torto nodded. "Good, Jack. Torto send. First, take off clothes, okay?"

"What?"

"Torto say take off clothes or no deal, don'cha know."

Jack hesitated, but when he saw the Identicals furrowing their brows yet again, he began to undress. After each article of clothing came off, he paused, hoping Torto would tell him to stop, but it wasn't until he discarded his briefs that a smile formed on the gnome's lips, along with the other Identicals at the same moment.

"Now, Jack lay on back."

Eyeing Torto suspiciously, Jack sat down on the floor and then lay back until fully prone. The wood planks were cold, which only added to his sense of humiliation and vulnerability.

Somehow, Torto got off the stool and waddled over. He opened his hand, which revealed a glowing pill, similar to the first, but purple this time. "Take pill, Jack. Take pill and start over."

Jack reached up and grabbed the pill, swallowing it without hesitation. Hardly perceptible, a heavy blanket of fog descended, much like anesthesia administered during an operation. He felt a pinprick on his leg, and then another, followed by several more. The room spun counterclockwise as he looked down at his body and tried to bring things back into focus. The pinpricks hurt, and the burn spread.

As his vision cleared, he watched the Identicals as their sharp teeth dug into various parts of his body, sucking and biting while making that odd purring sound. Jack shook his head and tried to move, but he was paralyzed.

Suddenly, a pair of hands grabbed his head and held it tight. He looked up, but he could barely see the outline of the old woman's stringy gray hair. She straddled him and started inching up. When she reached his chest, she leaned down and licked the side of his face before thrusting her tongue in his mouth.

"C'mon, pissant, give mama some sugar," she said.

Jack tried to scream just before he lost consciousness, but no sound came out of his mouth.

Chapter Twenty-One

Before settling on the idea he was in the grip of a massive hangover, Jack's first conscious thought was that he suffered a stroke or an aneurysm. That's how badly his head hurt. He rolled over and reached out for Juanita and found the smooth nylon fabric of her nightgown. She sighed softly, and he inched forward to spoon with her. There was a brief moment of contentment, but the pounding in his head worsened, as though he was waking up from a severe bender. After several more minutes of pure agony, he got up and sought out the medicine cabinet, where he gulped four ibuprofen caplets.

He walked back into the bedroom and said, "Alexa, off," within a nano-second of the alarm trigger. Juanita rolled over and stretched before raising herself up on one elbow.

"You have something important today?"

Jack paused. *That's odd. Did I know what she was going to say?*

"Yeah, I have to see Simmons. He's threatening to take his business elsewhere because Amtron gave him a better quote on equipment. That Gerry Rourke is a helluva salesperson, and the fact she's a knockout doesn't hurt with old lechers like Big Bob.

I can't lose that account. Walt and Hans will have simultaneous coronaries."

Jack stood for a moment and shook his head to blow out the cobwebs, but that only made the head pounding worse.

"Is something wrong?" Juanita asked while sitting up and taking notice of his obvious discomfort.

"No, I just have a massive headache. But..."

"But what?"

"I'm not sure, but I'm getting this feeling like I already know what you're going to say. After you say it, it's like I already knew it. I can't really explain..."

Juanita raised her hands and shook them. "Woooooo. Deja vu, Jack. Better watch out today."

He smiled. "Knock it off, wise guy." The pills began to take effect, and the headache eased a bit. She got out of bed and walked over to where he stood and put her arms around his neck.

"Hey," she said while looking into his eyes. "You may be the national sales manager, but you're still the best salesperson they have, and Walt knows it. You'll probably keep the account, but even if you don't, there's nothing that will shake my faith in you... Got it?"

He nodded, but there was that strange feeling again. A split second before she opened her mouth, he knew she would have some encouraging words about work.

After showering and shaving, he put on his lucky suit and started down the stairs, but even before he caught the first whiff, he knew Juanita

271

made French toast Guatemalan style, his favorite breakfast.

Bryson opened his mouth to speak, but Jack cut him off. "Fishing, tomorrow at Busse Lake. Roger on that." He turned quickly to Leighton. "Don't worry, we'll make it in time for your game." Finally, he looked at RosaMarie. "And you and I have a date with the characters tomorrow afternoon."

RosaMarie clapped her hands together. "Goodie! I'll have them all set up, Daddy."

Bryson put his fork down long enough to say. "How did you know what I was going to ask you, Dad?"

Leighton chipped in. "Yeah, me too. What's up with that?

Jack shrugged as he poured syrup on his French toast. "I can't say, exactly. I told your mom it seems like I know what's going to happen before it does today. Yeah, it's kind of weird." Leighton rolled his eyes, and Bryson just shrugged.

The conversation followed its usual course for a Friday: weekend plans, scheduling conflicts, friends, school and bonding. Naturally, Jack would remember the big events, but it was the small stuff, like breakfast as a family, that he enjoyed the most and would cherish forever. Bryson pushing to drive, Leighton trying so hard to be an athlete, and then there was RosaMarie. Jack looked at her and experienced a strong pang of anxiety. A strange and unsettling sensation washed over him.

There's something I need to remember about RosaMarie... What is it?

Jack kissed Juanita goodbye and made his way to the BMW. Just after pulling out of the driveway, he made a call to Stephanie to rearrange his traveling schedule, which turned out to be a mixed blessing. He would get to spend another few weeks at home, but that pushed his trip to Boston off until November.

The train ride gave him the opportunity to get psyched up for the Simmons challenge, but Jack was having difficulty getting motivated. Strangely, he already envisioned the outcome. Simmons would change his mind and keep his business at SPS. In fact, he was so sure of it, he leaned back in his seat and tried to sleep.

***

As Jack looked out the window with the expansive view of Lake Michigan, he barely heard Walt Offerman talking from behind. "Simmons canceled the meeting. He called before hours and left a goddamned voicemail. Said the offer from Amtron was too good to turn down. Said it would save him a million bucks a year."

"This is a catastrophic hit," said Hans. "Over twenty-five million in sales flushed. We're an independent distributor, and we can't absorb that kind of loss."

"Amtron has been a pain in our ass ever since they moved in here and started gobbling up all the smaller suppliers," said Offerman. "The exclusive deal they cut with Comfort King on equipment is killing us, and now they're ten percent lower than everyone else."

273

Jack looked back and said, "I'll handle it. Don't worry about it because I know exactly what to do and how it ends."

"What do you mean?" said Walt as a frown crossed his face. "How are you going to…"

The door was already closing before Offerman finished his sentence. Just before it shut, Jack leaned back in and said, "By the way, we're going to meet at O'Malley's to celebrate at two forty-five, so don't be late."

Offerman and Morris exchanged puzzled looks, but Jack just smiled, waved and left the room for good.

The actions that followed were almost robotic. He called Simmons' kid, Bobby, and squeezed him hard, even resorting to a hint at blackmail with some compromising pictures from Cabo. The kid, who had to be a major disappointment to his father, ratted his dad out, and Jack showed up at the old man's club to disrupt his lunch. At first, Big Bob played the hard ass. "It's business, blah, blah, blah," but Jack didn't hesitate to pull out the heavy artillery. He reminded Simmons that he saved his ass multiple times, and when Jack talked about a three-thousand-unit housing project contract that he controlled, Simmons melted into a blob of jelly.

Amtron and Gerry Rourke with her big boobs never stood a chance.

There was much backslapping, and Jack even got an ovation when he went back to the office, but today was not about that. As he pulled the door open to O'Malleys, where the celebration had already started, he looked around in anticipation.

Something was going to happen inside this place, and today, that's what it was all about.

The drinks were flowing and stories growing taller when she walked in. Jack never saw her before in his life, but he recognized her instantly. The dingy gray coat full of holes, the stringy gray hair and the lit cigarette dangling from her lips were unmistakable. He knew her from somewhere, even if he couldn't remember where.

"Tommy," he said while motioning the bartender over. "Get that woman a tall bourbon, neat."

The bartender grimaced. "Seriously? She's come in a couple times this week. I don't judge, but she has to be homeless." A look of curiosity crossed Tommy's face. "Hey, how would you know what she drinks?"

Jack shrugged. "I wish I could tell you, but I guarantee that's it: tall bourbon, neat."

Tommy turned toward the back bar and grabbed a bottle of house bourbon and did the pour. He was about to take it to the old woman, but Jack grabbed his arm. "Let me," he said. Tommy nodded but looked confused.

"Hey Jack, get back over here. Everyone wants to hear how you cut old man Simmons' balls off and mounted 'em like a large-mouth bass." Offerman shouted from across the pool table where, he was finishing off a game of eight ball with Tad Newsome. Jack waved him off and took the bourbon over to the back of the building, where the old woman sat at an isolated table.

She was hunched down and slumped over. Her tangled hair hung in a way that completely shrouded her face. He thought she might be sleeping or dead, until she said, "Well, what are you waiting for? Give me my goddamn bourbon."

Startled, Jack almost spilled the drink before recovering and carefully placing the glass on the table in front of her. She picked it up with shaking hands and guzzled about half the contents, dragging a coat sleeve across her mouth. Without looking up, she said, "Sit down, pissant."

"I'm sorry, have we met?"

She looked up and flicked the hair out of her face. Her eyes were ancient, but they burned with the fire of anger and defiance. "I said, *sit down*. I'm about done with you. Total waste of time."

Jack never broke her gaze as he took the opposite seat. *That smell. Familiar.* "Who are you? How do I know you?"

She grabbed the glass and took a smaller drink, but that sent her into a coughing spasm. He saw her pull a soiled handkerchief from her coat, and she covered her mouth and hacked into it for at least a minute. When she finished, Jack saw a smear of blood on the cloth before she shoved it in her pocket and regained control of her breathing.

Without saying a word, she thrust her arm out and opened her hand, which held a crumpled piece of paper. "Take it, pissant."

Hesitantly, Jack accepted the note and slowly unfolded it. Scribbled in writing that was faded and barely legible: *1233 Hardy RD, Des Plaines.*

I know this address, but from where?

He studied the note for several seconds, and when he looked up, he realized his headache had returned. "What is this?"

"Don't play dumb, pissant," said the woman as she rose from the table. "You know damn well what it is. Now, for God's sake, don't be late."

"I—I don't understand. What the hell is this about?"

She turned around and shook a finger in his face. "Don't you goddamn *dare* be late this time."

Her voice was loud enough that his co-workers' conversation at the pub table stopped as they all looked in his direction. Jack hardly noticed as he watched her lumber slowly over to the door. Once he knew she was gone, he shoved the note in his pocket and went back to the table.

"Jesus Christ, Jack, what the hell was that all about?" asked Offerman.

"No idea. You try to be nice to these homeless people, but some of them are really nasty... Anyway, where were we? Oh yeah, you should have seen old man Simmons' face when I told him I just got word that C.H.A. was releasing three thousand more housing units, and they wanted *me* to find the right contractor for the job..."

***

The train ride home seemed to take forever. The effects of the booze were wearing off, and an extreme weariness filled the void. That's how drinking usually affected Jack. For him, alcohol wasn't a sedative; it was like fueling an engine with nitrous. He would stay lit until the booze stopped flowing, and about an hour later, he would crash until the following morning.

The jiggling of his shoulder didn't wake him until it turned into shaking. He looked up and saw a large man standing in the aisle, staring at him intently.

Of course. The fat guy on the train. Something else I didn't remember until it just happened.

"Excuse me," the obese man said as he slid awkwardly into the seat next to Jack. "I'm sorry to interrupt your slumber."

Jack sat up and tried to focus as he cleared his throat. "Uh, there are several open seats in this car. It might be more comfortable for you to take one of them."

The man smiled, and the ample flesh on his face shifted. "Perhaps, but I would miss out on the pleasure of your company." He stuck out his hand. "My name is Tucker Lutz, but everyone calls me Tuck... I don't know why, but you seem familiar to me."

Jack grasped Lutz's hand and did his best to hide his revulsion at the transference of sweat. "Yes, I agree. I seem to remember you too, but I don't know from where. That's happening a lot to me today." He looked at Lutz for a moment. "My name is Jack Clausen... Wait a minute. You're a—a mind reader. Am I right?"

Lutz didn't appear to be particularly surprised at Jack's insight. "Close, but not exactly. I'm a clairvoyant. Sometimes, I can see the future."

"Ah, yes, the future. As soon as you said it, I remembered I already knew that."

Lutz looked away for a moment and ran a finger between his neck and the collar of his shirt. "Mr. Clausen. Can I call you Jack? This is going to sound

278

strange, but I assure you it's real. I came over to sit with you because your aura is very unusual. The resonance of your frequency is so unstable... It's like you don't fully exist in this dimension."

Jack chuckled. "Look, I admit to having a touch of deja vu today, but I seriously doubt I have any chance of slipping into a different dimension."

Lutz cocked his head to the side. "What is that?" He twisted around to look behind him.

"I—I don't understand. What is it you see?" Jack looked in the same direction as Lutz.

"Not see, hear. Something peculiar. I hear it and feel it. Another extremely low resonance... I can't identify where it's coming from. It's weaker and hiding underneath yours, but it's very disconcerting."

Jack turned away and rolled his eyes. "Look, Tuck, it's been a long day, and I'm trying to get some sleep."

Lutz turned back and placed his hand on Jack's arm. "I know things like this are difficult to understand, but I am concerned." He opened his overcoat and reached into his shirt pocket.

"You're getting off at Park Ridge, so you're about to give me a business card and tell me to call you if something that happens I can't understand."

"Yes," said Lutz, "those were my exact intentions. Where did that come from, Jack? Have you experienced this phenomenon before?"

"No. Just today, but I'm sure it will be gone by tomorrow."

The conductor called out, "Next stop Park Ridge."

"That's me." Lutz stood up and handed Jack his card. "Remember, call me if you find yourself in an uncomfortable situation you can't understand. I don't want to alarm you, but your frequency is resonating so low, it's imperative you keep an eye out for potentially dangerous situations."

"Sure, sure," said Jack dismissively as he glanced at the card. "Tucker Lutz: clairvoyant. I'll call you if I see any dead people."

Lutz didn't smile.

***

Jack woke up Saturday morning with an anxious feeling he couldn't explain. He rose later than he normally would when he had a fishing outing planned with Bryson. Once the coffee was on, he woke his son, and together, they started loading their gear into Juanita's SUV.

The spot Bryson picked was perfect. The location was isolated and had an abundance of the frogs, leeches and insects the bass liked to feed on. Father and son caught enough fish for a family fish fry dinner, but more importantly, Jack capitalized on the opportunity to learn more about the part of his teenager's life that would normally remain hidden.

Eventually, every perfect moment must end, and when Jack noticed two new arrivals heading toward their spot, he knew it was time to leave. The anxious feeling continued to grow, and he couldn't shake Lutz's words of warning.

Something terrible is coming… But what?

After watching the two amateurs struggle with their brand new gear, he clapped Bryson on the shoulder. "C'mon sport, let's get going." When one of the newbies dropped his tackle box, and the other almost fell in the lake, Bryson relented, and they began packing up.

Standing near his cooler, one of the men called out, "Hey, I hope we're not running you off."

"No," said Jack as the sensation of deja vu swept over him yet again. "We were getting ready to leave. The fishing is good; hope you catch a bunch."

"Okay, thanks." The man waved as he cracked open a beer.

As they approached the other fisherman, who was still trying to gather the spilled contents of his tackle box, Jack stopped suddenly. He waited a moment and then said, "Don't worry, I won't be late."

Confused, the portly man stood up and looked over. "What? Were you talking to me?"

Jack's head tilted a bit, and he shaded his eyes. "No, I guess I was talking to myself. Sorry."

The fisherman scratched his head, leaned back over, and continued to pick up his gear.

***

They made it to Leighton's game with time to spare. Even as his sense of apprehension grew, Jack fought through it and cheered on his youngest son. A strong suspicion that Leighton was going to get a hit today proved to be prescient.

281

At one point, he looked over and saw RosaMarie had disappeared from the nearby jungle gym, where she had gone to play, and yet, he felt no sense of panic. Without Juanita or Bryson even noticing, he left the bleachers and walked casually over to the playground and waited. Within minutes, an older woman with a warm smile walked up with his daughter in hand. Jack thanked her profusely, but his relief at recovering RosaMarie was short-lived. Deep in his gut, he knew something much worse was coming.

This isn't it. There's something else, but I can't... I just can't remember.

He leaned down and hugged her. "RosaMarie, you can't wander off like that. If we agree you're going to the playground, then that's where you better be, understand?"

RosaMarie nodded and looked at her father sheepishly. "Am I in trouble, Daddy?

Jack smiled. "No, pumpkin. Just don't scare me like that, okay?"

The whole family celebrated with video games and ice cream, and when they arrived home, RosaMarie bounded up the stairs. Jack knew exactly what her plans were, so he waited in his den until he heard her small footsteps approaching.

"Daddy, do you have time to play with me?" she asked.

"Sure, pumpkin. I promised, didn't I? And a promise is a promise."

The words echoed in his head as he said them. The sinking sensation continued and took him to a place so mentally bleak, Jack wondered if he was up to playing the game. He followed her to her room and took his usual spot on the floor, picking up Donald Duck and starting the adventure.

The game progressed as it usually did, with RosaMarie squealing in delight as the narrative she created unfolded. Jack tried his best to hide his growing anxiety, but the feeling crept through, until it enveloped him in a coffin of fear and dread.

"Daddy, are you okay?" RosaMarie set down Pooh Bear and looked at him with concern.

Jack tried to answer, but his vocal cords froze up. He couldn't move. It was as if someone injected him with a paralysis drug.

The doorbell rang as the clock struck three, and Jack brought his hand up to his chest as some invisible force grabbed his heart and squeezed.

RosaMarie walked over and touched his shoulder. "Daddy, are you sick?"

"Jack... Jack, can you come down here?"

With an enormous effort, he took a deep gulp of air, and his heart began to beat again in an erratic rhythm. He reached out to reassure his daughter. "I'm okay, RosaMarie. I just got dizzy for a moment.

Pausing to regain his balance, Jack rose on wooden legs, fighting the rising nausea and urge to faint. He walked out to the landing and looked down at the first floor.

"Jamal is here." said Juanita. "Could you come down and talk to him?"

Jamal is here. Of course Jamal is here...

Chapter Twenty-Two

Jack reached the front door, and moving on autopilot, stuck out his hand, which Jamal Egebe grabbed and shook heartily.

Here it comes. The mower. He's going to ask to see the mower, and I'm going to say yes, even though I shouldn't. I don't know why, but I know I shouldn't.

"Hey, Jack," said Jamal as his smile widened. "Do you have a few minutes to show me that new mower?"

Don't say yes. Tell him you're sick. Tell him anything, but don't go out of the house.

"Sure, follow me." Turning to Juanita, he said, "We'll be in the garage. Just a couple minutes."

After giving Jamal the complete rundown on his new riding mower, Jack watched and waited for Egebe to ask to ride it, which he knew was coming. Before his neighbor could get a word out, Jack crawled into the driver's seat and pulled out the key.

"Wow, Jack. That's great. I was just going to ask you if I could try her out."

Jack nodded and motioned for Jamal to hop on, and together they rode toward the Egebe house. The blackness hung on the fringes of Jack's peripheral vision, waiting to close in and squeeze out his consciousness. He swallowed repeatedly to keep the bile down. The day was pleasant, neither too warm nor too cold, but sweat poured off his body like he was in a sauna.

I'm having a heart attack. A panic attack, at least.

When they pulled onto Egebe's lawn, Jack quickly went through a list of the mower's operational and safety features. Throughout the mini tutorial, Jamal kept glancing over at him, each time with more concern.

"Jack, are you alright?"

"Yeah, yeah, I'm fine."

"Because you don't look so good. We can do this another time if you want."

"No," said Jack while wiping the sweat from his brow and somehow feigning a smile. "Go ahead, Jamal, get on. You're ready to ride."

"I don't know, Jack. You look awful. Are you sure..."

"I'm sure. Go ahead, ride it."

The bad is coming soon. It's almost here. RosaMarie...

"Jack... I don't think..."

"Goddamn it, Jamal, ride the mower!" Jack reached over and turned the key, and the engine roared to life. Egebe stepped on the gas, and the machine lurched forward, and he began cutting a beginner's ragged path through his front lawn. He was so consumed with controlling the mower that he didn't see Juanita running toward them from afar, but Jack did.

When he looked up and saw his wife, the memories returned, slowly at first, but ultimately as an avalanche. Jack's brain scrambled, and nothing made sense in the moment, but he knew every detail surrounding RosaMarie's abduction and how to prevent it. In a full sprint, he brushed past Juanita without saying a word, so he never saw her stop and turn toward him in desperation while screaming that RosaMarie was missing.

He ran into the house and grabbed his car keys, wallet and the hammer he brought the last time, but he didn't bother with the note the old woman gave him. Lattimores' address was something he could never forget.

1233 Hardy RD, Des Plaines.

Jack wouldn't need the GPS this time either. With the accelerator pushed to the floor, he squealed and smoked the BMW's tires as the car flew down Maple and turned onto Walnut.

He looked at his watch. At his current speed, he should reach Lattimores' house within ten minutes, which would leave plenty of time to rescue RosaMarie. Fortunately, the traffic on Northwest Highway was relatively light on a late Saturday afternoon, as people prepared their evening plans. He weaved around the slower moving vehicles but never felt in danger of being stopped.

The phone rang just after he glanced down at it. Juanita was calling, but everything outside of RosaMarie was a distraction.

"Juanita, not now."

"Jack, where the hell are you? RosaMarie… RosaMarie is gone…"

"I may know where she is. You're going to have to wait for me to call."

"How do you know? I'm losing it, Jack... For God's sake, I'm losing it. I need..." He ended the call and turned off the phone.

A slightly different conversation than the first time. So, not everything is the same.

By the time he turned down Courtland, Jack could hear the pulsing of his heart in his ears. The first time he rescued RosaMarie, he didn't know what to expect, but this time, the anticipation was almost too much to bear. He swerved and came closer to hitting the cyclist than he did during their first encounter. As he looked in the rear-view mirror and watched the slender young man holding his leg and rocking back and forth, Jack imagined he might be in a cast for several weeks.

The car veered sharply, and the tires squealed as he pulled up in front of Lattimores' house. Clutching the hammer, Jack jumped out and ran up the walkway. Remembering the front door was locked, he smashed the living room window glass and stepped inside.

His watch read 3:40. Last time, he arrived four minutes later. Subconscious familiarity trimmed minutes off the pursuit. Jack reached the end of the hall and kicked the bedroom door with such force it ripped out the striker plate. As he stepped inside the room, he immediately sensed something was different.

The first sensation was vertigo, almost like the spinning small children sometimes do to experience the buzz of dizziness. Then, a black gaseous cloud gathered in a corner of the room and rushed at him, passing through his body and leaving his skin feeling scorched. Feet frozen in place, he forced his head to turn to the left, even though he knew he shouldn't. For several seconds, there was no way to properly interpret the sight in front of him. His lungs collapsed; the air was sucked out of the room.

Jack fell to his knees, but his eyes remained glued to the disfigured body of RosaMarie. She laid on her stomach in a corner, wearing only her pink princess shirt. Angry, purple bruises covered her visible body. Her head was twisted grotesquely, and her dull, lifeless eyes were wide-open and stared deep into his soul.

There was no way to know how long he continued to look at her, as the confusion and shock obscured any other sensations. When he heard a whimpering from the opposite side of the room, he turned and looked at the trembling, pathetic figure crouching down, his head in hands, muttering to himself.

"This can't be," said Jack. "They told me they would make everything right. They promised..."

Pauley Lattimores looked up. His eyes were bloodshot red, and his face appeared puffy and bloated from crying. "I knew you were going to show up. I remembered from the last time. That's why I had to do it quicker and get it over with. Now, I'm supposed to get to leave. I'm supposed to get on with my life now."

The rage welled up from a place so dark, Jack was sure he tapped into a stream of vile bilge from the bowels of hell itself. He could feel the pressure building and knew it would erupt soon, but for now, it just smoldered. RosaMarie still stared at him, shredding his essence one filament at a time.

Carefully, he took off his shirt and covered her legs and lower abdomen.

"I don't understand," said Lattimores in a nervous, high-pitched voice. "They told me if I did those things and killed her, it would be over. We could finally live in peace. I took the third pill..." He looked up at Jack. "Don't you see, I can't live without Brandon. He's my only child. I had no choice."

"How did you think you were going to escape from me? I'm her father..." said Jack in a low monotone. His hand tightened on the hammer.

Lattimores seemed to shrink. His shoulders collapsed, and he doubled over, once again head in hands. "Oh God, no. Please, I didn't want to do it. I swear to God I didn't want to do it. Torto told me if I took the third pill... The girl... Your daughter. They said if I did it before you showed up, everything would be fine for us. I had to do it. My son and wife; I had to save them."

Lattimores rose to his knees with his hands clasped together. "Please. I begged them not to make me do that to her, but he said it was the only way. I should have killed myself... Brandon." Lattimores sobbed in a deep, mournful way, and in that moment, Jack didn't doubt his sincerity, and yet, none of it mattered anymore.

"You took everything from me. I have nothing left. I'm not sure where I exist or even if I exist at all. None of this may be real, but I only know that in that corner is the one thing on this earth I loved the most, and you've taken her from me. She died in pain, scared and wondering why I wasn't there to save her."

Jack's anger swelled until the rage finally boiled over, temporarily subduing the pain. There was only one purpose left: revenge.

Lattimores shuffled backward until he pressed tight against a corner. He looked up with a combination of fear and resignation. Jack inched closer and raised the hammer above his head.

"No, no, no..." Lattimores whined piteously as he shook his head and raised his arms. Jack stood over him for a moment, watching as a growing wet spot appeared in the crotch of the killer's pants. He knew that beating this piece of shit to death wouldn't change anything, and nothing would bring back RosaMarie. In a strange way, he pitied the pathetic character writhing on the floor. They both fell prey to the Identicals, and Lattimores was just another poor wretch who hoped their magic pill would change his life and solve all his problems.

"This is the cost we must bear, Lattimores. Neither one of us could accept our fate. We succumbed to the selfish temptation to change the past to lessen our own pain. The damage we have done is unfathomable."

The whining stopped as Lattimores looked up. "You understand. You know I didn't mean to kill anyone."

"Yes, I understand, but it doesn't change anything."

At that moment, Jack brought the hammer down on Lattimores, who did his best to dodge the blow. Instead of hitting his head, the hammer impacted with the murderer's shoulder, and he howled in pain and clutched the wound with his opposite hand. This only distracted him from focusing on Jack's follow-up strike, which landed flush on his jaw.

Lattimores straightened up and stared ahead with a befuddled look on his face. "Wait... Hold on a minute."

A third strike hit him directly on the crown of his head. The force of this blow was so severe that it broke his skull open at the impact site, and the head of the hammer sunk into the fissure. Jack let go of the handle as Lattimores teetered for a second, blinked several times and toppled over as a thick torrent of blood leaked out the top of his head.

With some difficulty, Jack freed the hammer, wiped it on his pants, and stuck it in his pocket. Fighting the paralysis of shock, he went over to RosaMarie and struggled to pull her jeans back over her tiny legs. Using the same degree of care reserved for delicate perishables, he gently picked her up off the floor and carried her to the car. She was heavier than he remembered, much heavier. He laid her in the back seat, and after putting his shirt back on, he got in, turned on his phone and sped toward the freeway.

Eighteen alert chimes rang out, a combination of texts and calls. When the final chime faded away, he pushed number one on the speed dial.

"Jack. Jack, tell me what's going on." Juanita picked up on the first ring. She sounded nearly incoherent. "Please, don't do this to me. Where is my daughter? Where is she? I'm out of my mind. Please Jack, please..."

"It's all going to be okay, Juanita. Listen to me carefully. I am in real trouble. What I've done... I wouldn't know where to begin. I just want you to know how sorry I am. It was all my fault. I shouldn't have left the house with Jamal without telling you. Please, whatever happens, don't blame yourself. Always remember, it was me. Totally me."

Her voice was subdued, and the crying stopped. "What are you trying to tell me, Jack? What are you saying?"

"RosaMarie is dead, Nita. She's been dead for a year and a half. It turned me into a drunk, a bad husband and a bad father. I drove you away, and you left me. I—I tried to fix it, but I only made it worse. I don't know, maybe there's a way... Please, remember how much I love you, and you make sure you tell the boys I love them too, okay?"

"Jack, I—I don't understand. You're... RosaMarie... What did you say? What?"

"She's dead, Juanita."

"Dead? No... My baby... No!" Juanita tried to talk, but her throat seized from dryness, and her voice caught. "Help me," she managed to croak out. Whatever was left of Jack's heart shattered at that moment. Before she could speak again, he punched the "end" icon and turned off the phone, this time for good.

Only one task awaited; only one place to exact revenge. Jack turned the car onto the freeway and sped past the different exits in a fog. All that he remembered over the past few days, or at least what he perceived as days, effectively scrambled his brain. He existed in three distinct realities with different outcomes, yet none of them was the one he hoped for.

Maybe the past simply couldn't be altered in a way that changed anything in the future for the better. The intensity of the pain he experienced, watching every member of his family die in different versions of the same scenario, made him realize the entire effort was folly. Now, he suffered pain even more overwhelming than losing his loved ones. He mortally wounded his family by isolating and forcing them to watch him self-destruct while they tried to deal with their grief and rebuild their own lives. As though somehow *his* pain was worse than theirs, he wanted to punish them because only *his* pain mattered.

Yet, everything changed when he saw Juanita's face as she came running to tell him RosaMarie was missing. In the two false realities, he paid attention to every detail, and each time he saw her terror, fear and anguish more clearly. She hurt as much as he did, perhaps even more, and yet, she still tried to keep the family together.

"Coward," he said out loud. "I'm nothing but a coward. A drunk and a coward." The realization stirred a sense of self-loathing so complete he would have crashed the car into the next bridge support if his final mission wasn't so important.

Jack knew he journeyed to the murky and shadowy dark underbelly of existence. A place that remained hidden, except to the few tortured souls who defied the will of God and sought it out.

After exiting the freeway at Marquette, he traveled west, reaching Ashland before turning onto 62nd. Slowly driving down Union Hills, Jack felt the same sense of apprehension and anxiety he remembered during his last encounter with the Identicals. Without hesitation, he exited the car and grabbed the hammer, still covered in blood and a few bits of brain. He stood quietly for a moment, allowing the energy surrounding the building to wash over him. From inside the house, the Identicals beckoned.

From what he remembered, the weather on this day was cool and crisp, and the sun was shining. Yet, he pulled up the collar on his jacket as an icy wind blew through the fabric and chilled him deep to the bone. The skies were rapidly clouding up and growing ever darker. As he made his way up to the porch, he hesitated before finding the nerve to reach down and open the door.

Standing inside the kitchen, he looked over at the child-creature sucking violently on the woman's breast as she sat on the floor as before. She reached out toward him, her face contorted into a mask of anguish; her eyes hopeless and pleading.

"Help me," she whispered.

He took a step towards her, but the creature disengaged from her breast and jumped down to the floor, snarling and snapping its jaws. Jack backed up and cocked the hammer, bringing it down hard on the monster's skull membrane. The sensation felt similar to crushing a melon, and some thick, green liquid splattered out the side of its head. The beast stumbled around and fell while the woman looked at Jack in shock.

"Run!" he said. "Get the hell out of here, and run as far away as you can from whatever brought you to this place."

She nodded and got unsteadily to her feet, moving stiffly while hunched over, fighting against the ravages of her captivity. Miraculously, she somehow made it out the door.

When he entered the dining room, he encountered an enormous beast, proportioned like a gorilla only larger, with a thick mane of long red hair covering its backside. A woman underneath the creature moved rhythmically and groaned while jerking back and forth. Somewhere from underneath the floor, he heard a series of muffled screams accompanied by sounds that reminded him of dental drilling machinery.

Jack entered the living room unnoticed as Torto and the other Identicals gathered in a circle, surrounding something he couldn't see. Together, they made a cacophony of sucking sounds, accompanied by that same purring noise he recalled from the dreams and his last encounter. As he grew closer, he looked between their spaces and realized they were feeding on the naked body of a woman, who appeared to be heavily sedated. She would flinch every so often, and Jack saw her eyelids fluttering, a sign she was in REM sleep.

"So, the dreams are real," he said. "How are you able to do that? I mean, transport people here and then back to their own rooms. How is that possible?"

Torto stopped sucking and turned toward Jack. "Jack stop Torto feeding. Not good, don'cha know." Jack noticed the deep, red circle, ringed by small bite marks, where Torto's pointed teeth had pierced the flesh on the woman's stomach.

"Why Jack come here? Old woman tell Jack how he pay other debt soon."

Jack smiled and strengthened his grip on the hammer. "I've come to kill you, you son of a bitch. I don't know what part of hell you come from, but I'm going to send you back. You've ruined my life."

Chapter Twenty-Three

Torto looked at Jack and grinned. "Why Jack mad? Torto do deal. Family saved, don'cha know."

"RosaMarie is dead. You let that bastard Lattimores kill her."

Torto shrugged. "Jack say he want dead family back, so Torto do it, but Torto need Jack to do his part of deal. Torto don't trust Jack. Not sure Jack kill Pauley if Pauley don't kill daughter. Torto has to make sure, Jack. All must square. Very big. Pauley dead, and Jack get family back. Boys, wife. Just like before. Torto do deal."

"That *wasn't* the deal. You were supposed to give me back my *entire* family. You never said that excluded RosaMarie. Give me another pill, or I swear..." He raised the hammer.

"Jack not good, don'cha know. Torto give Jack what he want. Bring back wife and boys, and now Jack threat Torto? Jack still *owe* Torto. Maybe Torto make Jack unhappy more."

As he spoke, Jack rushed the small creature, but almost instantly, he felt a sharp numbing pain that started in his shoulder and spread like melting butter down his arm and into his hand. The loss of feeling caused his arm to sink, until it was down at his side. His immobilized fingers opened involuntarily, and the hammer dropped to the floor. All sensation was gone, and the numbness spread quickly to his other extremities, which caused him to collapse. He lay on his back, unable to lift his head as drool rolled down both sides of his face.

"Now, Torto talk; Jack listen. Bargain not done; Jack still owe. Family not live if debt not paid." Torto waddled over and looked down at him. "Right, Jack?"

The numbness in his neck eased, and Jack nodded.

"Good. Torto give Jack more chance." He opened his hand, and a crumpled piece of paper fluttered down. "Old woman should say deals, but she... Go do deal, and Torto say all good, Jack. Family live, but not girl."

The feeling slowly returned to his body, and with difficulty, Jack sat up. He reached down and picked up the piece of paper and unfolded it.

Tucker Lutz, 1326 Mona Lisa, Berwyn — Sonia Williamson, 1215 Ridge Lane, Evanston

KILL THEM

"Why these two? I — I know Lutz, and you sent Williamson to kill me on the train in the last reality. Please, no more death."

Torto shrugged. "Jack must pay debt. If not want to pay, then *all* family die... for good." In his shuffling, wind-up toy way, Torto turned around. He licked his lips in anticipation of returning to sucking on the woman's body.

"Wait!" said Jack. "Okay, I'll do it. I'll kill them both. Just promise me there will be no more harm to my wife and boys."

298

Torto turned back and smiled. "Good. Go now; find them quick. Better hurry. Man police looking for daughter and Jack too, don'cha know." Torto kneeled down next to the woman, lying supine on the floor, and bit into her leg. He lifted his head long enough to say, "Gun in car box place, Jack. Bang, bang."

Jack nodded dully and stood up on wobbly legs. Somehow, he managed to stumble out the door and reach the car without falling.

I'm nothing more than a pawn. Just like the old woman said, the Identicals own me.

***

Once he pulled away, Jack forced himself into a single-minded purpose and compartmentalized the horror of the last few days. A sense of relief actually washed over him as he headed toward Berwyn. In a moment of clarity, a plan emerged, and as he fleshed it out, he realized there might yet be a way to escape this nightmare. An end to his torment and suffering, magnified a hundrred-fold since he swallowed the first pill, was in sight. Just two more horrible acts and the whole terrible episode might be over.

He pulled up in front of Tucker Lutz's house and waited. His hands were shaking violently, and it seemed like he was moving through a landscape in a dream. The scene outside was lit up in colors so vibrant they hurt Jack's eyes, and he squinted to keep from being blinded. Every so often the whole backdrop would flutter, and a kind of static would dull it momentarily, but then it flashed again, even more vivid than before.

Jack reached into the glovebox and pulled out his handgun. He didn't bother hiding it as he walked up the long cement pathway with purpose. The front door had a deadbolt that was engaged, so instead of knocking, he went to the back of the house and used the hammer to break the flimsy lock/knob combo. Jack reached down and pulled the throw latch out of the borehole and pushed the door open.

Apparently, he didn't create enough noise to gain anyone's attention because he was alone as he walked cautiously through the kitchen. In the main hallway, he heard muted voices coming from the living room. Once he came closer, he could make out what they were saying.

"It's okay, Sonia, you're not alone. I'm glad you contacted me. The more we communicate, the more we can understand this phenomenon. Perhaps in time we might even be able to defeat it." The voice clearly belonged to Lutz.

"Thank you for seeing me," a woman answered. "This has been such a horrific experience. I can't talk to anyone about it... No one would understand, and they would just think I'm crazy. Like I said on the phone, I couldn't kill Jack Clausen like they told me to, but after that, I lost everything... My wife *and* my son. I became so despondent, I tried to kill myself again, but that's when the one called Torto offered me a second pill. But this time, I was supposed to kill Clausen *and* place a bomb on a commuter train. I—I couldn't do either of those horrible things. I am terrified of what they'll do to me and my family next."

"I understand, Sonia. You're in a kind of personal hell no one could truly understand, unless they too were corrupted by the Identicals. But let's start with this. How did you find me?"

"I've been stalking Clausen. I was on the train yesterday, and I overheard you offering to help him. I'm so desperate, I hoped you might be able to help me as well."

Lutz stroked his chin. "So, it was *your* resonance I detected underneath Clausen's. I sensed there was someone else lurking. The frequencies were so distorted, my mind could barely cope." He picked up his coke and took a long swig. "You did the right thing, Sonia. Jack Clausen is in grave danger, and you cannot have this kind of blood on your hands."

"Can you help me, Mr. Lutz? Please…"

"Let me be very honest with you. I know little about these Identicals. I've encountered seven people affected by them, including Clausen. You are the eighth. A select group of colleagues may have come across several of the Identicals' victims without knowing it. You are the only one who speaks of a second pill and a third reality. However, I will say this with some certainty: Since you ignored their instructions again, you and your family are in extreme peril. You must get away from here, and I'm not sure if even that will help."

Jack froze. Somehow, both targets Torto wanted him to eliminate were in the same place at the same time. That couldn't be a coincidence.

301

Of course they're together. The Identicals probably arranged it.

"You're right," said Sonia. "Eva, my wife, cursed at me with the vilest language, and yesterday, she said she wished I was dead. She never swore in the original reality. Last night, I woke up at three in the morning and found her in the garage with the car running. She begged me to leave her alone. When I asked why she was trying to kill herself, she said she couldn't explain it, but her feelings were growing increasingly violent. She told me she wanted to kill me."

"Sonia, that's terrible."

"Then there is my son, Harris. He grows more sinister and vicious by the day. I'm a broken woman, Mr. Lutz, and I can't do this anymore. It's all happening again. I took the pills to save Harris and Eva, and yet, it's all much worse. What should I do?"

Lutz puffed his cheeks out and exhaled slowly. "I wish I could offer more... We've got to find these Identicals and at least talk to them. Could you arrange it?"

"I—I don't know. The old woman might be able to... Wait..."

"Who's there?"

She turned around and her eyes grew wide. "...*Clausen!*"

Jack stood under the arch between the living room and the front door. His face sagged, and his head drooped as he stared out menacingly from underneath half-shut eyelids. The gun was in his hand, but his arm lay against his side.

Hearing Williamson's voice and seeing her expression change, Lutz turned around and looked at Jack. His forehead creased as he tried to cope with the shock of seeing a second Identicals' victim standing there with a gun.

"Hello, Sonia," said Jack. His tone was dull and emotionless. "You had the knife in my gut. Why the *fuck* didn't you kill me?"

"I told you, I couldn't do it."

"But you took the second pill, and here we are. You're still supposed to kill me, and now I'm supposed to kill you. Which one of us gets their life back?"

Lutz struggled to his feet. "Wait, wait a minute. You took a second pill as well, Jack? You're in a third reality?"

"Bingo, give that man a prize."

"Look, Jack, what are you doing here? Whatever is wrong, we can fix it. Nothing is worth killing for, no matter what the Identicals have said or done to you."

Jack smiled, but his posture remained the same. "Yeah, let's talk it out, Tuck. Like we did the first time when you gave me your clairvoyant bullshit, or maybe that was the second time." He used the barrel of the gun to scratch his chin. "Why don't we start by going out to my car so I can show you my dead five-year-old daughter? You can see her disfigured body and then we can talk it out."

"Clausen, this isn't you," said Williamson. "The Identicals are doing this to both of us. Please, let's figure out a way."

"Sorry, Sonia, you're a dead woman walking, anyway. You should have killed me when you had the chance. Now, in this reality, you're fucked. If I don't kill both of you, the rest of my family dies."

"Please, Jack, for God's sake. Your aura, it's so black it's burning my retinas. Your frequency. The pain is too much. My eyes… I can't see…"

The first shot tore into Lutz's abdomen, and he doubled over. Williamson looked at him in shock and turned back toward Jack while making gestures that begged for mercy. "Please… Please, Clausen. My wife and son…"

"You should have paid your debt, Sonia." The second shot slammed into Williamson's chest, and she spun around like a marionette. The third shot hit her square in the jaw and ripped off half her face.

Lutz was squirming on the floor, looking much like a turtle on its back, flapping his arms and legs but going nowhere. Jack pumped two more slugs into the obese body until it stopped moving.

He counted five shots, and the .38-caliber revolver had one round left in the chamber. Calmly and slowly, he walked out to the car and opened the back door. He moved RosaMarie's legs so he could sit beside her. Her hair was becoming stiff, and the color was darkening, but he reached over and stroked the curls gently. In the distance, he could hear the wail of a police siren. By now, the nosiest neighbors were gathering to see where the loud crack of the firearm had come from.

"I love you, princess," he whispered as he leaned down to kiss her cold cheek. In a single motion, he straightened back up and put the gun to his head.

"What if Torto make better, Jack, don'cha know?"

Without looking, Jack grunted and screamed out. The gun shook as he pressed it harder into his temple.

"Torto fix if Jack want. Bring back *whole* family."

"No," said Jack in a voice that was heavy and laden with exhaustion. "No, you lie. It's another trick."

"No. Torto give Jack best deal this time."

Almost against his will, Jack slowly lowered the gun. He glanced around and saw the crowd of neighbors standing outside their houses, apprehensive, but growing bolder. One neighbor was carrying a handgun. The sirens grew louder.

"What deal? Every one of your *deals* just makes it worse for me."

"Old lady gone, Jack. Humans go old, don'cha know. She spoil soon. Torto send her to family so she say goodbye. Not see them for…" He seemed to struggle with the concept of time. "… for forty-two of things humans say is years. Torto need new human for work. Jack do deal, Torto make sure family live. *All* family."

Jack looked at the small, deformed looking creature. *How could something this wicked even exist?*

"You want me to take the old hag's place? To bring your horrible misery to others like she did to me? How would I even pull something like that off? Am I just supposed to disappear? A lot of people know me in Chicago."

Torto smiled, and his mouth opened so wide, Jack could see strings of white slime dripping down from the place his tonsils should be. "Torto

305

in places. *All* places. Chi-ca-go only one. Jack not be in Chi-ca-go much. Sorry. No one miss Jack for long."

"Hey... hey, what's going on over there?" The guy with the gun took a couple tentative steps forward. The sirens were very close now, probably only a few blocks over.

Jack looked out at the crowd and then back to Torto. "Alright. Alright, I'll do it. But I swear if this is a trick, I'll find a way to kill you, all of you. My entire family survives and lives long and happy lives. No accidents, no diseases, no premature deaths..."

"Yes, Torto make deal, don'cha know. Hurry." He held out his hand to reveal a bright red pill, fluorescent like the others, but even more vibrant, and it emitted a low humming sound. Jack grabbed it and shoved it in his mouth, swallowing just as the first squad car turned the corner.

"Why me?" he asked as consciousness faded, and the landscape grew increasingly blurry. "Why would you choose me?"

From a seeming infinite distance, he heard Torto's voice. "Because Jack buy Torto ice cream, don'cha know."

***

When he woke up Friday morning, Jack remembered everything almost instantly. He rolled over and pulled Juanita close, losing himself in the warmth of her skin, the feel of her supple curves and her intoxicating scent. As she stirred, his hands moved over her body, and she responded. By the time she turned over and looked at him, Jack was fully aroused, and he began kissing her body while removing her panties.

When they coupled, it wasn't sex. No, this was pure lovemaking. He looked deep into her eyes as he thrust, and he wouldn't allow her to look away for a single second. Their gazes locked, and Jack conveyed the love that came deep from his soul, along with the regret he had for all the sorrow he caused her. No matter how many times reality reset, her life would never be the same from this day forward. The spark and glint in her eye would be gone forever, so he took a mental snapshot of her face in this moment. He would always remember how full of life she once was.

His release was so powerful he thought he might leave a part of his soul inside of her. Her breathing was deep and rapid, and she muffled a scream while climaxing. A slick layer of sweat covered both of them, but Jack lingered inside her far longer than usual. This would be their last coupling, and he wanted it to last.

She reached up, and they kissed. It was a long and sensuous kiss, another memory Jack desperately grasped onto and filed away. Every detail of this day would be precious. If possible, he would have taken the day off, but he couldn't risk upsetting the balance or deviating too far from how events needed to unfold for everything to work as planned.

So, after kissing Juanita a last time, he got up, showered and dressed for work as he normally would. Glancing at his reflection in the mirror, he admired himself in his lucky suit. Downstairs, the kids were waiting, and their chatter was like a symphony. He spoke very little but simply smiled and watched their faces, especially RosaMarie. If all went well, and Torto held true to his word, Juanita would see her graduate and eventually marry. That was all that mattered right now.

When they finished the discussion about tomorrow's agenda, fishing with Bryson, Leighton's baseball game and playing characters with RosaMarie, Jack gulped the last of his coffee, straightened his tie and grabbed his briefcase. After kissing the kids goodbye, he held Juanita tight at the door.

"I love you," he said. "I don't care what happens to me, but I want you to know how much I love you and those kids. Nothing matters but that. Do you understand?" He used his hand to raise her chin so they were looking at each other again.

The life in those eyes. I must never forget.

"Jack, are you all right? The way you're talking… Is there something wrong?"

He shook his head. "No, everything is fine. For the first time, in a very long time, everything may be exactly right. I better get going. I've got an issue with old man Simmons."

"You'll fix it, and even if you don't, you'll still be a hero in my book."

***

The train ride into Chicago was routine. There was no sign of the old woman at Arlington or Ogilvie. Jack arrived at work and went through the motions, feigning indignation over losing the

Heating Experts account and then saving the day by confronting old man Simmons at Epstein's deli.

Later in the day, as the crew celebrated at O'Malley's, Jack reflected on his career and kept an eye on the table in the corner. He looked over frequently, but the old woman never showed up.

"Jack, buddy," said Offerman as he set his glass on the pub table. "You have a bright future with SPS Supply, a really bright future. Why, Hans and I were just talking about it. Who knows, there might be a partnership offer someday soon, Jack. Whaddaya think about that, buddy?"

Jack nodded and smiled. "That would be great, Walt, but on the other hand, have you ever considered a contingency plan if something happened to me?

Offerman pulled back. "Jesus Christ, Jack, are you leaving us? Did those bastards at Amtron make you an offer?"

"No, Walt, you misunderstand." Jack placed a friendly hand on Offerman's shoulder. "I just wanted to say thank you for the opportunity. It's been a great run. Still, if anything were to happen to me, I'd pick Jeff Franks. He's a rising star with a lot of potential."

"Okay, thanks for the advice," said Offerman while eyeing Jack suspiciously, "but just for the record, your ass ain't going anywhere."

***

Jack got up early Saturday with a sense of purpose. He woke Bryson, and together they gathered the gear and made their way to Busse

Lake. It was a gorgeous early fall day, even better than Jack remembered it in the other realities. They sat on the shore of the secluded spot Bryson found. Jack didn't need many words today; he just needed time with his son.

"Bryson?"

"Yeah, dad?"

"Whatever happens in your life, try to remember not to take the good times for granted. Hopefully, they'll all be good, but life can be harsh, and unexpected changes can hit you from left field."

Bryson reeled his line in a bit. "I'm not sure what you mean."

"It's called a New York minute. Everything can change in the blink of an eye. So, when it's going good, stop and appreciate it, okay? Hopefully, your good times will last a lifetime, but if they don't for whatever reason, hold on to the best memories, got it?"

"Okay, Dad... Is anything wrong?" Bryson looked over at his father quizzically for a moment.

"Nah. In fact, things couldn't be better."

They made it to Leighton's baseball game on time, and because he already knew a kind, older lady would be escorting a wandering RosaMarie back to her family, he completely focused on watching Leighton get his first hit of the season. It was a spectacular affair, and Jack soaked in every second of it. As the ball found a spot between the first and second basemen, Leighton sprinted like his hair was on fire. Jack watched as Juanita and Bryson leapt from their seats and cheered Leighton on. Pure love and emotion. It was wonderful to experience.

Juanita gasped as the younger Clausen boy slid into second base.

Safe!

Leighton jumped up and down and looked to the stands. Jack pointed at him and yelled, "You da man, Leighton!"

It wasn't until after the next batter doubled, and Leighton scored on an errant throw, that Juanita noticed RosaMarie was missing. Jack was still cheering and waving to his son when she pulled on his sleeve.

"Jack, RosaMarie. She's not at the playground." There was just the slightest hint of panic in her voice.

Without taking his eyes off the field, Jack pointed in the direction of the tennis courts. "Older woman, silver hair and a nice smile just found her. You can pick her up in front of court number one."

Juanita looked at him for several seconds. "What? How could you know that?"

"Hurry, Nita. The woman who found her is looking for a parent."

Chapter Twenty-Four

As they left the arcade after the ice cream celebration, Jack realized this would be the last time they spent together as a family. He did his best to hide his sorrow, and on the way home in the SUV, he once again did a lot of listening.

At some point, it seemed Juanita instinctively sensed there was something wrong, and she reached out and touched his arm gently and whispered, "Do you want to tell me about it?"

He patted her reassuringly and smiled, mouthing, "I'm fine."

The kids burst through the door as they always did, and Jack watched as RosaMarie bolted up the stairs, knowing exactly what she was preparing for. He used the intervening time to make sure all the bank, tax, insurance and investment records were in order so Juanita could find the information easily. She wouldn't be able to tap the life insurance policy for seven years, but they had enough money saved up so that she and the kids would continue to live decently without having to sell the house.

Jack experienced gut-wrenching pain as he imagined her struggling to make everything work without him. The light in her eyes would continue to fade, but he reminded himself that it was going to happen today, one way or another.

"Daddy, do you have time to play with me?"

For just a second, Jack stiffened. This was it. *Lights, camera, action!*

"Sure, pumpkin. I promised, didn't I? And a promise is a promise."

For the next half hour, Jack put his heart and soul into the characters game because he knew this would be RosaMarie's last innocent memory of him. Jumping from Mickey to Minnie to Pooh to Donald, Jack did his best impressions ever, which caused her to shriek and giggle with a sense of delight he had never seen before. As always, he did the acting while she created the scenes. This day, she seemed particularly engaged and set up her most intricate plot to date, which involved an alliance between Scar from the Lion King and Cruella Deville from 101 Dalmatians.

Jack played all the parts while RosaMarie filled in every now and again as Minnie and Owl. As he watched her play, he tried to burn her image into his brain. Every detail of the flow of her red curly hair; the freckles on her face; the way she moved her small hands, and of course, her smile. Those memories would have to last a lifetime.

The doorbell rang... Jack froze before steadying himself.

"Jack. Jack, are you up there? Jamal is here. Could you come down and talk to him?"

He looked over at RosaMarie, and for just an instant, he saw a sadness in her eyes that extended far beyond the end of the game. Almost as if she understood...

313

"It's okay, Daddy. Go talk to Mr. Egebe. I'll have to finish without you."

What she meant was, *I'll have to finish life without you.* Somehow, she knew...

Jack walked down the stairs and smiled at Jamal.

"Hey, Jack." His neighbor gave a friendly wave. "Do you have a few minutes to show me that new mower?"

Jack clapped Egebe on the back and motioned for him to follow. "C'mon, Jamal, you have to see this beast."

As he left the house, Jack turned and looked at Juanita. He studied her and soaked in the energy that came from the light in her eyes. She was smiling at him, and the intensity of her glow was so great, Jack thought for just a moment it might be the salvation of everything. Yet, inside, he knew that in just a few minutes, the light would dim, fade and never return. That was the cost, but it was far less than the alternatives. He gathered his last mental snapshot for safekeeping and left the house, leading Egebe out back to the garage.

The minutes that followed were a blur. Jack fought to remain focused and tried to maintain a demeanor that belied the churning inside of him. As he drove the machine down to the Egebe place, he kept looking over his shoulder, knowing this was it.

The end.

He fought the urge to run and then fought against the panic and blackness that tried to overwhelm his consciousness. Egebe climbed on the mower and started cutting his grass.

Any second now…

Almost on instinct, he turned and sprinted toward the house just as Juanita cleared the driveway. They almost collided as he grabbed her and held her at arm's length.

"Jack… It's RosaMarie…"

"Nita, don't worry. I'm going to get her. I know where she is, and she'll return safely to you. Don't call the police until you hear from me. Understand that I love you, and I always will. I'm sorry, but this is the best I can do. I tried everything else, but it just wouldn't work. Please remember, I did it for you and the kids." He squeezed her so tight he felt the air expel from her lungs.

"Jack, what are you talking about? I…"

She never got to finish. He was already running toward the BMW, which he parked in the street earlier that morning.

***

Jack smashed the front window, crawled through it, and walked with purpose to the back bedroom, where he knew he would find RosaMarie. When he kicked the door in, he found Lattimores sitting next to his daughter. She was still fully clothed but sobbing gently. When he saw Jack, Lattimores got up and retreated to the corner of the room.

RosaMarie ran to her father and hid behind him, hugging his leg tightly. Jack reached down and squeezed her reassuringly without taking his eyes off Lattimores, who was groveling and whining as his face grew increasingly red and puffy.

"RosaMarie, I want you to go wait for me by the front door. I'll be there in a moment."

"No, Daddy. Don't leave me. I'm scared."

"It's alright. Nothing is going to happen to you. I promise, and a promise is a promise, right?"

She nodded.

"Just walk down the hallway to the front door and wait for me there, okay?" He turned around and looked at her briefly, giving her a wide smile. "You have nothing to worry about now. Do you understand?"

She nodded again and let go of his leg, backing slowly out of the room and disappearing down the hallway.

"I—I don't belong here," Lattimores said in a trembling voice. "I'm already dead…" He fell to his knees and clasped his hands in front of him. "Please, please don't kill me again. I don't know if I belong here…"

"Pauley, you know we've done this before."

Lattimores' eyes widened. "What? Done what before? I don't feel like I belong here. There's no fourth pill. What does that even mean? I know there's no fourth pill, so why am I here?"

Jack approached slowly, with the hammer held high over his head.

"Please, please for God's sake don't kill me."

"I'm sorry, Pauley, but I can't take the chance you would come after my daughter again."

"I won't. There's no fourth pill. I have no one here… Why did I do it? I can't even remember… My son? Did I even have a son?" He looked up at Jack and pleaded, "Tell me why I did it? You can

316

trust me. I swear to *God*, I won't tell. You'll never see me again if you let me go. Tell me... Plea..."

The hammer impacted with the side of Lattimores' head as he tried to duck out of the way, but it stunned him, and he blinked several times and brought his hand up to the right side of his head, looking at the blood in a dazed stupor.

"Wait, you want your car today? We..."

The hammer crashed down on his skull a second time, shattering his forehead, which caused a thick grayish-red sludge to roll slowly down his face. Lattimores reached up and felt the hole in his skull. Just before he toppled over, for an instant, he looked puzzled.

Jack quickly checked for a pulse and then ran down the hall to find RosaMarie, who stood quietly next to the door. She had her hands over her eyes, and when she felt Jack put his arms around her, she burst out in tears and hugged him tightly.

He walked with her out to the car and set her in the front seat, strapping her in as securely as he could. They started the short trip back home, but RosaMarie wouldn't look at him. It wasn't until he realized his shirt was splattered with blood that he understood why. He glanced in the rearview mirror and saw several large dark red spots on his face, which he wiped off the best he could.

About halfway home, she finally spoke while looking out the window. "Did you hurt that bad man, Daddy?"

Jack thought about his answer carefully. "I made sure he could never steal you or any other little girl again. That's my job, RosaMarie, to protect my family. Everything I did was to protect my family. You'll remember that, okay?"

She turned, and they finally made eye contact. "I'll remember it, Daddy. I'll remember how you showed up and saved me from the bad man."

They drove for a while longer without speaking. As the BMW turned the corner onto Walnut, she said, "Are you going away, Daddy?"

Jack gripped the wheel tightly, and his jaw muscles clenched. "Yes, princess. I have to go away for a while. Never forget I love you more than anything in this world, and I'll always love you."

"But I don't want you to go." She started crying again, this time more from sorrow than fright.

"I'm sorry, pumpkin, but I have to. I wish it didn't have to be this way, but it does. I'll be back as soon as I can. Do you understand?"

RosaMarie continued crying softly, but she nodded.

Jack pulled up in front of the house and undid RosaMarie's seat belt. "Now, go inside and find mommy. Tell her I have some business to take care of. Can you remember that?"

"Business to take care of," she repeated.

Jack reached over and hugged her tight, savoring every second of the closeness. He leaned over and opened the door, making sure she got out safely. Watching her walk up the winding pathway without following was more difficult than he could ever have imagined. The temptation to reunite with Juanita and the boys to cry and hug their way through this crisis was almost too much to bear, but he knew the consequences.

About halfway up the walkway, the front door opened and Juanita came rushing outside. Jack gunned the engine and pulled away, glancing in the rearview mirror to make sure mother and daughter were together again.

He checked the glovebox and confirmed his .38 was loaded. One more debt needed to be repaid to the Identicals. In about half an hour, Tucker Lutz would open his door to greet Sonia Williamson. Jack grabbed the pistol and headed to Berwyn.

Chapter Twenty-Five

He sat under a canopy at the farthest table from the street, hidden from the world by a thick beard, dark glasses and a worn, wide-brimmed Fedora. Slowly, he sipped a tall, neat bourbon. Southern Spain was delightful this time of year, and Cordoba's Historic Centre was bathed in the sweet sounds created by the wandering musicians. As he watched the children playing and listened to the birds singing, he pictured the entire scene on the front of a postcard.

Take a snapshot because everything here will be burning by tomorrow...

"Excuse me, have we met?" A tall, slender woman with flawless olive skin walked up to his table. She was dressed smartly in business attire: tan slacks and a blue button-down blouse. He said nothing and continued to stare out into the street.

"My name is Isabella," she said in a perfect Castilian dialect.

He looked up at her and took off his sunglasses. For just a moment, she recoiled. "You don't need to introduce yourself," he said. "I know who you are."

"Do you mind if I sit down?"

He motioned to the chair across from him.

"Tell me how we know each other," she said as she smoothed out her slacks. "You look very familiar."

He picked up his smoldering unfiltered cigarette and took a long drag. "I already said I know who you are."

The woman sipped at her drink nervously. She tried to make small talk, but he was fixated on something in the road and virtually ignored her. Finally, as she ticked off a list of places they might have met, he leaned in and made a quick slashing gesture, which caused her to stop mid-sentence.

"When it happens, you must be on time," he said.

She looked confused and pulled back. "I don't understand. What are you talking about?

"When it happens, you must understand how important it is that you pay your debt."

She got up quickly, almost overturning her chair in the process. "I think I better leave."

"Did you hear me? When the time comes, you must be on time and pay your debt. You need to know that you can't get away from it. They all need you to show up on time."

She began backing away, but he got up and closed the distance. She gasped as he grasped her hand and stuck a folded piece of paper in her palm, closing her fingers around it. "Don't be late. Whatever you do, don't be late, you *pissant*."

Isabella ripped her hand away while still clutching the note. Her heels clacked on the cobblestone pavement as she hurried away from the café.

Jack sat back down and lit another cigarette, gesturing for a refill. He glanced at his watch. He had an hour before he needed to be in Shanghai.

END

Sign up to my email list:
https://authorwbk.com/contact/
Visit my website:
www.authorwbk.com

Facebook:
https://www.facebook.com/WilliamBrennanKn
ight1

Twitter:
https://twitter.com/Williambrennank

Instagram:
https://www.instagram.com/wbkauthor/

Other Books by William Brennan Knight

The Suicide Society Series:

Prequel: Desolation (novella)
Book One: The Suicide Society
Book Two: Rational Insanity
Book Three: Kill it to Death
Book Four: Resurrection of Death

About the Author

William Brennan Knight is originally from Chicago and settled in Arizona in the 1980s. In his life, he has been a father, musician, salesman and business owner. His passion for writing began early in his childhood and flourished as he grew older. He enjoys reading horror, thriller and science fiction as well as memoirs and biographies.

Knight currently lives in Southern Arizona and spends most of the summer in Ruidoso, New Mexico.

If You Liked the Book, Please Leave a Review

If you enjoyed this book, would you mind taking a few minutes to leave a review on Amazon? The process is very easy. Scroll down on the book page until you see the reviews section. On the left side, underneath the ratings, you'll see a button that says, "Write a Review." Simply click the button and a box will pop up where you can leave your review. If you're uncomfortable with writing, not to worry. Most review readers are just looking for your general impressions and how much you liked the book.